FINDING ORIEL

ADRIAN CHAPMAN

EMER PUBLISHING

Published by Emer Publishing
Contact author: adrianchapmanauthor@gmail.com

This is a work of fiction. Names, characters, places and incidents either are the product of the author's imagination or are used fictitiously and any resemblance to actual persons, living or dead, events or locales is entirely coincidental.

A catalogue record for this book is available from the National Library of New Zealand.

ISBN 9780473742898 (paperback)
ISBN 9780473742904 (EPUB)

Cover design by Jeroen ten Berge, jeroentenberge.com

For Nicky and Eimear

1

THEY SAY WORSE THINGS HAPPEN AT SEA. BUT IF YOU'VE never been taken from behind by a hairy-arsed sailor, then you're not really in a position to comment. Morgan had never even been on a boat, but he knew one thing. A worse thing had never happened to him.

Going north was his first mistake. The shops in Newry offered cheap toilet rolls and electrical goods, as well as the opportunity to buy condoms without a prescription and a note from your mother. But the cost of getting there in terms of time and petrol meant that only a significant purchase made it worthwhile. Morgan was only looking for one reasonably priced item, which he could have picked up in Dublin for a fractionally higher cost and within a ten-minute stroll from his front door.

But curiosity and a vague sense of adventure led him to point his car northwards on that Saturday morning in February 1986 and head towards the border. A late winter frost brought a glistening sheen to the fields and daffodils were peeking their optimistic heads above the hedgerows. He sang along to the New Romantic songs on RTE Radio 2 on his car radio until it faded out north of Dundalk. A Flock of Seagulls' 'I Ran' was the last song he heard on RTE before the Northern stations kicked in and the music was replaced by urgent security alerts and statistics on the previous night's road accident deaths.

Slieve Gullion appeared before him, dark and brooding and staring endlessly south, like a humourless security guard at an Orange Order cake sale. Army watchtowers dotted the mountain's slopes and Morgan immediately had the sensation of being watched and tracked.

As he crossed the border, he instinctively fiddled with the temperature control and moved the lever a few notches to the right. He passed the burned-out shell of the border custom's post, its 'HM Customs and Excise' sign dangling in the breeze as a memory of distant times when normal commerce took place here, and he snaked his way towards Newry.

The concrete monolith that served as the British Army's first checkpoint in Northern Ireland stalled his progress temporarily, but the bored soldiers on duty seemed more interested in the long queue of cars trying to escape to the South than the shoppers heading north. He edged through the chicane created by the concrete bollards and came out the other side as though he had passed through a vortex. The skies seemed darker, the people more huddled and their step more urgent. He turned the heating up a notch again and soon he was driving through the dirty streets of Newry.

Morgan parked his battered and rusting Toyota Corolla on an almost deserted street. As he turned off the ignition, a gloomy shadow appeared at his window and tapped aggressively on the glass. Morgan wound down the window and tried to identify the stranger beneath the dark hood of his anorak. He noticed three-day-old stubble and gapped and blackened teeth.

"Is there a problem?" Morgan asked.

"You're not leaving that yoke there, are you?"

"Why not? There are no yellow lines."

"It's a control zone, ya eegit. If you park a car with no one in it, the Brits will have the boot blown off it before you get back. An empty car round here usually has a bomb in it. See all these cars here with a little old lady in the passenger seat? That's what we're reduced to these days in the wee North. If you want to come shopping in Newry these days, you have to bring your granny with you to mind the car."

"My granny is in Tipperary," Morgan replied. "I don't suppose you rent out spares?"

The stranger laughed in the low guttural way of a lifelong smoker.

"You could park up in the northern part of town, but there would be a brave few Union Jacks on the poles up there and they mightn't like the look of that southern reg of yours. I can't supply a granny, but do ya see that laneway up there on the right? A buddy of mine owns the place up the back of that lane. If you give me a couple of bob, I can let you park up there."

Morgan looked at him suspiciously. He had only been in Northern Ireland for ten minutes and he felt like he was being ripped off already.

He fiddled in the cup holder beside the gear stick.

"I only have punts," he muttered, as he thrust a few lonely coins in that stranger's direction.

"All the same to me, horse. I do most of my drinking in the South these days anyway, as there's fuck all craic in Newry."

He gestured towards the alleyway and Morgan followed, parking his car beside what looked like an abandoned stable. He fixed the steering lock tightly before he locked up and, with no particular destination in mind, headed towards the town centre.

The rain had eased but the sky was still battleship grey, so

Morgan pulled the hood of his parka up and fished around the inside pocket for his Walkman. He pulled out the headphones and with wind-scarred fingers started to unknit the cord. He was humming the tune to a Kajagoogoo song that had been playing as he parked the car and was trying to remember the lyrics as he danced around the oil-stained puddles that littered the pockmarked footpath.

"Watch where your goin, ya fuckin twat."

Morgan looked up to find he was toe to toe with a British soldier who didn't look in the mood for getting out of the way. The soldier's face was smeared with green and brown camouflage paint that made his eyes sparkle like cat's eyes caught in headlights. Morgan had stumbled into an army patrol and, being a Southerner, this was a strange and unusual occurrence.

He reached inside his parka jacket and felt a frisson of tension stir within the soldiers. Their rifles were raised to firing position, their bodies tensed, while the outliers formed a circle, monitoring the street for secondary threats. Old ladies ducked into shop doorways and those with no option of cover froze. Morgan took the Walkman out of his pocket and attached the headphones. 'Too Shy' was the Kajagoogoo song he was trying to remember. The lyrics suddenly came to him as he weaved his way through the soldiers and headed towards Market Street.

There wasn't much sign of a market today, however. He passed a lonely and ragged plastic Christmas tree, its branches torn bare by the artic winds. It was beside a burned-out and buckled metal bin. A faded plastic police tape tried to guard their indignity and Morgan wondered if the excitement that caused the bin's demise had happened the previous Christmas or was it so old that it didn't register with the locals any more. A helicopter passed overhead, on its way to harass the mourners at a Catholic funeral, but Morgan didn't notice. He had slipped a Christy

Moore tape into his Walkman and was singing along to 'Ordinary Man'.

The streets were packed with dark overcoated Southern shoppers, battling the sideways rain and bone-shuddering wind to spend their savings in shops advertising 'Your Irish punt is as good as sterling here' and selling exotic items not available in the Republic of Ireland, such as Curly Wurlys and Spangles.

Morgan found a small electrical shop on Hill Street and studied the window display. It was mainly portable television sets and top-loader VHS players festooned in tacky tinsel, but a sign for 'Specialists in Word Processing and other office requirements' made him think that he had found the right place.

He opened the door and entered the brightly lit shop. Wham!'s 'Careless Whisper' was playing on a multi-deck stereo system and twelve colour TV sets with the sound turned down were showing the same snooker game. Surprisingly, given the busyness of the street outside, the shop was empty apart from one assistant who was studying the *Racing Post* while leaning on the counter.

Morgan waited for some acknowledgement of his presence, but when none was forthcoming, he coughed and whispered, "Excuse me." The assistant lifted his head slowly and grunted.

"What can I do for you, horse? Is it a telly you're after?"

Morgan shuffled his feet. He was only ninety kilometres from his home, but he could have been at the other side of the world. The accents were different, the street lights a darker shade of orange and the air heavy with unresolved history. He felt his palms sweating and he fiddled nervously with his collar.

"No, it's something a bit more specialised than that," he blurted.

The assistant's eyebrows rose conspiratorially. "If it's them dirty videos you want, you'll have to come back in March. I had a fierce run on them these past few months. You couldn't keep up with you Southerners trying to get your sticky fingers on them. But I'll be getting a brave few in soon. I've ordered a fresh load from over in Germany. Me brother's taking a load of cattle over and said he'll bring a few back. There are some wild dirty bitches over there."

Morgan looked around. The shop was still empty. He could sense humiliation coming and as a stranger in a strange land he didn't want witnesses.

"I'm not after that sort of stuff. I'm doing family history research. Walking around old graveyards and that kind of thing. I was thinking of getting up to date with the new technology. I spotted a couple of Yanks in the National Library and they had these fancy gadgets for recording their thoughts and whatever. The sort of thing you can slip in your pocket."

As he said this, the memory of previous conversations came flooding back. All those times when he had felt embarrassed about using a book token or a record voucher and found himself explaining that it wasn't for him; he was picking up a book or cassette for a cousin. All those times he'd been served Guinness when he wanted lager but found it impossible to say anything else apart from "Thank you, that's lovely." He had spent his life apologising to shop assistants and waitresses and he didn't know why. He was a working-class boy who had climbed the ladder to a low-level suit-wearing job in an insurance office, but he retained some of his class cringe when he bumped into people from his own background. Here he was again, explaining his personal business to an ignorant shop worker.

The assistant looked at him blankly. "You'll have to give me more information than that, boss. Are you looking for a tape recorder or a typewriter?"

"I want a Dictaphone."

"Can't you use your finger to phone like everybody else?" The assistant coughed up a low, rasping chuckle as he turned and waddled into the back room.

While he was gone, Morgan noticed that the snooker had finished and the twelve televisions were now showing a newsreader with a worried expression, mutely explaining some tragic event for which Northern Ireland was becoming sadly familiar. The war, which the locals liked to downplay by giving it the childlike name of 'the Troubles', had been raging for seventeen years and had settled into a dreary and desperate muddle of tit-for-tat killings interspersed with the occasional major atrocity. Morgan had watched these same TV pictures from the safety of his flat in Dublin, but here in Newry they seemed more visceral, more tangible, as though he was in the midst of its suffocating embrace. The TV switched to a reporter in a sheepskin coat who was standing in front of a badly damaged army post. Sirens and the flashing lights of a Sea King helicopter illuminated the scene behind him.

"Your boys have been at it again, I see." The assistant had returned with several boxes.

Morgan turned with a look of confusion written across his face.

"I'm sorry, what boys?"

"You're not from the border counties then, boss?"

"No, I'm from Tipperary, but I've been living in Dublin for the past few years."

"Ah, a soft Southerner. Don't they have electrical shops in Dublin? Not much point if you don't have electricity, I suppose."

Morgan's face reddened. He knew that this was only piss taking and that he was expected to retort with a witty reply. But thinking on his feet was never his strength.

"I'm the customer," was all he could manage. "Haven't we got the dynamic wrong here? I don't want to question your sales technique, but you'd think you were trying to keep your products secret."

"I couldn't give two shits about selling ya somethin, horse. I only work here. I don't earn commission. But look, here's the dog's bollix of a machine if that's what you're after."

The assistant placed a small cardboard box on the counter.

"It's an Olympus Pearlcorder. Never mind your Dictaphone shite. This is the real deal. Olympus are the boys who invented these yokes."

He took out the recording machine and pressed a button and a miniature tape popped out.

"Smallest tape ever," he said. "About the size of your dick but, unlike your dick, this one is popular with the ladies. They can slip this into their handbag and record all the gossip they hear at the hairdressers. Or they can hide it in the hubby's coat and find out what he was saying in the pub. Very discreet little machine, if you know what I mean. We've only just got them in, but I could let you have one for a hundred quid. I'd throw in a few free tapes and the batteries."

He pushed the machine towards Morgan and lowered his voice. "You could record all your dirty little secrets in here."

Morgan coughed and looked at his shoes. He did plan to use the recording device for family history research, but he also thought it would be useful to capture his random musings. Lines of poetry that came to him when he was lying on his sofa thinking about Orla, doggerel that popped up while he was strolling alongside the Grand Canal, or jokes that he thought of when there was nobody around to tell.

"Look, that's a wee bit above my budget. Do you have anything cheaper?"

The assistant muttered something under his breath. Morgan

couldn't make it all out but thought it contained the regular anti-Catholic barb "tight-arsed taig".

A small box with Asian writing was pushed across the counter.

"This is one of those Dictaphone things you were looking for," the assistant muttered. "It's more in your price range. I could do that one for forty quid."

Morgan picked it up and searched for some writing in English. He eventually found something on the side panel. He showed it to the assistant.

"It says 'Dicktafone' here," he said, pointing at the box. "It's not a rip-off, is it?"

The assistant shook his head. "It's forty quid, mate. Costs more if you want correct spellin'. Look, it comes with a cable that you can copy onto a normal tape deck."

"Okay, what will it cost me in punts?" Morgan asked, conscious that it was getting dark and he had a long trip back to Dublin.

The assistant brought out a small calculator. He tapped a few buttons and said, "Rounded down I could let you have that piece of Taiwanese electronic wizardry for fifty punts."

"But everyone else in Newry is doing punt for pound parity," Morgan said pleadingly.

"Fair enough," said the assistant. "If you want parity, I can do fifty pounds or fifty punts." The word "punts" was filled with contempt for the weak Southern currency and its pathetic bearer.

"I've heard that you Free Staters are so tight that you peel oranges in your pockets. But I'd say you'd be too mean to buy oranges in the first place. You probably save it up for the collection plate at chapel."

Morgan handed over the cash and grabbed the box before turning for the door. As he got there, he turned one last time towards his nemesis, who had returned to studying the racing form. "The less I have to do with anything orange the better," he said and exited sharply before he could be barbed with a response.

Morgan smiled as got back to his car. It wasn't often that he had the last word in sparky conversations. He was a master at conjuring up a witty response ten minutes after the event. He opened the box and noted that the instructions were in twenty-six languages, none of which was English. But there were only three buttons to press, so he figured it couldn't be that difficult.

He hit the large red button that looked most like 'record', held the device close to his lips and said quietly, "Testicles, testicles, one, two." He giggled to himself like a guilty teenager and pressed the other buttons until his flat Southern voice was replayed.

Flushed with success, he placed the machine in the space underneath the car radio and decided to narrate his journey home, so that he could replay it in the comfort of his flat later that evening and perhaps preserve it as a social narrative that he could leave to future generations who searched for him in their family tree.

"Just pointing my trustee steed towards the South," he said in the manner of a TV narrator. "Away from this godforsaken land of terrorists and religious bigots." It would take him nearly two hours to get back to his ground-floor bedsit in Ranelagh and he could fill that time recording his musings on the Troubles, the depreciation of the punt and the never-ending recession in the South. Morgan had an opinion on most things but lacked the confidence to express them publicly. But a recording device couldn't sneer or roll its eyes, so he welcomed the opportunity to get things off his chest. And if he ran out of things to say on those subjects, he could start on a critique of 80s music and why the 90s would be so much better.

Just south of Newry the army checkpoint at Dromad rose from the mist like an ugly pimple on the landscape. It was camouflaged against the dull grey sky and Morgan joined the queue of cars waiting to snake through the chicane. He had come through here before with little problem. A smile was usually enough to appease the waiting British squaddie, who was equal parts cold, bored and terrified. But as he approached the checkpoint, he noticed that something was up. A helicopter sat in a nearby field, its blades rotating angrily. Sirens screeched and flashlights danced around the early-evening darkness.

A soldier raised his hand, ordering Morgan to stop, just as the helicopter took off and flew overhead, sending the February puddles into widening circles across the oily tarmac. As it did, a flash of red caught Morgan's eye in the downward beam of the helicopter's searchlight. It was blood, fresh blood, and a knot of anxiety began twisting inside his stomach.

"Gimme your fuckin' driver's licence," the soldier shouted into Morgan's ear in a broad Glaswegian accent. The tension was knife-cuttingly clear. The helicopter, the sirens, the blood. It all suggested something nasty had happened here. Probably a bomb and probably a dead soldier. The image on the TV screens earlier jumped into Morgan's head. This was the blown-up army base and he had stumbled right into it.

Morgan decided that witty repartee was probably not his best option. He fumbled in his glove compartment and produced his Irish licence, wrapped in a dirty plastic cover. He struggled to extract the small pink form from its cover, and he felt the soldier edging closer. Finally, he managed to pull it clear and passed it through the open window. The soldier shone his torch on the paper and pointed a gloved hand at the name. "What the fuck is that?" he screamed.

"Seamus Ó Muireagáin," Morgan explained. "It's my name. In Irish."

The soldier stuck his head inside the car and brought his

automatic weapon up to Morgan's ear. "Are you a Provo then?" he growled.

Morgan moved backwards, but the soldier's gun followed him to the point where he was almost sitting in the passenger seat. "You're not automatically a terrorist just because you have an Irish name," Morgan muttered. "That's like assuming you are a child molester just because you have a British name."

Morgan struggled when under stress and tended to blurt out the first thing that came into head. As soon as he said this, he regretted it. The soldier flung open the door and dragged Morgan onto the tarmac. Morgan slipped on the oily surface and fell backwards. His elbow hit the ground and a sharp electric pain shot up his arm. He pulled himself into a tight foetal position and could feel the fear-induced adrenalin racing through his body.

"One of my mates got killed today by you bastards and now you have the nerve to call me a fuckin paedophile." As the squaddie said this, he dug his -boots deep into Morgan's rib cage.

"I want to see your superior officer," Morgan moaned while he lay huddled on the wet ground.

"Oh, do you?" the soldier said. "Well, here he is," as he drove the butt of his rifle into Morgan's stomach. "And this is his footman," he screamed as more kicks rained down on Morgan's motionless carcass.

In the distance, the lights of another car were approaching, so the soldier dragged Morgan into a nearby hut where two policemen were engrossed in conversation. They stopped as the soldier flung Morgan to the floor. Morgan lay there shaking, his arm throbbing with pain and his face devoid of colour. One fearful eye watched the soldier in anticipation of further blows.

"I think this one is a terrorist," the soldier explained.

"And what makes you say that?" the older of the two policemen answered.

"He's got an Irish name on his driver's licence and he called me a child molester when I challenged him."

The policemen exchanged a weary glance. "How long have you been here, son, and is this your first tour?" one of them asked.

"Two months," the soldier replied. "And, yes, it's my first."

"Well, let me explain something, sonny," the policeman said as he placed a comforting arm across the soldier's shoulder. "The terrorists here are usually smart enough not to use Irish names on their licence and they don't pick fights with squaddies at heavily armed checkpoints. Particularly after they've set off a bomb that killed four of his mates. Now if I was you, I'd get a couple of chums to write up a report saying that this guy attacked you and you had to smack him a few times to protect yourself. And get an ambulance to take him to hospital. The press will be here soon and the last thing we need is a bloodied Fenian lying around the place."

The soldier looked crestfallen but recognised authority when he saw it, even if it was the dreaded Royal Ulster Constabulary, which his senior officer had warned were almost as dangerous as the IRA.

"I'll sort that out, sir," he said. "But what about his car?"

"We'll take that back to the station. We came on the helicopter and it left with the last of the injured. So, if he wakes up, tell him he can pick it from there when he gets out of hospital."

The soldier summoned two of his mates and the three of them manhandled Morgan's unconscious body onto a chair before one of them went off to call the ambulance. Then they huddled in a corner and quickly coordinated their stories.

The two policemen watched them from the other side of the room.

"Following the best traditions of the British Army, I see," the taller of the two said. "As soon as things go to shit, get out a statement saying the other side started it."

———

Morgan woke up two hours later on the starched white sheets of Daisy Hill Hospital. He coughed and a nurse came over.

"Where am I?" he asked.

"You're in hospital in Newry. An ambulance brought you and said you'd been fighting with soldiers." She leaned closer and whispered. "Next time you do that I'd suggest you have an Armalite with you."

"When can I get out?" he asked.

"As soon as the doctor's been round and had a look at you. They said your car was up at the police station but if I was you, I'd leave it there for a day or two. Those bruises will just arouse suspicion."

"I wasn't in a fight. I was dragged out of a car by a British soldier and beaten up," he said meekly.

"Well, good luck getting that story past the RUC. They don't have much sympathy for Catholics complaining about the security forces."

Morgan tried to focus on her through his puffy eyes. "How do you know I'm a Catholic and why does it matter?"

She held up his chart which was dangling off the end of his bed. "You weren't in any state to answer questions when you came in, so they got your name from your driver's licence. There aren't many 'Seamus Ó Muireagains' who aren't Catholic. It mightn't matter where you come from but up here it's important."

She leaned in to puff up his pillows and her breasts, encased in a starched white uniform, almost pressed into his face. The thought struck him that this was the closest he'd got to a woman's breasts in a long time.

She noticed his eyes widening and smiled. "My name is Sinead by the way. That's a good Catholic name too. All the nurses here are Catholic and all the doctors are Protestant. That pretty much sums up Northern Ireland. You might notice up here that when people ask you your name, they are a doing a wee mental check. If it's not obvious what religion you are from your name, then they'll ask you where you live and that will usually be a giveaway. Every village or housing estate up here is segregated. As a last resort, they'll ask what school you went to.

"The funny thing is, we don't put patients' religion on their chart but everyone can tell from their name and address."

Morgan didn't understand any of this and to be honest he wasn't really listening. His attention was focussed on her breasts and the intoxicating allure of perfume and hospital detergent.

"Hi Sinead, my name is James Morgan, actually. The Irish name in my licence was just a joke to be honest. It took me four goes to pass my driving test and when I finally did the lady at the licence office took the piss out of me. She said she wouldn't trust me with a toy truck. So, I wrote down the Irish version of my name on the form and then watched her take four goes to type it properly on my licence. I live for little victories like that. The truth is that I've only ever heard my Irish name before when the roll was called at school. And I had to ask the guy beside me to give me a nudge when my name was read out. That happened every day for thirteen years. I never remembered it."

Sinead placed the clipboard at the end of the bed and tucked in the blankets.

"And there was me thinking all you Southern boys were fluent in Irish. The nuns beat it in to us up here."

Morgan pushed himself up in bed. Sinead's attention had

made him momentarily forget about his injuries and he winced in pain as he raised himself up on his elbows. "My school just prepared you for emigration. Learning Irish wasn't going to get you a job in Birmingham. We were treated like cattle that were being fattened up before being put on the boat to England."

She sat at the end of the bed. "Jeez, we're fighting away for a United Ireland up here. You're not exactly selling it as a land of milk and honey."

"Do you go down south much?" he asked.

"Ach, we're probably down most weekends at one of the discos. Every Northern girl is looking for a Southern fella. Didn't you know that?"

Morgan noticed a twinkle in her eye and he had to adjust the bedclothes to disguise a growing embarrassment that was expanding in his groin department.

"So, what's wrong with the fellas up here?" he asked.

"The lads here are all into cars and heavy metal music. It's a macho culture."

"Bit different to me then," he said. "The first two years I was driving, I thought the gear stick was for stirring the oil. And I'm more of a female country kind of guy. You know the sort of songs where all the men are bastards except one guy. And he's dead by the end of the song."

Sinead leaned closer and whispered. "It sounds like you've got in touch with your feminine side."

Morgan had to adjust the bed clothes again and coughed. "I'm not sure. If I had a feminine side, I think I'd stay at home all day playing with it."

She threw her head back and laughed outrageously, causing the heads of all the other patients to turn and the ward matron to stare disapprovingly. It had been a long time since a girl had laughed at his jokes and he turned himself in the bed to get closer to her. Unfortunately, he had also forgotten about his bruised ribs and he had to force a smile to show her he was interested in her response.

"That's good to hear," she said. "I was worried you might be gay."

Morgan leaned closer. "I'm not gay; I just help them out when they're stuck."

Sinead looked at him quizzingly and furrowed her brow.

"I don't get it."

Morgan blushed. Yet again, he had tried too hard and ruined a perfectly good conversation with an inappropriate comment. "I'm sorry. I think whatever drugs you gave me are starting to wear off. My head and elbow are a bit sore. I'm not thinking straight."

Sinead stood and wrote some notes on Morgan's charts. "I'll get you a wee painkiller," she said. "And when the doctor discharges you, I'll give you a lift down to the police station and I'll go in and ask for your car back. They won't give a nurse a hard time."

With that she was off, and Morgan watched her walk away. Her leather-soled shoes sang as they danced across the polished floor.

Morgan lay back and pondered his predicament. A simple shopping trip had ended in a beating and a trip to the hospital. And worse than that, he might have to spend more time in this Northern hellhole. If only he had his recording device now, he thought, he could record a few choice anecdotes. How he had single-handedly taken on the might of the British Army. How he had won the battle of repartee with both the soldiers and the surly shop assistants of Newry.

But he didn't have his recording device. It was still in the space below the radio in his car, which was now sitting in the car park of Newry RUC station. The two-hour tape had run its course and the machine had turned itself off. If anyone had cared to play it back, they would have heard fifteen minutes of Morgan's self-aggrandising dialogue as he drove out of Newry. Ten minutes of shouting and beating at the checkpoint and one hour of distant and meaningless car park noises until the tape ran out. And, in between, thirty-five minutes of conversation between two senior police officers as they drove back to the station. The contents of that conversation would make the tape extremely sought after and Morgan's life a lot more complicated than he could ever imagine.

2

The letter arrived by registered post three days later.
Seamus Ó Muireagáin had been badly and probably deliberately
misspelled, but it was clear that the name and address had come
from his driver's licence nonetheless. The crown in the top right
corner gave an ominous clue to the letter's contents. Morgan's first
thoughts were that it was a speeding offence. But his battered car
could only test the speed limit if it was going down a steep incline
while towing a ten-tonne trailer.

So, it was with some trepidation that he tore the envelope
apart and spilled its contents onto the kitchen table. Morgan's
hands trembled as he read the officious and grandiose words. He
was summoned to Belfast Magistrates Court on 28 February to
face charges of assault against an unnamed British soldier. He sank
back into the only comfortable chair in his sparsely furnished
living room. He had taken the day off to catch up on personal
admin. To get through the list of bills gathering dust on a clipboard
attached to the fridge. To empty out six months' worth of half-
eaten takeaways that he had optimistically stored in his freezer and

to rearrange his record collection into alphabetical order. But it was lunchtime and he had only made it as far as his kitchen.

He had tried hard to forget about that chilly February day and his ill-fated trip. Clearly the British hadn't. They were a nation of form fillers and bureaucrats, and the soldier had followed orders and got a few of his mates to lie on the official report. A form had been lodged, so they needed to follow protocol and press charges.

Morgan checked the calendar in the kitchen. It was still on the page for January and after a moment's confusion when he thought that the 28th fell on a Sunday, he flicked the page over and noticed that 28 February was just four days in the future.

"Shit" was the first thought in his head. It normally took him a week to organise buying a postage stamp. In four days, he would have to arrange time off work, find a solicitor in Northern Ireland, get his one and only suit dry cleaned and figure out where exactly the court was.

His head ached as he catastrophised each scenario. To begin with, he didn't even know where to start in asking for time off work. His boss had the emotional sympathies of a great white shark and treated all leave requests as an act of treachery to the company. One of Morgan's colleagues had asked for time off to go to his mother's funeral and the boss had asked what time the service was at and whether he would be able to make it back to the office in the afternoon.

Trials were open ended and the last thing Morgan wanted to do was make his Northern adventure public. He would have to come up with a plausible alternative story for why he would be out of the office for an indeterminate amount of time. And he would need several more cups of tea before he could manage that.

In the meantime, he gathered all the coins he could find and headed up to the phone box at the end of the street, clutching the letter from the Belfast court.

He eventually got through to a lady with an accent that would not have been out of place on BBC radio in the 1950s. He mumbled through his dilemma and how four days was unreasonable for him to organise himself.

He heard an audible sigh on the other end.

"Sir, justice delayed is justice denied. We look on each case on its merits and this looks like a pretty straightforward affair. The Crown Prosecutor is happy that all the evidence is at hand and the case will be heard before a judge with no need to procure a jury, so we feel that the notice is quite adequate."

"That sounds like you've already decided I'm guilty."

"Sir, I would remind you that this case will be heard under the high principles of Her Majesties Crown services. Things may be different down there in Eire, but I can assure you that everyone is innocent until proven guilty up here."

Morgan was agitated. He shuffled nervously inside the phone box and gripped the hand set tighter.

"I read an article about the Crown services in 'Magill'," he blurted.

"Apparently you guys arrange these trials quickly so that the defendants don't have time to organise their case and sort out witnesses. It's all part of your anti-Irish bias."

As he said this his face reddened. He wasn't good on confrontation and was already regretting his outburst. The odds were already stacked against him and accusing the judge of prejudice wasn't going to help his cause.

"Goodbye, Mr O'Whatever your name is. We'll see you on the 28th and don't be late."

She hung up and Morgan looked out onto the busy streets of Ranelagh. Life was carrying on in the rest of the world, while he was trapped in a small box wondering how his existence had just become so complicated.

He decided to call in to see his boss rather than ring him. The office was only a ten-minute walk away and he hoped he could win more sympathy with a face-to-face meeting than a phone call.

"Afternoon, boss."

The boss lifted his eyes slowly from the paperwork he was studying and eyed Morgan suspiciously.

"Why are you dressed like a tramp, Mr Morgan?"

"I'm on a day off, but I wanted to have a quick chat if you have time."

"A day off? What idiot signed that off?'

"Eh, you did, boss. Last week. Remember I caught you just as you were heading out to play golf?"

"Hmm. You have a knack at picking your moment to ask for things, don't you, Mr Morgan? Anyway, unless this is about work can you get on with it. I don't have all day."

"Well, it's just that I'm going to need some more time off. Something has come up that I can't get out of."

"Well, this is very inconvenient, Mr Morgan. We're doing the annual commission run next week and we need all hands on deck. How many days are you talking about?"

"That's the thing, boss; I don't know. Might be just a day or it could be a couple of days."

The boss pushed his chair back and took on the expression of somebody sucking a lemon.

"This is all very suspicious, Mr Morgan. Sounds like an impending court case."

Morgan blushed and he looked around hurriedly to make sure nobody else was in earshot.

"No, no. Nothing like that, boss. It's a, em, medical issue."

"Do you have a doctor's note?"

"Well, not quite, boss. It's a bit difficult. I have to go and see someone on the 28th to get it assessed and then there might be follow-up stuff."

"You're being exceedingly vague, Morgan. What exactly is wrong with you?"

Morgan slipped into the office and closed the door quietly behind him. He could feel his story stretching beyond his powers of imagination. Somewhere in his mind he calculated that an embarrassing condition might end the conversation.

"It's a bit delicate, boss. It's sort of personal. It's a downstairs issue," he whispered while instinctively glancing at his groin.

"Good God, man. You don't have that Aids thing, do you? I was just reading a report on it today. Apparently, it will be the death of the insurance industry. It would be a bit embarrassing if one of our own employees made the first claim."

Morgan started sweating. His mind was a tumble-dryer of thoughts.

"No, no, boss. It's nothing like that. It's a urinary thing. I've been peeing every five minutes."

"Sounds like the clap," the boss replied in a disappointed voice and resumed reading the papers on his desk.

"Make sure you drop a doctor's note into HR when you get back and don't let the door hit your arse on the way out."

Morgan walked home, relieved at least that he had overcome his first hurdle, even if his dignity had taken another battering.

He brewed up a pot of tea and thought about his options. He could ignore the summons. Northern Ireland was a different jurisdiction after all, and they were unlikely to pursue an expensive extradition process for a small case like this. And if they did, he could always throw himself onto the mercy of the Southern media who would champion his case as a rebel fighting the imperialist British machine. Few extradition processes had been successful in the past, even for people who had done nasty stuff like killing people. And if the worst came to the worst, part of Morgan's twisted outlook on life would enjoy the thought of him being driven to the border in handcuffs and then handed over to the RUC under the glare of TV lights and the scribbled notes of the international media.

He sat imagining himself as an Irish Mandela or Havel. Imprisoned unjustly by a cruel regime and writing long and insightful pamphlets from his prison cell, smuggled out on toilet roll hidden in his foreskin.

That thought woke him from his comfortable dream, and the harsh realities of his predicament suddenly became clear. He could end up in prison with a bunch of terrorists who he would then be forced to associate with for protection. He'd lose the job he hated but needed for social comfort and to pay the rent on his miserable bedsit. And his mother would never forgive him. And nothing was more terrifying than the wrath of an Irish mammy.

He paced around the flat, desperately seeking a solution to his dilemma. The recording machine sat on the kitchen table, unused since he had retrieved his car from Newry police station. It made him remember that day and the inane recording of his own voice that had kept him occupied on the way south. Then he suddenly remembered that he had never turned the machine off and that it would have recorded his conversation with the soldier and the sound of him being dragged violently from the car.

Giddy with excitement, he played the tape back from the beginning. Fifteen minutes in, he found what he was looking for and he turned the tape off when it got to the part when you could hear his unconscious body being dragged away from the car. That proved that the British soldier had started the fight and that he was an innocent abroad, bruised and battered by the military industrial machine.

He brought his tea into the living room and his eye caught a

John le Carré novel resting on the coffee table. He had bought it as a Christmas present for his friend and unrequited love Orla. Morgan had been meeting her on and off for two years, without even a snog or a fond look. They usually met when she was bored and needed a chat and never when he wanted to. Months would go by without hearing from her and then he would get a call out of the blue asking if he wanted to meet up. This was usually when she'd broken up with a boyfriend or was having problems with a colleague at work. Sometimes those events would combine and he would be entertained for two hours by tales of some senior partner at her law firm and her evening adventures with him on a walnut desk illuminated by a green lamp. Orla had an unfortunate ability to describe her trysts in such intimate detail that Morgan could not help but find himself in the room she described.

Nevertheless, he would always agree to meet, hoping against hope that this date would be the big one, but knowing that it probably wouldn't.

He hated himself for being so compliant, knowing that if he acted like more of a bastard, he would actually stand some chance of success. But she gave him just enough signs of hope, holding his hand sometimes as they walked down Grafton Street or staring at him for an age as they nursed pints in Kehoes.

In the two years that Morgan had known her, he had never met her at the weekend. That's when she lived the exciting part of her life. He met her in the dull dreariness of Wednesday evenings when his only competition was *Coronation Street* on TV.

Their last meeting was before Christmas in O'Donoghue's Bar, and after a beer or two, he had managed to swing the conversation away from Wham! and Duran Duran and onto his preferred topics of Second World War and spy novels. Part of Morgan's love for Orla was that she could morph from South Dublin goddess, with an eye for fashion and flash cars, into something that could best be described as a bloke. She could hold her own on football and even knew more about the workings of the internal combustion engine that Morgan could ever aspire to.

It turned out that her grandfather on her mother's west Brit-leaning side of the family had worked for the Secret Service in London during the war. They spent the rest of that night (before she left him with the standard one-armed hug and peck on cheek) talking about spies and subterfuge.

The next day, while nursing a hangover and a desperate sense of longing, Morgan had made his way to Eason's bookshop and purchased a copy of *Smiley's People* by John le Carré. It was also available in hardback and Morgan had considered buying that for Orla. But he was a star-crossed lover, not a fool, and he figured that until he got a decent kiss he wasn't going to splash out £9.99.

The novel now sat untouched, awaiting wrapping that Morgan never got around to. But it made him realise the intrigue of the situation he now found himself in. There are spies everywhere, he thought, and you can't be too careful. He realised that the tape was his only way of proving his innocence and that the nasty British with their surveillance cameras and network of informers would be keen to get their hands on it.

He resolved to make a copy, but technology wasn't his forte either. Making a mixed tape for Orla had proved to be a testing process that took three months and seven discarded cassettes. In the end, the finished product, *Tales of Melancholy*, hadn't been a huge success. Leonard Cohen and Miles Davis didn't appeal to her fun-loving side.

Morgan shook out the recording box and a cable fell out. Rather miraculously he found that it connected into the back on his rickety old stereo and through a process of random button pressing, he discovered that he could copy the tape onto a standard cassette. Flushed with pride at this achievement, he then proceeded to search the house for the best hiding place he could find. Old jars and shoe boxes were tried but discarded for being too obvious. The spies that Morgan now imagined were setting off in smart suits and sunglasses for his humble residence and were probably already peering through the window.

Then he remembered the extractor fan in the kitchen. During a storm two years ago, it had fallen off and in his handy-man ignorance, Morgan had never gotten around to properly fixing it. It came away easily from the wall, exposing a large cavity littered with mice droppings. Morgan had used this space before to hide his pornographic magazines whenever his mother came to visit. If she couldn't find them, the combined forces of the British Secret Service would also fail. He wrapped the cassette in a plastic bag and placed it carefully into the cavity.

———

The morning of 28 February was cold and icy, so Morgan set off early for his return visit north. He had thought about hiring a solicitor to represent him, but money was tight and he was newly emboldened from having spent the three days leading up to the trial engrossed in the Rumpole novels his Aunt Mary had bought him for Christmas. The law seemed pretty black and white to him on that icy morning, and he had his tape safely tucked into his inside pocket. Morgan had decided on self-representation and after watching *To Kill a Mockingbird*, he pictured himself as a modern-day Atticus Finch.

He planned to sit there stoically while soldier after soldier got up on the stand and told barefaced lies. He would let them present their case before getting to his feet, clearing his throat in a dismissive manner and making an objection. Reality, as with many things in Morgan's life, was much more mundane. When he announced that he would be representing himself, the judge called him and the prosecutor into a side room to discuss the evidence they would be presenting. Morgan rather sheepishly produced the tape and after an hour or so of faffing around, the judge finally found a machine to play it on. While it was playing, the prosecutor blushed and desperately scribbled notes, unable to make eye contact with the now fuming judge.

They stopped when it reached the sound of Morgan's beaten-up body being dragged into the checkpoint office.

"I'm dismissing this case outright," the judge said. "And furthermore, I will be contacting the RUC to ask them to carry out a thorough investigation into this outrageous perjury and the attack that was carried out on this innocent man. Mr Morgan, can I ask you to hand over this tape so that I can pass it on to the police? It will be an important element in their investigations." Morgan was happy that the original was safely tucked away in his flat in Dublin. He complied and shook hands with the judge and prosecutor before taking his leave. As he marched confidently towards the exit, he passed the soldier who had assaulted him, buttoned up in his dress uniform with the tam-o'-shanter of the Royal Regiment of Scotland proudly on display. Beside him sat two similarly attired comrades, ready to perjure themselves for the cause.

"Looks like you might need a lawyer, mate," Morgan blurted out with as much toughness as his voice could muster. "Guess you didn't know that I was taping the whole thing."

The soldiers didn't reply but looked at each other with worried expressions. Morgan left quickly, suddenly aware that he was acting in a hostile manner towards three trained killers. Morgan avoided conflict with his boss, with all the women he had ever known and with his mother. He wasn't about to take on the British Army.

He raced towards his car and headed south again. The recording machine was on the passenger seat, refreshed with a new blank tape. Morgan hit record as he turned his car onto the Lisburn Road. "The Lone Ranger lives to fight another day," he exclaimed. "They thought they had him trapped but with one bound he was free."

The cold, grey countryside of South Ulster was laid out before him and as the evening grew dark at five o'clock, sleet and rain battered his windscreen and he fumbled constantly with the temperature lever, as though jiggling the control would make the air warmer. In the distance the red flashing lights of the Dromad checkpoint appeared. Morgan remembered his last visit to this unwelcoming spot and his stomach tightened as he approached. Suddenly above his head, the thunderous sounds of a Sea King helicopter broke the monotony of rain. It seemed as though it was about to land on Morgan's car but at the last minute it veered left and came down in the adjoining field. Twenty black-faced British soldiers jumped out and ran towards Morgan's vehicle. He gripped the steering wheel and waited for the assault, but it never came. The soldiers filtered out around his car and disappeared over a nearby stone wall. The Sea King roared its engine and lifted itself into the charcoal sky. In a moment, it was gone and the road was silent again, save for the relentless tapping of rain on the windscreen and the booming cacophony of drums within Morgan's heart.

He drove slowly to the checkpoint and, with shivering hands, passed his licence to the waiting soldier.

"And what brings you to Northern Ireland today, Mr O'Muireagáin?" the soldier asked.

"I had to see a man about a dog," he meekly answered. The soldier looked at him with a puzzled expression, but he had heard a lot of strange things since his tour of duty in Northern Ireland had begun and a Calor Gas heater in the hut was calling him. "Thanks very much Mr O'Muireagáin, safe home," he said as he handed back the licence.

"Happy New Year," Morgan said as he wound the window up and slipped the car into first gear.

"Same to you, sir" the soldier replied as Morgan's car disappeared towards the horizon. These Irish are a funny lot, he thought. Some of them are trying to kill you but most of them are decent folk just getting on with their life. The soldier suddenly felt homesick and wished that he could be spending the late days of February with his mates in Cardiff and not standing on a miserable dark road in South Armagh, asking complete strangers what they had been up to today.

———

Morgan made it back to Dublin in time for the evening news. A soldier had been killed that day in a roadside bomb attack in County Tyrone. Morgan thought about the squaddie he had just wished Happy New Year to. Much as he wanted to hate the British Army for what they had done to him in Newry, he didn't really have it in his heart to feel that way about anyone. Morgan was an idealist and made excuses for all the people who had ever done him harm. "Forgive them Lord," he would often say, "for they know not what they do." He said this whenever Orla refused his invitation for a drink and whenever his boss told him that his office attire would be more suited to a tramp with self-esteem issues.

"The meek shall inherit the earth," was another quotation that Morgan liked to comfort himself with. Even though he knew, as a fully signed-up member of the meekness society, that if offered this inheritance, the meek would simply hand it back apologetically while muttering about how they couldn't cope with something so large and complex and how it would be much better in the custody of those who are strong and self-confident.

Morgan got back to work on the Monday after the trial. He poked his head into his boss's office but it was empty. As he turned around, he found that Dunne from the sales team was behind him and grinning broadly.

"How's the itch, Morgan?"

Morgan blushed.

"What are you talking about, Dunne?"

"The boss was saying you had to take Friday off to have the little fella cleaned out. Did they use a scrubbing brush?"

Morgan recalled the boss's mention of the clap when he asked for the day off. He didn't really want to tell Dunne the truth about his adventures, but he couldn't think of a good compromise story.

"It's a urinary thing, Dunne. I don't really want to talk about it."

"Are ya taking the piss, Morgan? If you don't mind the pun. The boss doesn't believe your story and I don't either."

Morgan shuffled off wondering what was being said about him behind his back. He wanted to challenge Dunne but didn't have the courage. Dunne was brash and self-confident and that was exactly the sort of personality that Morgan found most intimidating. He had been sent on a confidence-building course by his employer, with limited results. He was now able to look at other people's shoes while talking to them, rather than his own. But he was a nervous soul and no amount of soft management skill courses was going to change that. The insurance industry in which he worked wasn't particularly cruel, but Morgan could create imaginary demons at the drop of a hat. A memo from his boss saying that all client correspondence should now begin with "Dear Sir/Madam" rather than the long-established tradition of "Dear Sir" would wound Morgan like an arrow to the heart. He would take it as an attack on his work practices and an opportunity to beat himself up for not suggesting the change earlier.

He wandered down to his desk and found a pile of correspondence that nobody had bothered to look at while he was away.

"How long have you been here now, Morgan?"

O'Leary from Accounts had swivelled his chair round for his regular morning chat. They had a shared awkwardness that created an odd friendship that could stretch to five minutes of conversation each day.

"I'm the longest-serving staff member at this branch, actually. And I probably know more about the company's policies and internal workings than anyone else, present company excepted," Morgan replied.

"I'd say you've seen a fair few changes in that time."

Morgan lay back in his seat and put his hands behind his head.

"I've been doing pretty much the same job since I left school in 1979 and entered the exotic world of general insurance. There have been technology changes in the interim of course. When I started we had rotary dial phones and they've now been updated to a sleek touch-button model and you no longer have to walk to the stationery shop on the corner when you want a document copied. The biggest leap forward is in the typing pool where the secretaries no longer use typewriters and have migrated onto slick new IBM PCs. But I still like to hand them my handwritten letters to type. I'm old fashioned, particularly when it comes to avoiding work."

"But you've never put yourself up for promotion or even used your length of service to land a better desk when the branch goes through its regular reorganisations," O'Leary replied.

"I'm happy being stuck down the back, behind the telex machine and the dot matrix printer. And if you stand on a chair, this window looks over a car park onto Winton Road with a view of Fitzwilliam Tennis Club. My ideal day is to get through my work early and enjoy watching pensioners mishit backhanders."

"I thought you liked it down here because the boss can't be bothered to navigate the office furniture to call down to your desk personally, and I notice you often leave the phone off the hook in case he's calling you."

Morgan smiled. "That gives me the benefit of avoiding the boss while also making it seem as though I'm really busy."

"It's funny but the boss was down here on Friday. We haven't seen him here much since Mary, that good-looking young one, left last July. He used to be a regular visitor before then."

"What was he looking for?" Morgan asked as leaned forward with a worried expression.

"He didn't say anything. He was looking for something on your desk and in your drawers. He was muttering something, but I couldn't hear."

Morgan instinctively checked around his desk, but nothing seemed to have moved. He felt uneasy that the secret world he had stepped into outside work seemed to be seeping into his office.

He decided to crack on with work and tried to not think about what his boss might and might not know. His experience meant that he finished his daily workload, which consisted of correspondence to unhappy claim applicants and monotonous premium calculations, by 11 am. He then turned his mind to the monthly commission report that he was required to provide to Head Office. This involved sending a report to the dot matrix printer and waiting three hours for it to finish.

While this was running, Morgan turned his hand to what he considered more productive purposes, including completing the Crosaire crossword in *The Irish Times* and designing a cassette cover for a mixed tape he had made for Orla. When these tasks were exhausted, he stared out the window and watched the planes taking off from Dublin airport. Most of his school friends were in London working on building sites or in pubs. They came home at Christmas with tales of free-loving English girls and easily accessible pornography. Morgan was tempted by the bright lights of London, but despite many drunken boasts about his emigrant intentions, he had never managed to get around to going.

3

IN A BOMB-PROOF OFFICE 160 KILOMETRES FROM MORGAN'S flat, Inspector McGuinness slammed his office door shut and pulled the blinds. It was 8.30 am on Monday at Special Branch headquarters in Belfast, and Detective Anderson had just won the weekly sweep. Each week the three constables who sat outside McGuinness's office would try to guess their boss's Monday-morning mood. Whistling and patting backs after a win by his beloved Glentoran was one option. Pensive and deep in thought was a more common expression. But this morning's winner was the full-on rage usually brought about by a Sunday night call from the chief.

The three cops exchanged knowing glances. "What do you think is up?" McLaren asked. "There was no action over the weekend. The wires are pretty quiet."

"I reckon it's HQ," Anderson answered. "He probably got a call from the chief about his dodgy expenses, or the amount of unaccounted cash he's handing over to touts. The chief goes to church on Sunday and has a sudden outpouring of guilt about all the shifty stuff we're doing down here in Special Branch. Then he calls the boss and gives him grief. I reckon that's all there is to it.

"I'd give it about thirty seconds before he calls one of us in. It will take him that long to dream up a reason for it being our fault. But I win, I picked grumpy bastard as his mood this morning, so get you two down to Kinneys bakery and get me a filled bap. I'll deal with his mood swings while you're away."

Anderson leaned back and awaited the summons from his boss's office. His desk was a jumble of overflowing manila folders and he had no enthusiasm for opening any of them. He looked around the office at his colleagues. There were a few upright ones who went to Free Presbyterian services on Sunday and probably made love to their wives through a hole in a sheet. There were also huddled dishevelled ones with rosy cheeks that betrayed their high-functioning alcoholism.

Anderson fell into neither camp. He was an old-fashioned cop in a world that despised and ignored that type of policeman. It was very different when he joined the force. Back then he was interested in forensics and righting the social wrongs of society. But an incident several years previously had drawn him towards the darker side of the law.

Like many of his colleagues, Anderson lived in a 'safe' suburb dominated by policemen huddled together for security. Across the street from his house was a burly copper called Evans. He was good company in the pub and a regular on the force's rugby team, but like many officers he escaped from the stress of the job by hiding in the fumes of a whiskey bottle.

Most weekends Anderson could hear the fighting from across the street and the sharp, cracking sound of a hand hitting soft skin. Anderson had been in enough interviews to recognise the sound of a fist meeting somebody's cheek. Evan's wife was a quiet English woman who walked around with the quizzical look of somebody who had ended up in Belfast and couldn't quite remember how she got there.

All Northern Irish policemen were trained in how to avoid being killed. One key check was to look under your car each morning to make sure that some nasty terrorists hadn't come to visit during the night. They liked to attach a motion-sensitive device to the bottom of the car which would explode once the vehicle moved.

Anderson was checking under his own car one bright March morning when he saw Evans emerge from across the road, unshaven and with his uniform jacket half on. His wife had followed him to the front door, shouting about unpaid bills and lack of sleep. Evans ignored her and jumped straight into his car.

Anderson was thrown against the front wall of his house before he even heard the sound of the explosion. He got to his feet and the street was silent apart from the pinging in his ears. The burning wreckage of Evans' car stood before him and Anderson found himself looking directly into Evans' wild eyes that stared back at him like a zombie from the shell of his scorched corpse. It was an image that would never leave him.

Evans' wife lay still in a pool of her own blood and Anderson stayed with her until the ambulance came. While he held her hand and watched the life disappear from her eyes, he re-evaluated his life in the RUC. He suddenly realised that traffic work and common or garden forensics were meaningless in a country where a civil war was ongoing. His talents could be better served going after the people who had killed Evans and his wife.

He submitted his application to join Special Branch that afternoon.

Anderson's colleagues returned with his bap, but he didn't have time to enjoy his prize before he was summoned into McGuinness's office by an urgent howl. He sat staring at the barbed-wire fence that lined the police station while his boss paced the room.

"Do they have any vacancies at the local garden centre, Anderson, or maybe in the slurry industry in Fermanagh?" McGuinness asked as he lit his fifteenth cigarette of the day.

"Why do you ask?"

"Because creating shit is all you're good for."

Anderson twisted uncomfortably in his seat. He had no idea where this conversation was headed, but he was sure it wasn't going to be a fun destination.

"There was a tape recorder in the car, Anderson. Did you know that?"

"Hmm, no I didn't," Anderson replied as he desperately tried to recall which car McGuinness was talking about. They rarely travelled in the same vehicle twice. Their job required them to rage against routine. Terrorists lurked outside waiting for the same car to make the same trip. McGuinness's office was lined with pictures of fallen Special Branch colleagues who had made the mistake of slipping into routine.

"The Fenian that the soldiers beat up in Newry, we drove his car back to the barracks and it turns out that he had a bloody tape recorder going that recorded our whole conversation."

"So what," said Anderson. "It was probably just you ranting on about Glentoran and dodgy refereeing decisions."

McGuinness stared out the window at the rain and the grey huddled masses scurrying down Knock Road. "We weren't talking about Glentoran that day. We were talking about Oriel and you used his real name."

Suddenly it all came back to Anderson. The mangled bodies of the dead soldiers, the deafening sound of helicopters ferrying the wounded to hospital and, in the midst of all this, an idiot

Southerner giving back chat to troopers who had just seen their buddies killed.

He also remembered the conversation in the car about Oriel, the RUC's prized spy in the headquarters of the Southern Gardai. Except Anderson didn't mention his real name. Until that day he didn't even know it. McGuinness was the one shouting his mouth off, bragging about how he was running a prized informer, an asset sitting right in the heart of Gardai headquarters and feeding back priceless intelligence on Garda activities and strategy and in particular the information from informers that the Garda hoarded and refused to share with their Northern colleagues.

But Anderson thought it prudent not to mention this. McGuinness wasn't fond of being told that he had done something wrong. He already had a wife and the Chief Constable to do that.

"So, what do you suggest we do?" Anderson asked.

"The tape he produced in court was a standard cassette. That means he still has the original mini tape from the recording device. There is no evidence that the Fenian knows the importance of the tape. If he did, he would have used it by now. Tried to blackmail us or would have given the tape to the Gardai. Which reminds me, call Oriel and see if there is any talk in Dublin about it. Don't mention that we've announced his name to the whole bloody world. The last thing we need is for him to go loco on us. Then see if you can contact those soldiers who beat the Fenian up. They need our help to get them off the assault charge. Call in a favour and get them to go south and see if they can find the tape. If we can get it back, we might be able to keep this thing under wraps."

Anderson took a moment to digest this request from his boss, which was essentially to break several laws and carry out a secret mission in a foreign country.

"If we're going to try to get the tape back, shouldn't we use

Special Branch? We've done jobs in the South before and know how to do tricky stuff like that."

"No," McGuinness thundered. "The fewer people in Special Branch who know about this the better. Let's keep this between ourselves. Oriel is our prized asset and I'd rather the Gardai found out about him than the fuckers in this office. Do a nice quick, clean job and move on. You and I are the only people who know about Oriel, and I want to keep it that way."

Anderson retreated to his desk and the remains of his bap. The fillings had gone cold and soggy, which reflected his mood. He dialled a Dublin number and said, "I have some information about graffiti." He could detect a faint sigh on the other end of the line.

"I'll call you back in five minutes," the voice said. It was going to be a long day.

———

Anderson was waiting by the payphone on Knock Road when it rang. He picked up the receiver and heard the familiar sound of coins dropping into a box when the person calling you was also on a payphone.

"How's the weather in Dublin?" he asked.

"The weather? Same as it is in Belfast. How big do you think this fucking island is?"

"Alright, Oriel. I was just making small talk. I just wanted to catch up, see if anything was going on."

He heard a slow exhalation of breath coming from the other side. He wondered if it was because it was Monday morning or if Oriel was always a grumpy bastard.

"Look, I told that boss of yours that I would contact you if anything came up. I don't like being contacted out of the blue. It's not a good look if I just slip out of the office. I work in Special

Branch. They are trained to be suspicious. And do you know how hard it is to find a fucking phone box in Phoenix Park?"

"No, I don't," said Anderson. "I haven't had the pleasure of visiting your fine city. Maybe I could meet you down there for the next rugby international. It would be pretty inconspicuous. And it would be good to put a face to a name."

There was another pause and for a second Anderson thought the line had gone dead.

"I'm more of a soccer man," Oriel said. "And to be honest I'd prefer to keep whatever bullshit relationship this is at arm's length."

"You're starting to sound like my wife."

"Look, I'm sure you didn't call up to talk about the weather and your wife," Oriel said. "I'm busy, so if there is nothing specific you want, I'm going to head back to work."

Anderson wondered how much he should disclose. He didn't want to make Oriel nervous because his experience of touts was that the more nervous they became, the more likely they were to do something dumb.

"I was just wondering if there was any chatter about a lad called James Morgan from Dublin. He was in court up here recently for assaulting a soldier at a checkpoint. We were wondering if he had any IRA connections and if your informers were talking about him. Maybe his name came up in your office."

"Look, most of the guys here are more interested in finding Shergar than they are about lads beating up soldiers. And Shergar has been missing for three years. I haven't heard anything about a chap called Morgan. We don't pay much attention to Southerners in court up the North. If they are dumb enough to go up there, then they deserve whatever they get. We're more interested in the ones from your part of the world that we want to get into court here."

"Alright," said Anderson. "I won't keep you. If you hear anything, you know where to find us."

He stepped back onto Knock Road and remembered that he still had to contact the soldiers. He knew he would have to do a bit of background research to find out their names and where they were based. But that was standard stuff and wouldn't arouse suspicion. Calling them from his desk phone was a different issue. He took it as a given that his phone and that of every other RUC officer was being recorded. As a result, he had tracked down a number of payphones in the vicinity of his base that he used for conversations which he categorised as sensitive.

As he headed back to the office to look up the soldier's contact details, a dark cloud appeared over Black Mountain, as it did most days. The rain was coming and Anderson lost his appetite to go back out and hunt down a payphone on Knock Road. He would take his chances and call the soldiers from his desk phone. And if the spooks were listening in, then good luck to them. There were worse things going on in Northern Ireland that day than a policeman asking three soldiers to break into a flat.

Anderson went back to his office and found out the names of the soldiers and that they were based at Crossmaglen army barracks. He knew the army were sticklers for protocol, so rather than asking for the soldier he wanted, he went through the commanding officer first.

The British Army were suckers for praise so Anderson knew that a little buttering up would do wonders.

"Major, pleasure to speak to you. Detective Anderson here from Head Office Special Branch. I'm working on that attack at Dromad checkpoint just before Christmas... yes that one. Tragic loss for your regiment. You have my sympathies. But listen, your lads did a great job in the clean-up. Very professional indeed. A credit to their regiment.

"Anyway, look I have to take statements from everyone who was there. You know what the paperwork is like in situations like this. I managed to speak to most of them on the day, but there was one guy, a Sergeant Hastie I think his name was. He was busy trying to keep morale up that day so I didn't want to interfere. He was doing a tremendous job. But I just need a quick chat with him to tie up all the loose ends."

Ten minutes later, Hastie had been dragged out of the snooker room and summoned to the phone.

"Sergeant Hastie. I'm with RUC Special Branch in Belfast. I believe you're in a bit of trouble with the beaks up at the courthouse."

There was a pause on the line before Hastie answered. "Look, if this is about that business in Belfast the other day, then I'd prefer to leave it to the Army brass. No offence bud, but I'm not going to say anything to the busies."

"Sorry Sergeant, I think you have the wrong end of the stick. I'm not here to question you. I'm here to help. I've seen the paperwork and the uniformed boys are going to lay charges on you and your two amigos any day now. And as the sergeant, they are going to come down on you like a town of bricks."

"Why is that? I never even touched the wee fucker."

"It's not the assault they are interested in; it's the cover-up. And they will hold you responsible for that."

Anderson let that sit for a moment. He guessed that Hastie was a career soldier who had reached the rank of sergeant through hard work and licking the arse of senior officers. And he wasn't likely to throw that away easily.

"But listen, Hastie. We're Special Branch. We see the bigger picture in this war against the IRA. And we can help you and your mates. If you help us, we can help you. Get these charges swept under the carpet and your top brass in Crossmaglen don't need to know anything about this."

"Alright, you got me listening. What can we do to make this go away?"

Anderson sensed that he had his man. Years of turning informers had taught him to recognise the point at which the adversary has given up hope and throws himself at your mercy. The mistake most officers make is to put the boot in at this point. Anderson was different. He knew that a kind word now would gain him a greater advantage. The informer would still turn but at this point he needed a friend more than anything and friends are far more yielding in the long term than enemies.

"The funny thing is, Hastie. You stumbled on a serious player last November. That Morgan guy you beat up is one of the most senior intelligence officers in the IRA. Through your actions, we had a big breakthrough in a case we've been following for three years."

"Fair enough. But what is it you want from us to get us off the hook? We might be army, but we're not hitmen for hire, in case that's what you're thinking. I know you busies think we're just a bunch of thugs, but some of us just want to get out of this shithole with as little hassle as possible."

"Hastie, I think you might have a misconception about me. I know that lots of shady shit goes on in Ulster, but I'm an old-fashioned cop and like to do things the right way. I just thought you could do us a favour. We have information to believe that this Morgan chap is sitting on a small tape that contains information that could be very useful to us. And we reckon he has hidden it in his flat in Dublin or his office. We want you and your two mates to go down there and turn those places over and find the tape. Make it look like a burglary."

"Why don't you just hire a couple of goons to do that?"

Anderson laughed, "I saw what you boys did to that Morgan chap at Dromad. Where would I find bigger goons?"

The line went silent again. "I'm pulling your leg, Sergeant. Look, we need a favour and you're in need of a bit of help. That's the way we like to work. We do something for you and you do something for us."

"Alright," said Hastie. "How do we do this?"

"I guess you guys socialise in Lisburn. There is a pub there called McEntegarts. Ask for Sammy behind the bar. He's on most nights. I'll leave a letter with him with all the addresses and any other information you need. It will have a phone number that you can reach me on. Call me when the job is done."

"Cool, we'll do this and then we're quits, yeah?" asked Hastie.

"Yep, I'll talk to the uniform guys and we'll find a way to make your little problem with the judiciary go away."

"Fair enough, big man," said Hastie. "But I didn't catch your name."

"That's because I didn't give you my name," said Anderson. "This is Ulster, remember. You are better off not knowing people's names."

With that, he hung up and headed back to McGuinness's office to fill him in on the calls.

———

"Okay, let's keep our heads down and act normally," McGuinness said. "We'll meet again next Monday when I hope you've got some good news for me. There is a tout down in interview room 4. He claims he knows the leadership structure of the Ballymurphy IRA. See if it tallies up with our list."

Anderson picked up his notepad and headed downstairs. Talking to touts was his least-favoured part of the job. It was hard to respect a person who would sell out their friends for a few quid. But they were a necessary part of the ugly business he had signed up for. He opened the door of the interrogation room and sat facing the unkempt and red-eyed figure of Joey Matthews. Joey wore a sweatshirt that was as grey as his face. "How's about ye?" he said as Anderson shuffled a chair in place.

"I'm grand, Joey, how are you?"

"I'll be better when I get out of here. The longer you're in here the more the boys assume you've been turned. So, if we can get this out of the way sharpish like, I'd really appreciate it."

Anderson paused, sat back and enjoyed Joey's increasing discomfort. "And what exactly is it that you want me to be sharpish about?"

Joey's eyes betrayed panic. He had explained all this to the cop who had arrested him and assumed the information had been passed on. Now it looked like he'd have to go through the whole thing again and he could be stuck here for hours. There were at least three IRA guys in the pub when he was lifted and they would have recorded the time he entered police custody and the time he got out. If you're not in front of a judge within six hours or back on the streets, then the IRA assume you are singing your head off to the police. If this dragged into a two-day interrogation session, he could picture the reception he'd get when he was dumped back on the streets. He even knew the house they would take him to in Ballymurphy and the assortment of medical and engineering instruments they would use during the discussion. The prospect terrified him.

"I've got information," he stuttered. "Stuff that could help ye boys. But I'm only squealing if you agree to drop the charges. The peeler who lifted me said that I needed to speak to Special Branch. That's you, I expect?"

Anderson nodded but again let the silence hang.

"So, what do you think?" Joey said. "You scratch my back and I'll scratch yours so to speak. I mean it's all rubbish that I was lifted for anyway. That wee lassie is just making up yarns for attention. I mean, I'm her uncle. I'd never touch her. I mean I've had a cuddle and all that, but I was only being friendly."

Anderson leaned across the table. "I'm not interested in what you did or didn't do with your niece, Joey. You said you had information, so let's hear it."

"So, we have a deal?" Joey said.

"Give me something interesting and I'll see what I can do."

Joey looked down at the handwritten sheet in front of him and pushed it across. "That's the full command structure of the IRA in Ballymurphy."

Anderson looked at the barely legible scrawl in front of him. "How do you know this?" he asked.

"Cause, I'm in second battalion. I've been to all the meetings. Saw all them boys there."

Anderson lifted the page and scanned the entries. "You realise you've just confessed to being a member of the IRA, a proscribed organisation, membership of which carries a four to seven-year prison sentence. Let's assume you get another five for fiddling with your twelve-year-old niece, then you're looking at about ten years in Crumlin Road jail where you'll be marked as a nonce from day one. Not a pretty outlook, Joey."

Joey's face turned a whiter shade of pale. "What? I thought we had a deal. I'm not going to prison. I can't. They'd kill me in there. Look I'll sign this, stand up in court and accuse this lot of killing Jesus Christ or anything else you want. I'll be the biggest grass you've ever seen. Please, mate. I can't go to jail."

Anderson leaned forward. So close that he could smell Joey's bad breath and see the individual beads of sweat on his forehead. "This is shit, Joey. I could get these names from last week's *Belfast*

Telegraph. They are so well known they should have their own TV show. I need you to tell me the secret ones. The ones that don't turn up to IRA funerals. The ones who don't drink in Republican clubs. The ones who don't provide security to Sinn Fein. You know what I want, Joey. I want to know about the guys that the IRA doesn't want me to know about. Now you'd better start giving me proper names or I'll have you in Crumlin Jail so fast, you won't have time to undress before they drag you into the showers to rape you."

Joey gulped. He needed to think fast, when the truth was that he was useless at even thinking slow. "I haven't got any more names, I swear. Those are the only folk I ever saw at meetings or on jobs. I was pretty low down the chain. I didn't get to meet any of these special agents you're on about."

Anderson walked to the back of the room where he had hung his jacket. He reached into the inside pocket and took out a pistol. He placed it in the centre of the table.

"Do you know what that is, Joey?"

"Is this a game?" Joey asked. "You're going to threaten to shoot me or ask me if I fancy playing Russian Roulette?"

"I thought you might recognise it," Anderson said as he circled the room. "It's an IRA gun. Was used on a bank job that I believe you took part in. The robbery was still going on when we turned up. The IRA boys scarpered, but in the confusion, they dropped this gun. I was first on the scene and I picked it up. I was mad with myself because I didn't follow procedure. I should have worn gloves, but I ended up getting my smudgy fingerprints all over it. Then I thought, what's the point in handing this into evidence. We'll never convict anyone for a bank job anyway and my fingerprints will invalidate any evidence the gun gave us.

"So, I stuck it in my pocket and thought that it would come in handy someday. And I reckon today is that day. See, what if I release you today. Send you out the front door so that the IRA knows you are on the outside. Then I pick you up later and bring you to a quiet country road near the border. I let you make your peace with whatever God you have. Let you apologise for being a dirty terrorist scum and a child molester and then quietly put a bullet in your head, just behind your left ear."

Anderson was standing behind Joey at this point and pointed his index finger into the sweaty skin behind Joey's ear.

"I know the IRA codes," Anderson continued. "So, I can phone it in. Say that you were a tout and you were executed in accordance with Central Council's standing orders. I'll say that a booby trap has been attached to your body. So, they'll let it lie there for two or three days while the rats nibble at your fleshy wounds. Then they'll do an autopsy and when they dig the bullet out of that undersized brain of yours, they'll trace it back to a known IRA gun. Special Branch will brief journalists behind the scenes to say that you were a tout, killed by your own people and that, consequently, Special Branch have zero interest in investigating the case. We'd be quite happy if the IRA kept shooting their own people, to be honest.

"Even the IRA will assume that they did it. You being a known nonce and all that. That's the great thing about the IRA's secretive cell structure. If something like this happens, everyone will assume it was done by another unit and because they are not allowed to talk to each other, that assumption will stay alive. It's the perfect crime, Joey. I get to get rid of a low life like you and the IRA get blamed for it."

Joey looked at the gun and then reached across it to retrieve the sheet of paper. He looked mournfully at Anderson. "Do you have a pen?" he asked. "I think I remember a few more names."

———

Anderson brought the sheet back to his desk, took a copy and then passed it to a constable to carry out some background checks on the names Joey had provided. He took no pleasure from turning criminals into informers. He leaned back in his chair and stretched his hands behind his head. The conversation with Oriel was replaying in his mind. How do the cops in the South not know about Morgan? He had been involved in a high-profile case with three British soldiers. The RUC Special Branch in Belfast keeps a close eye on court cases in the South that have a vague connection to the North. It prompted him to dig out a file from the bottom of his desk drawer. It had been given to him by McGuinness when he had first invited Anderson into his secret world.

The file contained notes of all the calls between Oriel and his masters in Belfast, going back to 1982. Anderson decided to read them from the start to try to gain an understanding of the spy he had never met. He was curious to try to understand what motivated Oriel. It wasn't money. Anderson had been responsible for dropping a quarterly envelope into an abandoned cottage just outside Dundalk and it contained less than they would pay a low-life drug dealer to spy on movements in the Divis Flats. Experience had shown him that people turn for a multitude of reasons. Perhaps Oriel had been passed over for promotion and wanted vengeance against his masters. Or was the IRA the real subject of his ire? Gardai had been killed by the IRA and Oriel may have been affected by this.

But the more Anderson read, the more he became convinced that Oriel was doing it simply because of the thrill of the game. Ireland in 1986 was full of spies, chancers and amateur adventurers. Oriel was just another one, trying to suck some blood from the beast that was the Northern troubles.

———

McEntegart's Bar in Lisburn was a favoured drinking haunt of British soldiers, off duty RUC men and the mysterious spooks of MI5, who would try desperately to fit in with the locals, while looking to the entire world as though they had just got off a bus from Basingstoke.

McEntegart understood his clientele, so the walls were lined with Glasgow Rangers posters and recruitment advertisements for the Ulster Defence Regiment. Tennent's was the only lager available and the pork scratchings were imported from Bradford.

Monday nights were generally quiet. A few policemen who had finished a weekend stake-out were huddled in one corner and two noisy helicopter pilots took out their aggression on the pool table.

Nobody noticed the three Scottish soldiers who slipped in and sat as far from the bar as possible.

Sergeant Hastie was the leader of the group and the one whose career was hanging most precariously after the incident at Dromad. He had just picked up the letter from Sammy behind the bar. He was now tasked with winning over his colleagues.

Private Burr went to get the beer.

"What's this about, Sarg?" said Private McMillan. "Are we in trouble again? You don't butter us up with beer unless there is bad news coming."

"Let's wait till Burr gets back," said Hastie. "He's not the brightest tool in the box and I'm going to have to explain things slowly to him. I don't want to do it twice."

Burr returned with the beer and three packets of crisps wedged between his teeth. "I gave the barman a fiver and got £1.20 back. £3.20 is not bad for three pints and three crisps," Burr said.

Hastie and McMillan exchanged a knowing look. Burr was a fearless soldier who would put himself on the line for his colleagues, but God forbid that he was left in charge of map alignments or ammunition allocation. Chances are they would end up in the Faroe Islands with two handguns and a ground-to-air missile.

Hastie cleared his throat. "You remember that business at the Newry checkpoint last month? The brass are looking at a court martial and there is the possibility of a court case for assault. And needless to say, none of us want to spend any time in a Northern Ireland jail. British soldiers would be as welcome there as Celtic fans at Ibrox. So, our only chance of getting off is to get those RUC guys to back up our story."

"What story is that?" Burr asked. "He gave me lip and I hit him. What's wrong with that?"

"Why did you join the army, Burr?" Hastie asked.

Burr leant backwards, furrowed his brow and caressed his philtrum with his lower lip.

"To shoot people and wear cool clothes I suppose."

"So, you didn't join to learn a trade or to see the world?"

Burr stared at the sergeant like he was a lunatic. "I joined after the Falklands," he said. "It looked brilliant. Going in a ship half way across the world to shoot Argies. Maybe getting to go in a helicopter. I joined up and what did I get? A poxy hut in a camp outside Edinburgh and a tour to this shithole. So no, I haven't learned a trade, unless toilet cleaning is a trade. That's the only thing I've got better at since I joined the army."

"Well, if you want to stay in the army, you'd better listen up. Those Pollis guys want a favour if they are going to stand up in court and say that Paddy hit you first. They want us to go down to Dublin and see if we can find a tape at the Paddy's flat."

"What sort of tape is it?" Burr asked. "The Police maybe. Do you get it, Mac? The police asking us to a find a tape of The

Police." Burr laughed so loudly that the helicopter pilots stopped and stared.

Hastie leaned closer. "It's one of those small Dictaphone tapes. I don't know what's on it, but it must be pretty saucy if the busies are this concerned about it. But that's not for us to worry about. We just need to get in and get out as quickly as possible. The Pollis man who called me gave me the laddie's address in Dublin and the place he works at. I can swing us a bit of leave for this weekend, and it turns out that there is a rugby match in Dublin, us against the Micks next week. So, three Scottish lads in Dublin wouldn't look amiss. I reckon if we pick up a few kilts and a couple of cheap rugby tops, we'll fit right in."

Burr interrupted, "I'm no wearin a fuckin dress man. I'm a Weegie, it's only soft tuechters that wear kilts."

McMillan smiled. "Have you heard the stories about the lassies in Dublin on rugby weekends? I hear the cannie resist the sight of a Scotsman's legs. Even a dolly like you could get off with one. Come on, it'll be a bit of fun and we can have a few bevvies if we get the job done quick."

"But Sarg, wouldn't this Mick have made a few copies of the tape? I know I would if I was in his shoes."

Hastie looked around the room. The pilots had moved on and the police in the corner were busy discussing their own torments. "The Pollis don't think he understands the importance of the tape or he would have been making noise about it. They think he's holding on to the original until our court case is held. I reckon if we can find this Dictaphone machine thing, we'll probably find the tape inside. Anyway, we only have to find one tape. I don't care if the wee fucker has thousands of copies."

Burr suddenly blurted, "Why don't we just kill him?"

The police group in the corner suddenly stopped talking and to a man turned to face the soldiers.

"We're just talkin about our CO," Hastie explained while forcing out a fake laugh. "He's a bastard but we love him really."

Then pulling Burr in closer he said, "Keep your mouth shut, Burr, before I shove my fist in it. We're already in enough trouble. I've got the meat heads taking statements from everyone in the squad and they are particularly interested in you Burr and those times your ammo didn't tally up when you got back to base. You have more skeletons in your cupboard than there are in Necropolis graveyard. So many, I wonder where you store your fuckin kit. You don't need any more attention. We'll no kill anyone. We'll make it look like a burglary. You're from Paisley, so that should be second nature to you."

Hastie went to get another round. The bar was empty now and McMillan and Burr had moved on to talking about football and what they would and wouldn't do to the honour and virtue of the Dublin women they intended to meet next weekend.

Hastie stood at the bar and thought how his career had ended up like this. Four years earlier he had received commendations for his actions at Port Stanley. His CO had talked about a commission and a cushy job back at headquarters. And here he was in a dingy bar in Lisburn with two idiots, planning a break-in to avoid being thrown out of the army altogether. He ordered a large Johnnie Walker while he waited for the pints to be served.

The next day Hastie met the other two squaddies in the canteen at Crossmaglen.

"I've got the kilts," he said. "And the laddie threw in a couple of sporrans as well. My aunty works for Jenners in Edinburgh. She said she'll knock off three rugby jerseys for us and post them over. I should get them tomorrow. So, we're all set for this weekend. We can get a lift on one of the choppers going up to Belfast and then get the train to Dublin from there."

Burr joined the army to fly in helicopters but too many

windswept flights over the South Armagh drumlins had dulled his enthusiasm.

"There's a train station in Dundalk that's only five miles away," he said. "Why don't we just go there?"

"Dundalk's in the South, ya dolly," said McMillan. "How do you propose we get there? Walk five miles across the border with our army crew-cut hair and Scottish accents? Or maybe we can ask the RAF boys if they'll land a chopper in the car park of the train station in Dundalk."

"We could get a taxi," Burr offered.

"You've been here five months, Burr," McMillan retorted. "And you haven't noticed that the local taxi firm doesn't take bookings from the British Army? Believe me, if three British soldiers got into a South Armagh taxi, we wouldn't be going to a train station. We'd be on a one-way trip to a meat factory in North Louth."

Hastie intervened. "I spoke to one of the officers. Had to bullshit him that I was interested in rugby when the truth is that I think they are all a bunch of posh poofters. He told me that there will be a boatload of Scottish fans coming into Belfast on Friday and getting the train south. We'll not be noticed if we mix in with those. We'll scope out his flat and his work on the Friday night. I wanted to use our walkie talkies but it's too much hassle trying to sign them out. So, we'll have to find a couple of phone boxes to stay in touch with each other. I'll go to his work and if he leaves there and looks like he's heading into town for the night, I'll phone you boys and you break into his flat. We want to make this look like a normal burglary, so don't hold back on smashing the door in and that sort of thing.

"Then if we can't find it at his flat, we'll hit his office the following night when nobody is around. With a bit of luck, it will turn up quickly and we can spend the evening on the beer. That officer I spoke to said that Leeson Street was the place to go. Apparently, the lassies will be dying to see what's under our kilts."

"And what will be under out kilts?" Burr asked, his face suddenly a mask of confusion.

"Nothing," McMillan answered. "That's the mark of a true Scotsman."

"Are ya nuts man?" said Burr. "I'm no swinging my willie around in March. Do you know what the cold does to your willy?"

It was Thursday afternoon in Morgan's office and things were starting to wind down. St Patrick had done them a favour and was celebrating his birthday on a Monday this year. That meant a long weekend to look forward to and traditionally that started with Thursday-night booze. The culchies, which was everyone who hailed from beyond Dublin, would normally head home for the weekend, particularly a bank holiday like this. So, Thursday was the night when his office crowd traditionally went out drinking.

Morgan knew that this would be a big night out and he impatiently watched the office clock crawl towards 5 pm, when he knew that somebody, not always the same person, would suggest going for a quiet pint. Morgan was seldom the direct recipient of this question, but he would tag along with the drinking party that quickly assembled and make his way to one of several establishments that they frequented.

This week, the crowd picked Neary's Pub as the starting point of their revelry. The city was humming with overseas visitors and rugby fans who had arrived early for Saturday's game.

"Let's start in the city centre tonight," said O'Leary from Accounts. He tended to be the alpha male on these outings and as long as it didn't involve crossing the river, the others were happy to go along with his plans.

"Town will be full of American cheerleaders who are here for the parade on Monday," he continued. "We can have a bit of craic with them. Pretend we're their long-lost cousins and that sort of thing."

"They are not going to shag you if they think you're a cousin, ya eejit," said Dunne from the sales team. He was a brash Dubliner, who saw drinking with the commoners from his office as an occupational hazard that had to be endured.

"Maybe shagging your cousin is acceptable in West Cork, where you come from, O'Leary," he said. "But we're a bit more sophisticated up here in the big smoke. Besides, it's not Americans with their big teeth and bad clothes that we should be chasing tonight. There is the small matter of a rugger game at Lansdowne on Saturday. It's Scotland, and you know what that means?"

"Five jocks sharing a pint because they are too mean to buy a round?" ventured O'Leary.

"No, ya bleedin' spanner. Town will be full of well-spoken, well-educated Scotsmen in kilts. And for reasons that I can't fathom, nothing attracts your well-heeled South Dublin princess into town as much as a man in a skirt. The nice girls of Rathgar and Foxrock will be putting on their best Brown Thomas frocks as we speak and lining up the bottles of Satzenbrau in Neary's waiting for the first train from Belfast to arrive."

O'Leary stopped on the corner of St Stephen's Green. "Let me get this right, Dunner. You want us to go to a pub so that we can watch good-looking women ogle at hairy-legged jocks?"

Dunne smiled in that patronising way that Dubliners have when addressing their colleagues from the provinces.

"Let the hare sit, boys, that's all we need to do." He scanned the crowd and registered only puzzled looks.

"You're all culchies. I thought you'd recognise an agricultural reference. If you want to catch a hare, you don't chase it around the field like a mad man. You just need to get close enough and then stay still. Eventually, the hare will get curious. Stop and slowly come towards you. These princesses from Terenure are the hares. We just need to be in the pub when they realise that underneath the kilts, these Scotsmen are all accountants and estate agents and not only that, they've been drinking since seven o'clock this morning when they got the ferry to Larne. We'll be there when that crushing sense of disappointment kicks in. It always pays to meet a woman when she's at a point of weakness."

Morgan listened to all this from his favoured position at the back of the group. He knew that Dunne was all talk and no action, but he could be funny at the same time and his heart was in the right place.

The quiet pint quickly descended into several noisy beers and Morgan was tolerated as a sometimes-amusing dour wit, but he found himself gradually drifting to the edge of the crowd when it became more interested in chatting up women than conversations on the merits of First War World poetry or the music of the Furey brothers.

At midnight, the pub closed and those still with a thirst for alcohol or the opposite sex drifted off to the basement clubs on Leeson Street, where a hefty entrance fee would gain you the right to buy expensive wine that would normally be used in mainland Europe as stock when making stew. Morgan hated those places, full of desperate men and women in their late thirties trying to fool the world that they were only there for a casual late drink.

Most weeks, he would find a way to slink off in the circuitous route between pub and nightclub. He knew he wouldn't really be missed. While his belly was full of beer at this stage, he always seemed to have enough room to squeeze in some fast food and Ranelagh had plenty of opportunities to satisfy his desires. This was where he had first tasted pizza and kebabs, but his favourite stop was the Golden Duck Chinese takeaway. Chicken and mushroom with chips was his go-to meal and he would finish it off back at his flat before setting his alarm clock to get up for work on Friday in five hours' time.

Morgan struggled into work the next day with a feeling that somebody had stolen his tongue while he slept and replaced it with one three times bigger. To his annoyance, he had spent the previous day with the auditors and nobody had looked at his correspondence while he was away. As a result, he had two days' worth to catch up on. It took him until 1 pm, by which stage he was starving and needed more nourishment than the standard cheese and tomato sandwich that he had brought in that morning could provide. He ventured over to Leeson Street, which offered pub grub to a level not found elsewhere in Dublin at the time.

Just as he rounded the corner from The Appian Way, a familiar voice called his name. He turned and there was Orla, fashionably adorned in a hand-knitted scarf with matching hat. Her cheeks glowed red in the March cold.

"Well, if it isn't my old buddy Mr Morgan. What have you been up to? I haven't seen you in months."

Morgan was momentarily stunned. He tried to find a witty response, but he needed advance notice and a team of writers to pull that off.

"Oh, nothing much. Spent Christmas Day with my family, just to remind myself why I left home in the first place. And I had to go to a court case in Belfast. But that's all sorted now."

Morgan felt that he had lost her attention at "Oh", but the

mention of the court case brought it back. Until then she had been looking over his shoulder while nodding absentmindedly.

"Wow, are you one of those diesel smugglers or are you secretly in the IRA?"

"Why don't you come for a drink tonight?" he said. "And I can explain everything."

For once his nervous enthusiasm worked and the hint of danger and excitement was enough to prick her interest.

"Okay, how about Kehoes on South Anne Street at 7 pm? I've got lots to tell you about. I met this new guy and he's lovely but he's wrecking my head. I want your advice on how to dump him."

She gave him the now-standard moisture-less peck on the cheek and jumped on a passing Number 11 bus. Morgan smiled. All he had to do was make his life seem interesting and Orla would come willingly, even on a normally out-of-bounds Friday night. He found a pub and ordered lunch and started to plan how he would present his court appearance. Turning it into a James Bond novel might be a stretch. But he could be a little liberal with the truth. His fight with the soldier could become a mass brawl involving Morgan and five; no let's make that twelve, soldiers. His interrogation could be remodelled on the Russian Roulette scene from *The Deer Hunter* and his discovery of the tape could be blown up into a technological masterpiece.

Morgan finished his Chicken Kiev and headed back to the office so that he could count the minutes down to 7 pm. He decided not to go home first, even though it was only a ten-minute walk. He had nothing better to change into and, besides, it would make him seem busier and more career minded to Orla.

———

Earlier that day, the soldiers caught a lift to Belfast and joined the throngs of drunken Scottish lawyers and accountants at Central Station. Hastie didn't want them to drink so that they would have clear heads for the job ahead. But Burr would find it easier to pass a kidney stone than an off licence and before Hastie could intervene, he had stocked up on a dozen cans of Special Brew and six packets of exotically flavoured crisps.

The train ride to Dublin was uneventful. The kilt and jersey trick worked and they blended into the blob of Caledonian drunkenness with only the occasional problem of having to make up a fictitious fee-paying rugby playing school when questioned about their rugby lineage. Hastie had found out from his officer friend that the only time a Scottish rugby fan would ever visit Glasgow was to catch the train to Stranraer. So, he made up a Glasgow school called St Cecil's and would embellish his tale with a rich history of his school's exploits in the West of Scotland rugby leagues.

They arrived at Connolly station and caught a taxi to the B&B that Hastie had booked in Ranelagh, just around the corner from Morgan's flat. They identified a call box nearby and Hastie made a note of the number. He left the other two there and made his way to Morgan's workplace. There was a call box across the street, but a ten-pence piece was wedged in the coin slot and despite his best efforts, Hastie couldn't budge it. After a momentary panic, he noticed that there was a payphone in the lobby of a pub nearby that offered a clean view of the front door of Morgan's workplace. He figured he would look less conspicuous if he bought a drink. "A pint of Tennent's, please" he said. The barman looked at him with an air of resignation, brought about by having served a hundred Scottish rugby fans that day.

"We don't do Tennent's, but I can do you a pint of Harp," the barman answered. Hastie had heard about Harp from a few of the soldiers who had been out in Belfast and who told tales of its stomach-churning capabilities. But he figured that one pint couldn't kill him so he ordered it and brought it to the window where he could keep an eye on the insurance office where Morgan worked. Ten minutes later a frail figure emerged buried inside a parka jacket and turned towards the city. Hastie caught a glimpse of a pale face beneath the parka hood and recognised it from the court case in Belfast. He ran to the payphone to alert his colleagues, only to find a heavy-set, balding figure hunched over the phone and engaged in a heated and evidently drunken conversation about horses.

Hastie waited for a second before tapping the drunk on the shoulder.

"Excuse me, big man, but I need to make an important call."

The drunk turned his head slowly and met Hastie's gaze.

"Is it more important than who is going to win the 4.10 at Leopardstown tomorrow? If it's not, you can fuck off."

The drunk turned back to face the wall and continued his incoherent muttering.

Hastie felt his temples begin to throb. He had told the guys he didn't want any violence, didn't want anything that would draw attention to them. But this dickhead was putting their whole plan at risk. He remembered the training he received before setting sail for the Falklands. The top brass were expecting a lot of hand-to-hand combat with the Argies, once the British ships had landed. They brought in a few Gurkhas to teach them the nasty arts of dealing with an enemy when you got too close to use your gun. Hastie thought the Gurkhas were mad bastards, but one trick they showed him had always stuck in his mind and he had the opportunity to practise it once or twice in the trenches above Goose Green.

He looked around to ensure that no one was watching and

then silently moved forward and pinched the drunk at a particular point on his neck. He discovered that the crucial artery was a little harder to find among the folds of fat on the drunk's head than they were on the skinny Argentinian conscripts he had met in 1982.

But eventually the pressure point was found and the drunk slumped to the floor. Hastie tidied him up so that he looked like just another Dublin alcoholic sleeping off his afternoon excesses. He took the piece of paper from his pocket on which he had scrawled the other phone box number.

Burr answered on the second ring. "We're good to go," said Hastie. "You two start and I'll be there in fifteen minutes."

A minute later, Burr had smashed the front door and was busy tearing open drawers.

In the meantime, Morgan was ordering his first pint, oblivious to the chaos into which his world was about to be thrown. He glanced at the TV in the pub. A newsflash was asking all key holders on Prince William Road in Lisburn to return to their properties and to check for explosives.

The occupier of the neighbouring stool turned to Morgan and said, "Things might be shite down here but at least it's not as fucked up as up there."

"You're right," said Morgan as he nuzzled his pint. "Sometimes there is a lot to be said for a quiet life."

He had left the office at 6.45 pm, making a point of passing his boss's office to say goodnight and so as to register that he was working late. He had almost made it to the front door when the boss called him back. He was on the phone and motioned with a single raised index finger that Morgan should wait in the doorway.

As Morgan took up station as requested, the boss turned his back to him and started speaking into the phone in hushed tones. Morgan was irritated at being kept back for no obvious reason but was also curious as to who his boss might be speaking to. It couldn't be Head Office. They rarely worked late any night and certainly not on Fridays. And Morgan was pretty sure it wasn't a client. His boss was a political player, adept at licking the backside of any senior internal executive who could oil the wheels of his career development. He saw clients as an irritation to be avoided whenever possible.

Morgan caught the eye of his boss in the window reflection. It was a cold and scornful look and Morgan suddenly had the sensation that whoever the boss's secret conversation was with, he was the subject. He was filled with a sense of unease and racked his brain for the reason. Did his boss know of the events in Newry and the subsequent court case or, worse still, did he know about Orla and was sabotaging Morgan's only Friday-night date?

The minutes ticked by, interspersed with regular forced coughing from Morgan to try to catch the boss's attention. Finally, the boss put his hand over the receiver.

"Morgan, that commission run was a disaster. I need you to stay late tonight and reconcile it."

"It looked alright to me, boss. I can give it another look over on Tuesday."

"Do you know what the fucking unemployment rate is in Ireland? If you don't want to be adding to that number, get back to your fucking desk and do that reconciliation."

Morgan slunk back to his desk like a puppy who had been chastised for peeing indoors. He opened the commission file and pondered what was more important. Job security or watching Orla laugh and throw her hair back as he regaled her with his witty tales. His experience in the Belfast court had sparked a flicker of rebellion in his otherwise conservative heart. He closed the file and skipped down the back stairs and left by the fire exit.

He didn't notice the gentlemen with a crew cut staring at him from across the street. He headed towards the city centre and the sparkling Christmas lights that still adorned Grafton Street, even though it was mid-March.

He made it to Kehoes early so he could he pick a seat that meant Orla would have to look at him or the blank wall behind. He wasn't confident that she wouldn't find the wall more interesting. Orla arrived late as was her want and launched into a breathless summary of traffic and weather-related issues.

By 10 pm Morgan had consumed enough Guinness to overcome his nervousness. Unfortunately, his new-found exuberance came at a cost. Flatulence is a by-product of Arthur Guinness's popular beer and Orla didn't appreciate being downwind in these situations. She made some motions to leave, picking up her handbag and biting her lip as she mentally rehearsed her excuse for disappointing Morgan for the umpteenth time. They had spent the night discussing her latest boyfriend. How he was too clingy and had ridiculous dress sense. Morgan had done his best to offer a consoling ear while internally burning with desire to swap places with that soon to be dumped boyfriend. In his mind, a night of being Orla's lover would be worth a cruel break-up the following morning.

As they made their way through the busy Friday-night crowd and headed for the exit, Orla suddenly remembered that she hadn't heard Morgan's court story. The cold night air hit Morgan with a bang. Suddenly the beer was swirling around his brain and his nostrils were filled with the alluring aroma of Charlie perfume (which Orla had received as a Christmas present from her soon to be ex-boyfriend). He felt giddy and before he could talk himself out of it, he blurted out a suggestion.

"Why don't we grab a takeaway and go back to my place so that we can discuss it?"

To his amazement, Orla accepted and soon they were sitting in a beaten-up Ford Cortina taxi and heading for Ranelagh. As the car rocked its way along the canal, Orla placed her hand tantalisingly close to his. He thought about reaching out to touch it, but his confidence suddenly deserted him and he felt the benefit of the alcohol seeping from his body to be replaced by nausea and a rumbling stomach. He stared out the window at Kavanagh's canal-bank seat and tried to rehearse some poetry that he would use to impress Orla once he had her settled on his settee.

"Do you normally leave your front door open?" Orla asked as they descended the stairs to his flat. Morgan froze. He was fastidious about security ever since his bicycle had been stolen in primary school and he had a compulsion to descend the stairs and return to his flat every time he left just to check that the door was locked.

He inched his way gingerly down the steps until a sound from inside the flat made him freeze.

"They are still inside," he whispered to Orla who was stationed at the top of the stairs with her hands planted on her hips.

"Well, what are you going to do?" she asked.

Morgan looked confused. He always considered himself more of a lover than a fighter and a crap lover at that. His last physical fight was in primary school when he just about got the better of a kid from his class who had polio and had his left leg in a brace.

Orla didn't wait for a response, she strode purposely down the steps, past the now shaking figure of Morgan and stood in the doorway. Then she looked back and called out loudly.

"What was that, Sergeant? You have twenty armed Gardai on the way? Ah yes, I can see them coming down the road now."

The door was flung open and three dark figures raced out. Orla stood to the side but Morgan was still transfixed on the steps. The first figure pushed him aside and as he fell, he tripped the second burglar and they landed together in a heap. As they struggled apart, Morgan noticed that his head appeared to be trapped inside a skirt. But he could see in the tangerine street light that the skirt wearer wasn't sporting any underwear. And the view only added to Morgan's confusion.

The burglar forced himself forward and pushed Morgan aside. As he did, the third figure appeared in the doorway. As Morgan stumbled to his feet, they came eye to eye.

"We'll be back, big man. We're no leaving till we get what we came for."

With that, the strangers were gone and Morgan stared at them as they ran down the street. Orla appeared by his side and squeezed his hand. But Morgan was too numb to register this momentous development in their constant false-dawn relationship.

"Looks like you've been burgled by three men wearing kilts. That's not something you see every day. I wonder what they were wearing underneath?"

The blood had drained from Morgan's face and he suddenly felt the late-night chill.

"Trust me, Orla, you don't want to know. I've got an image lodged in my head that no amount of alcohol will ever force out."

The flat was in darkness and as he reached for the light switch, he was suddenly engulfed with fear, realising that other intruders might still be within. As the light came up, he readied himself for a confrontation. But none arose. Morgan's muscles relaxed but his heart sank as he surveyed the chaos before him. His lovingly collected LPs lay cracked and broken, with their sleeves scattered to distant corners of the room like leaves in a storm. His TV lay smashed on the floor like a beached whale that had been plundered by hungry natives.

It clearly wasn't a normal burglary. The only things of value that Morgan owned lay broken before him.

"I didn't realise you were this untidy," Orla remarked with a casual air that roused Morgan from his shock.

"They were looking for something," he replied and as he said these words, he suddenly thought of the tape secreted in his kitchen-wall cavity. He stepped carefully over broken glass and crockery towards the extractor fan. It looked untouched and when he peeled it back a comforting cloud of dust wafted out. The tape was still there and Morgan let out of deep breath of relief.

"If that's what they were looking for, you know they'll be back."

Morgan turned and Orla was standing behind him. His secret was no longer his alone.

5

"Well, I'd better call the cops," Morgan said. "Although I'll be lucky to get anyone to answer the phone at this time of night. There is a phone box at the end of the street. I'll be back in a minute."

He suddenly felt a pang of guilt. "Maybe you'd like to come with me; it doesn't feel particularly safe here."

"No, I'll wait here," Orla said. "Your door is busted, so somebody needs to mind your stuff."

"I'm not the luckiest guy in the world. But I doubt if I'd be unlucky enough to be burgled twice in the same night."

"It's cool," she said. "I'll wait here and I'll be careful not to touch anything. The cops will probably want to sweep the place for fingerprints."

Morgan looked at her. She was beautiful and clever but at the same time she could also be incredibly dumb.

"I work in insurance," he said. "I deal with burglary claims every day. The Guards don't have it on their priority list. They are too busy tailing anti-American protesters and people trying to smuggle in contraceptives. If you get burgled, you just call them and give them a list of what was stolen and they type it up and give out a file number for your insurance claim. You could say that you were minding the Mona Lisa on behalf of the Musée de Louvre for the night and they wouldn't bat an eyelid. I doubt if they ever bother to visit the crime scene, never mind look for fingerprints. Anyway, this place would be covered with prints from all the friends I have visiting."

"You don't have any friends," she said bluntly, in that way she had of not intending malice but inflicting it nonetheless.

Morgan frowned. "You've been reading too many of those spy novels," he said. "I don't know if it's even worth reporting this to the cops. It doesn't look as though anything was taken."

He picked up his Walkman from the coffee table and checked to see that his prized Stockton's Wing tape was still inside.

"No, it seems that your burglars came to the perfectly understandable conclusion that your stuff isn't worth nicking or they were looking for something. That tape perhaps. I have a cousin who is a Ban Gardai. She works in Head Office in Phoenix Park. I meet her every Sunday at Mass. If you want, I can mention it to her. She might know a special unit that looks into stuff like this."

Morgan looked at her suspiciously. Orla always seemed to have a friend or relation in a key role that could be called upon in case of emergency. It was how she'd landed a job at one of the city's biggest law firms. It was how she was always able to get tickets for rugby internationals and could mysteriously conjure up a taxi in the city centre at 2 am when the rest of the population were wandering around like the lost tribe of Israel trying to find some transport home. It was the social capital that came with growing up in the right part of South Dublin and it always made Morgan feel like an interloper and vaguely inferior.

"You still go to Mass?"

"You have your messy little bachelor pad here. I still live at home with Mammy and Daddy. They don't make many rules but no carnal knowledge under their roof and weekly attendance at St Patrick's is still in force."

"That's a shame," he said. "I was looking forward to an invitation to Chez Orla's."

She didn't answer, which was her stock response when Morgan tried to be risqué.

"I stopped going to Mass when I spotted too many inconsistencies in the Bible," he said. "Like, why did Saint Paul keep writing to the Corinthians, when there is no evidence that they ever wrote back."

She flung him a withering look. His attempts at being clever never worked with Orla.

Nevertheless, he soldiered on. "I mean he never starts any of his letters with 'I refer to yours of the 14th inst.' Or says 'It was great to hear about your holiday in Crete'."

Orla sighed and her eyelids drooped. Morgan identified the sign language clearly. Yet again, she was telling him that he was trying too hard.

"Sorry," he said. "It would be great if you could speak to your cousin and maybe she could call me at work."

After Orla went home on Friday night, he tried to barricade his front door as best as he could. He slept fitfully, waking with every cat cry in the alleyway outside or the meaningless mutterings of drunks stumbling past his window.

Friday night drifted into Saturday morning and he woke late feeling as though his life had taken a wild turn on the road and he wasn't in charge of the steering wheel. He lay in bed for an age, torn between the desire to snuggle deeper under the warm duvet or to tiptoe across the frozen lino to the bathroom where he could relieve his aching bladder.

The only source of heat in his meagre flat was a Superser Heater in the kitchen, which even when lit gave no benefit to the bedroom. The cold seeped in through the cracked window frames and on March mornings like this, the bedroom felt like a fridge.

He eventually got up around lunchtime, to discover that his kitchen was hopelessly under-resourced in the matter of basic food provisions, and this spurred him into a trip into the city centre with the intention of stocking up on groceries and perhaps adding an item or two of clothing to his meagre wardrobe. His stock of five white Dunnes Stores shirts were gradually fading to a dirty, pigeon-coloured grey with collars so frayed they could grate cheese.

In the event, he made the mistake of visiting Hodges Figgis bookshop on Dawson Street first and got lost in their history and poetry departments. He emerged three hours later with an obscure paperback but with his kitchen and wardrobe sadly not replenished.

Saturday nights were the toughest time of the week for Morgan. He left Tipperary for the bright lights of Dublin with the intent of discovering a world that didn't really exist. Or, at least, did not exist in the orbit in which he moved. He had few friends outside of work and even they were not the kind who would tolerate his company outside of the defined environment of Thursday night. The bus to Tipperary was always an option, but he saw that as an admission of failure, turning up in his local pub to be met with raised eyebrows and muttered mocking. Besides, the bus was full of students and he couldn't stand their endless enthusiasm and youthful energy. He was only in his mid-twenties, but the bus to Thurles on a Saturday evening had a way of making him feel old.

He could find things to do during the week, but Saturday night was a gaping hole waiting to be filled with self-doubt and regret.

He tried occasionally to go to the movies on his own, particularly if the Classic Cinema in Harold's Cross was showing something European. But he struggled to get over the awkwardness of being penned between passion-filled couples who were using the dark interior of the theatre to fondle each other in ways they couldn't do at home in front of their parents.

Luckily on this occasion a distant cousin from back home had called to say he was in Dublin for the weekend and asked Morgan if he could show him around. They arranged to meet in Kehoes at 8 pm and Morgan spent the afternoon planning the evening itinerary.

He thought about going home to freshen up first, but the events of the previous night weighed heavily on his mind and he couldn't face the prospect of wading through the wreckage of his possessions and wondering who had violated his flat and why. Orla's doom-laden prediction that if they didn't find what they were looking for, they would almost certainly be back was troubling him, particularly as the city was full of kilt-wearing Scotsmen, all of whom seemed to be staring suspiciously at him.

He called into a bar for a beer and to try to formulate his thoughts. Before he realised, it was 7.45 pm and the decision was made for him. He would avoid his flat until he was inebriated enough to face it.

He liked to impress visitors with his detailed knowledge of Dublin's nightlife. Where to source the best burger after midnight, where to find impromptu Trad sessions and most importantly, where to secure late-night alcohol in a thirsty city where closing time was officially 11 pm.

He gathered this knowledge, not from experience, but from the pages of *In Dublin*, which he bought each week to plan nights out that he never went on.

However, it came in useful when he met his cousin. They

started in Kehoes, sampled some Irish music in O'Donoghues, had a few tasty pints of Guinness in Mulligans and then ended up in Lansdowne Rugby Club at midnight when the Saturday-night disco kicked off.

The queue to get in was full of frauds. Giddy teenagers trying desperately to look older than they actually were and rugby fans who hadn't made it home from that afternoon's game and were gently swaying in the breeze and clinging to the last vestige of sobriety until they got past the bouncers and were safely inside.

Scottish accents were plentiful, so Morgan didn't particularly notice the three kilt-wearing gentlemen standing further back in the queue. Their hair was shorter than anyone else around them and they lacked the wild abandonment that was etched on all the other faces. But with their kilts and dark blue jerseys, they looked like just another group of Scottish rugby fans ready to tease the females of South Dublin with the mystery of what may be beneath their kilt.

Morgan and his cousin paid their admission charge and entered into the dark and sweaty interior.

The cousin took to the dance floor with the enthusiasm of a boy from the country that had just discovered the music of Culture Club and Duran Duran. Morgan wasn't really into dancing, so he found a perch at the corner of the bar and took up station there where he could survey the assembled mass of drunken Scottish rugby fans, students in faded chinos and earnest woollen tank tops and thirty-somethings desperately trying to cling to their youth.

The soldiers reached the front of queue when a large tattooed arm blocked their path.

"What's the problem, big man?" Hastie asked.

The bouncer pointed to Hastie's footwear.

"Sorry, bud. No trainers."

"Are ya fuckin serious, man? We're rugby fans. This is how we dress. It's part of our culture."

The bouncer took a step to the side so that he completely blocked the door. Two of his colleagues edged closer to offer support. They stood together with their arms folded and glowered at the soldiers.

"I don't know much about your culture, buddy. But all your other mates that turned up in skirts had the decency to wear black shoes and socks. You muppets are wearing Adidas Rom trainers. And I'm pretty sure they weren't around three hundred years ago when you were fighting the English. Now, fuck off before you get a toe of my boot up your hole."

Hastie made a quick assessment and figured that discretion was the better part of valour.

"Come on, lads" he said. "I wouldn't give my money to this bunch of spud eaters anyway."

They regrouped on the training pitch beside the clubhouse.

"There's more than one way into a club," McMillan said. "There's probably a fire exit or a toilet window round the back. We should have a look."

The fire exit was locked, but there was toilet window slightly ajar.

"Right, Burr. You're the smallest," said Hastie. "We'll give you a hoosh up and when you get in, you can open the emergency exit and let us in. Go in feet first. There will be a sink or something like that on the other side."

Hastie and McMillan lifted Burr up and pushed him through the window, Adidas Rom trainers leading the way.

"Bollix. Stop!" Burr shouted. His kilt had caught on the window latch. But it was too late. The momentum pushed him forward and he could hear the sound of fabric ripping as he landed on the bathroom floor. He turned around to face three open-mouthed young ladies standing at the sinks. They screamed simultaneously in a pitch that could be heard over the throbbing rock music coming from the disco in the main hall.

It didn't take long for the news to reach the bouncers at the main door.

"There's a bloke in the ladies with nothing on."

The bouncers raced inside and found Burr huddled in a cubicle trying to hide his embarrassment from a group of giggling girls who had gathered in the bathroom.

The head bouncer recognised the trainers straight away. "I thought I told you pricks to fuck off. Right lads, let's teach this Jock a lesson. We'll take him out the back through the fire exit."

Hastie and McMillan were listening on the other side of the window and they didn't need to confer. Burr might be an idiot, but he was their idiot and one thing the army beat into you was that you never abandon a colleague. They got to the emergency exit just as it burst open and the three bouncers emerged with Burr.

"Right lads," Hastie said. "We can do this the easy way or the fun way. You probably realise that we're soldiers. You might be big cunts, but we're trained for this shit. So, you can let our buddy go and we'll tiptoe off into the night. Or you can come and have a go and see what we did to those Argie conscripts when we came across their trenches. I've had a shitty week and I honestly don't care which of those options you take."

The head bouncer stared at Hastie for a moment. His gut wanted him to fight. He could picture future nights in his local pub when the Republican songs were being sang. He could regale his friends with tales of the night they kicked the shit out of three British soldiers. But his head told him that he had a job to do.

He flung Burr towards Hastie. "Fuck off then. And the next time I see you, I hope it's down the barrel of an Armalite."

The soldiers walked back to their lodgings. Burr had found a bin liner and had fashioned a temporary kilt for himself.

"I'll tell you what, lads," he said. "I'd rather face a terrorist than face those lassies laughing at me again."

They stopped at the corner of Appian Way and Hastie checked a hand-sketched map that he had in his pocket.

"Let's do one more job, lads. Then we can get out of this fuckin' dump for good."

———

Morgan had watched Burr being dragged through the disco. He had a vague recollection of seeing that face before, but he couldn't remember where. A girl stood beside him waiting to be served and threw him a shy smile. He was desperate to say something witty or vaguely intelligent, but his confidence had gone into hiding. He realised that he could only talk to girls if he had hit that sweet spot between drinking enough to work up Dutch courage and not drinking so much that he would be incoherent. As he swallowed his ninth pint of Guinness of the evening, he realised that he was comfortably in the latter category, but not so far gone that he didn't have the wits to realise this.

At 2 am the lights came up and the national anthem was played. Morgan stood to attention and along with everyone else he pretended to know the words and sing along. He found his cousin wrapped in the arms of a pretty little nurse who was doing a detailed inspection of the inside of his mouth with her tongue. Morgan left him to it and queued for his coat before joining the throngs outside who were looking for a taxi.

He gave up after twenty minutes when he remembered that in the regulated world of the Dublin taxi industry, a cab at 2 am on a Saturday night was as common as Hayley's comet.

He set off on foot as another shower of rain raced in from the Irish Sea and the wind whipped up crisp packets and plastic bags. As he turned the corner into Appian Way, he passed his office and thought he saw the flicker of torches through one of the windows. He stopped to see if he could see them again when a car passed at speed directly through the puddle that Morgan was standing beside. The water soaked his trousers and made him instantly forget the torchlight.

He raced home, spurning even the tempting lights of the Golden Duck, and was asleep before his head hit the pillow.

Sunday morning was surprisingly warm and the first signs of spring crept through Morgan's bedroom window, reminding him that he'd forgotten to close the blinds again. At least the lino felt snug under his feet as he stumbled sleepily into the bathroom for his morning bladder evacuation.

He thought about going back to bed, but the sunlight put a spring in his step and he quickly dressed and headed to the corner shop. He bought milk and the *Sunday Independent*, and as he walked back up the hill to his flat, he heard the sound of bells from the Church of Mary Immaculate and it momentarily brought him back to his childhood. He had stopped believing in God around the time of his break-up with his childhood sweetheart when it dawned on Morgan that God showed no obvious signs of believing in him. But he still liked the rituals and comfort of the Church. The smell of incense on a dark night, a choir singing 'Ave Maria' on a Christmas morning or the comfort of a handshake with a stranger during the sign of peace.

He thought he might go to Mass, but then the sports section of the paper caught his eye. They were doing a colour preview of the 1986 World Cup and that was much more enticing.

While the drawstrings of the Church weren't strong enough to pull him into Mass, they were still sufficient to tickle his inherent guilt. And he knew that the only way to satisfy that itch was to ring his mother. He walked to the phone box at the end of the street, but the floor was covered in vomit and discarded takeaway containers. Two pigeons were greedily working their way through the contents and Morgan's stomach wasn't up to the challenge. So, he headed to Smyth's Pub in Ranelagh, ordered a pint of Guinness and settled on a stool behind a payphone.

His father answered, but being a Tipperary farmer, his conversation didn't extend beyond hurling. As it was the off-season, that didn't last long. His mother took over and started by listing the people who had died in the locality since they last spoke. "You'll never guess who died," she said. "Mini Sorahan, and her only seventy-four."

Morgan had no idea who Mini Sorahan was. After a few fruitless guesses, his mother gave him a clue.

"You know Mini. She lived in the house with the green roof at the crossroads. You and your brother used to prog apples there every September."

"You mean Mini Callan," he said, calling her by her married name. "She would have got married about fifty years ago; how would I know her maiden name? Anyway, what did she die of?" Morgan asked. The line went silent, but he was sure he could hear wheels turning in his mother's head.

"I think she died of a Tuesday," his mother replied. "But it was a couple of weeks ago, so I don't remember."

Morgan changed the subject to his siblings and spent ten minutes listening to his mother's complaints about lack of phone calls, waster boyfriends and his brother buying a new car when he didn't have an arse in his trousers.

He was going to mention the court case and the break-in but knew that would result in his mother appearing on his doorstep the next day. They exchanged the usual banalities about weather and general health and then said goodbye.

Morgan brought his pint to the counter. He passed the snug where the three soldiers were huddled over half-finished pints with the hoods of their coats pulled up. Morgan didn't notice them. He was thinking about Orla and how magnificent she had been on Friday night. He thought about calling her, but he remembered that her family always had a formal Sunday dinner and he didn't want to interrupt.

He had planned to have only one beer, as a hair of the dog cure. But it went down very easily and he realised that he had the 'gooh'. That inexplicable urge to drink beer that comes after three nights of overindulgence.

"Have yous no home to go to?" the barman roared as he turned off the TV and casually threw a dirty tea towel over the beer taps. It was 2 pm and the start of 'Holy Hour'. The Church-imposed rule that shut pubs for two hours every Sunday to force all the patrons to go home for their dinner. Morgan cursed his timing. The Guinness had gone down very smoothly and he was gagging for another.

The barman moved behind him, tidying the stools. He leaned over and whispered into Morgan's ear.

"If you want to stay on, there is a card game kicking off in the back room. But don't let those feckin students see you, or they'll all want more gargle."

Morgan nodded without making eye contact. Pubs were dens of conspiracy and Morgan realised that his attendance at the monthly table quiz and purchase of tickets in the turkey raffle at Christmas was paying dividends. He put on his coat and headed for the toilet. Then at the last minute, he turned left and entered the back room.

The three soldiers immediately rose to follow Morgan but were stopped by the barman before they could get past the bar.

"Where do you boys think you're going?" he asked.

"Wherever he went," said Hastie. "I presume it's where you get more beer."

"Are you lads from Scotland then?" the barman asked, noting their accent.

"We are, yeah," said Hastie. "Just over the match."

"Well, you can fuck off then. It's regulars only in the back room."

Hastie edged closer until he could smell the beer from the barman's apron.

"Look buddy, I'm a bit pissed off at people telling me to fuck off in this city. If you don't get out of the way, I'll shove that fuckin' apron up your arse."

The barman looked over at the only other customer left in the pub, a middle-aged man staring into a beer as though it was his only source of affection.

"Sergeant Duffy. Will you give your colleagues a call down at the Garda Station and tell them we're having a few problems with some of our Scottish visitors?"

Duffy looked up with hollowed eyes but dutifully slouched off towards the phone box.

Hastie exhaled slowly and shook his head. "Come on lads," he said. "I know when we're not wanted."

In the back room, the curtains were drawn and four older men were spread around the room, each drinking alone and nursing a pint of Guinness as though it were a newborn calf.

"Is this where the poker game is taking place?" Morgan asked as he stood in the doorway.

"Were you born in a feckin field, ya eejit? Come in and close that feckin door and keep the heat in. Poker? Sure, we don't even have a deck of cards, ya amadain."

The other three didn't even look up and clung to their pints as though their life depended on it. Morgan ordered a beer and found a corner table to take up his lonely station. This is what I've become, he thought. The sort of person who craves a lock-in on a Sunday afternoon, so he could drink alone and contemplate his navel. Mind you, he had a lot of contemplation to do. His simple life had been turned upside down with the court case, the tape and the break-in. He looked around the room and realised that his companions probably had their own stories to tell. Broken marriages, unemployment, or struggles with their sexuality in a country that had only just come to terms with heterosexual sex. But he guessed that they were in no mood to talk about it and Morgan certainly was not going to ask.

He knew the unwritten rules of the back room of pubs during Holy Hour. That its true meaning was in its name. It was where men who had no Sunday dinner to go to came to reflect and confess their many sins. But instead of doing it to a priest, they did it silently to the disappearing suds in a dirty beer glass.

At 4 pm the doors were opened again and the pub filled with students and tourists. Morgan took up station at his stool at the bar and watched TV with the sound turned down. He stayed until closing time and then gorged on takeaway food on the way home when he remembered that he hadn't eaten since breakfast.

By Monday, he had drunk enough to float a battleship, so he wandered into town to watch the parade and to grab some fast food to sooth his hangover. St Stephen's Green was filled with fifteen-year-olds greedily gulping down cans of warm Harp Lager. The smell of beer caught in Morgan's throat and for a moment he thought he was going to throw up. He found a bench in the park and buried his head in his hands. That didn't work, so he figured a brisk walk might clear his head and he forced his weary bones off the bench and headed down to see the parade.

———

"What's the plan now, Sarg?" McMillan asked as the soldiers drank tea beside Christchurch Cathedral and looked out on another grey Dublin morning. "We're due back at base tonight."

"I don't know, boys. I'll talk to the busies and see if they'll leave it as it is. We've done our best, I reckon. We've torn his flat and office apart. I thought by following him all weekend he might lead us to a lock-up garage or something, but how was I to know the wee laddie would just go on the piss for three days? We Scots can put away a brew or two but he takes it to the next level. Anyway, drink up lads and we'll head back to the train station."

The soldiers headed down Dame Street towards Connolly Station. The street was lined with people, festooned with shamrock and adorned in various combinations of green, white and orange. They were awaiting the parade which they could hear approaching from the distance.

"It's like being at a fuckin Celtic home game," Burr muttered as they strode purposefully towards the city centre.

Morgan was coming from the opposite direction. He came down Grafton Street and met the parade as it passed through College Green. A group of leotard-wearing American majorettes were just passing, twirling batons into the damp air as they gritted their teeth against the crippling cold. Toddlers were chasing green balloons through oily puddles while miserable-looking leprechauns distributed sweets to the crowd.

The forced gaiety was cloying and Morgan had had enough. He was about to leave when he noticed the Tipperary float coming around the corner. Four guys in tattered GAA shirts stood around a large grey papier-mâché blob.

"Morgan, is that you? Jaysus, I've haven't seen you since school. How's it hangin? It's Benny Toland here. Do you not remember me?"

Morgan had very few memories of school. He had drifted on the periphery most of time, smart enough to avoid too much hassle from the teachers, but not sporty enough to fit in with the pupils. He preferred poetry to hurling and that was enough to get him lined up in the sights of the likes of Benny Toland.

"Jump on board, Morgan. You're a pale imitation of a Tipp man, but one of us all the same."

"Ah, it's not really my thing, Benny. I was just heading home."

"Come on man. We're heading in the same direction anyway. We'll give you a lift."

Morgan reluctantly climbed up on the float and shook hands with the other occupants.

"So, are you a Pats man, like Benny?" one of them asked. "They'll be shite this year now that Tobin has fucked off to Boston."

Morgan had no idea what he was talking about but nodded affirmatively anyway.

"What's that thing in the middle?" he asked.

Benny looked around and then back to Morgan. "That's the Rock of Cashel, ya eejit. How long have you been away from Tipp?"

Morgan looked at the crowd and noticed small children and tourists waving at him and wondered what sort of character they assumed he was. The rain started to come down in sideways sheets and while the papier-mâché rock seemed to wilt a little, they all huddled below for protection.

The soldiers were passing the Central Bank when McMillan stopped and pointed at an oncoming float.

"Sarg, look. It's him. What will we do? This could be a secret handover of the tape or something like that."

He pointed at the Tipperary float where Morgan was huddled with his hands buried in his jean pockets and seemed deep in conversation with his companions.

Hastie bit his lip and tried to quickly assess his options. The police contact had stressed that they should not arouse suspicion. To make the break-in look like a normal burglary and to do nothing that would spook Morgan and encourage him to contact the Dublin Police. But Hastie was a soldier, trained to react to changes on the battlefield. Besides, he was sick of trailing Morgan around Dublin like a third-rate private eye and he was also worried about returning north with nothing to show for the trip south other than a possible kidney infection derived from wearing a kilt all weekend.

"Fuck it, let's grab him," he said. "We'll jump on the float behind his and wait till he gets off. Then we'll grab him once we get away from this crowd."

They let the float pass and then jumped on the one behind it. Hastie climbed up first and was met by a heavy-set guy squeezed into a Brazil football kit.

"Where are you going, bud?" he asked.

Hastie did a quick reconnaissance of the float. It contained a large multi-coloured football with 'World Cup '86' painted on the side and was surrounded by men in football kits who looked nothing like footballers.

"We're the Scottish delegation. We thought the float would benefit from people who have actually qualified for the World Cup. Unlike you muppets."

"Is that right, buddy?" the guy in the Brazil shirt said. "We don't want a Scottish delegation, because that would mean we'd have to have an English one and God forbid, a bloody Northern Ireland one as well. This float is to celebrate all the nice countries going to the World Cup. So, you lot can fuck off."

"Look pal," said Hastie. "I've had a gutful of wankers like you telling we where I can go." He brought his face so close to the other guy's face that he could smell stale nicotine and Guinness.

"Now, get out of the fuckin' way, or I'll introduce you to a Glasgow kiss."

The other football-kit wearers gathered at the front of the float to offer support. They glared at Hastie with arms folded, waiting on him to make the next move.

"Look Sarg," McMillan shouted. "He's getting away."

Hastie turned to see Morgan slip off the front of the Tipperary float and disappear into the crowd. The road had narrowed and the floats were backing up. The audience pressed tightly against the sides and they were hemmed in.

Hastie jumped onto the Tipperary float and the others followed. He could just see Morgan's bobble hat in the crowd and he strained to keep his focus on it. That meant he didn't notice the looming Rock of Cashel approaching. He crashed straight into the papier-mâché construction. Burr and McMillan followed and their momentum destroyed what was left of the rock. They ended on the floor surrounded by grey cardboard and sticky tape.

When they looked up, Benny and his mates were standing over them, hurleys in hand.

"You ruined our fucking float," Benny said. "Now you're going to pay for it."

Hastie pulled himself to his feet. He scanned the crowd but the bobble hat had disappeared. They would go back to the North empty handed. But first, he would have to negotiate with a group of angry stick-wielding Southerners.

Morgan wandered aimlessly around town. He thought about calling Orla to see if she wanted to meet up, but he had never once been honoured with two meet-ups in the same week, so he wasn't going to assume that it would happen now. When it got dark, he headed home. He found an old pork chop at the back of the fridge that hadn't yet developed mould. So, he fried that up with some boiled potatoes and retired to his sofa. Work was looming tomorrow, but he didn't feel sleepy. Three lie-ins in a row had messed up his sleeping pattern. He flicked around the channels until it was time for the late-night Channel 4 movie. He liked to pretend that he watched these for their dark European film noir qualities, when in fact it was the copious amount of nudity that really attracted him.

He fell into a restless sleep on the sofa, dreaming of dark forces outside his flat. He woke at 8.30 am with one arm, which had been trapped under his body all night, asleep and tingling with pins and needles. When he stood up, he realised one of his legs was asleep as well and he stumbled into the shower and got himself ready to face the day.

———

It was 9.30 am when he turned into Winton Road and found his colleagues standing on the footpath outside their office. His boss approached him as he drew near.

"Morgan, nice of you to join us today. I trust you had a nice rest."

"Sorry, boss," Morgan said. "I had a bit of trouble finding matching shoes this morning."

"That's no excuse for turning up half an hour late."

"I'm sorry, which would you prefer? That I spend time looking for matching shoes or get to work on time?"

The boss shook his head. They played this game most Mondays and it made no difference. The boss was never going to push the issue because Morgan was good at his job, if tragically non-ambitious.

"You might be wondering why we are all standing in the street," the boss said.

"Hmm, fire drill maybe, or have you organised another of those fun-filled team events?"

"No, we had a break-in over the weekend. Head Office are concerned that some client files might have been stolen, so they are in there doing an audit and the police are here checking things out."

Morgan thought about how quickly the cops responded to a break-in at a business address compared to their lack of interest in his dilemma.

"It's funny," the boss continued. "They seemed to be mainly interested in your desk. They pulled it apart. I'm afraid your *Star Wars* poster was collaterally damaged in their attack. It seems that not even Darth Vader could repel them."

The boss tossed Morgan a fake smile of condolence and turned to meet a detective that had just left the building.

Morgan moved closer to eavesdrop on their conversation.

"It's odd," the detective said. "They don't appear to have taken anything. The computers and printers are still there and the boys from your head office say that the files are in a mess but seem to be intact. It's a mystery, but I'd say they were looking for something. We'd like to interview some of your staff, particularly this Morgan guy whose desk has been pretty much wrecked."

Morgan started putting two and two together and was coming up with numerous answers. He needed time to think, so he slinked away when nobody was looking and found a phone box. He called

Orla at work, and she answered as the ten-pence piece dropped into the coin box.

"Hi Orla, James here. I was wondering if you'd had a chance to speak to your cousin yesterday at Mass?"

"Hiya, Morgan. She gave me the bum's rush, actually. Got all snooty with me and went on about how she works in the special investigation unit in Head Office and doesn't have time to look at common or garden burglaries. That side of the family have always been very competitive. I mean she's a cop; that's only one branch up the evolutionary tree from teacher. Her parents are worse, always going on about how they have a fixed mobile home at Brittas Bay when everybody else has a caravan. But I remember when they didn't have an arse in their trousers...."

"Orla, sorry to interrupt. Your family history is fascinating but something else has happened. I got to work this morning to find that it had also been broken into over the weekend, and they seemed mainly interested in my desk. I'm getting a little scared, to be honest. Do you think your cousin might be more interested now?"

"Yes," said Orla. "This is fantastic. She always drops little hints that our family do boring jobs. I'll show her. I'll give her a call back and fill her in on developments. And keep me up to date, Morgan. This sounds like a fascinating case."

Morgan headed back to work. The Head Office staff and police had left and the staff were gingerly working their way through the debris. The office looked worse than it did the morning after the previous year's Christmas Party, albeit with fewer stains on the carpet. Morgan found his way to his desk. The drawers had been tossed around the room like acorns on a windy day. His desk had been turned over and his phone had even been dismantled and sat on the floor with its guts exposed to the world.

"Do you think you can tidy it up and be ready to start work by 11 am?"

Morgan turned and his boss was behind him.

"We've a backlog of client queries already. We're an insurance company, Morgan. It's a bad look if we can't recover quickly from adversity. Good man."

He patted Morgan on the shoulder and turned to walk away before stopping and turning. "Oh, by the way. That detective asked you to call him. Here's his number."

Morgan put the number in his pocket. He needed to practise his story before calling the cops. Would he tell them that he had kept a copy of the tape? What was so special about the tape anyway? He had listened to the whole recording, including the largely boring conversation between two Northern policemen. He resolved to listen to it again that evening when he had tidied up at work and home. Tidying wasn't one of Morgan's key skills and it took him all day to get his desk space back to a reasonable state.

As he sellotaped his *Star Wars* poster back together, he thought how the client queries and the detective would just have to wait. He was confused but he had finally managed to get Orla excited. Every cloud had a silver lining.

6

Morgan's doorbell rang at 8 pm and he undid the newly installed locks. One advantage of working for an insurance company was the contacts it gave you in the locksmith and general repair business. Morgan had been able to call in a favour from a tradesman who he regularly recommended to clients and his front door was now guarded by a deadbolt and a security chain.

It took him five minutes to figure out how to open everything while the sense of anticipation grew as to who was standing on the other side of the door.

Eventually the last bolt was released and the door flung open to reveal a smartly uniformed young woman with auburn hair tied back in a severe bun.

"Hi, I'm Garda Tina Reynolds, Orla's cousin." She proffered a hand which Morgan took and shook weakly.

"Ah yeah, come in. I'm just tidying up."

Morgan walked ahead of her and tried to conceal the pizza box and empty beer bottles that littered his coffee table.

"Take a seat," he said as he cleared the scattered supplements of the previous week's *Sunday Independent*.

Tina sat on the edge of the sofa, her dark stockinged legs primly together and her hands resting on her lap.

"I understand you've had some problems with break-ins here and at your work. I took the liberty of checking out the files and I see that you were also involved in a court case in Belfast just after Christmas. Do you think these events could be connected?"

Morgan was facing the sudden realisation that he was strangely attracted to women in uniforms and had processed little of what Tina had said but had spent his time studying the perfectly knotted tie that hugged her neck.

"Hmm, sorry, what did you say?" he spluttered.

"The court case and the break-ins. Do you think they are connected? I mean they were obviously looking for something. What do you think it was?"

"A tape," he said before he even had a chance to think about whether he should mention it or not. It seemed to him that the fewer people who knew about that damned tape the better.

Tina took a notebook from her inside jacket pocket and as she did so she revealed the perfect curve of her tightly buttoned breast. Morgan found himself staring and had to turn away and seek sanctuary in the kitchen.

"Would you like a cup of tea?" he said. "The kettle's boiled."

"No thanks," she said as she placed the notebook on her lap and started writing.

"What's on this tape that is so special? Have you listened to it?"

"It starts off with three British soldiers beating me up and then it records two RUC guys having a conversation." He went on to explain how he came to have a tape running in his car and the incident at the border and the subsequent court case.

"So, you left the copy with the court in Belfast. I'm guessing you kept the original and they, whoever they are, are keen to get their hands on it. I don't suppose I could have a listen?"

Morgan froze. He didn't know why, but it seemed that the tape was his only security. "I've hidden it," he said. "Somewhere away from here and my work and I'd rather leave it there to honest, if you don't mind."

Tina stared at him and Morgan felt his knees weaken. She stood and walked slowly to the kitchen and stood directly in front of him. "I can only help you if I know everything, James. If these guys haven't found the tape yet, the next thing they are going to come looking for is you. If I know what's on the tape, I can protect you. She placed her hand on his arm and squeezed gently. Morgan stared into her clear blue eyes and tried desperately to think.

"Can I get back to you?" he said. "I'm struggling to remember where I put it."

Hastie wasn't happy. He was sitting with a half-finished pint in McEntegarts when Burr and McMillan turned up, and he made no move to buy them a drink. They sat in silence for a few minutes before Burr spoke up.

"We might not have found the tape, but I did find the laddie's porn collection. He's got some interesting mags."

"I'm glad you found something to amuse yourself, Burr," Hastie replied. "I was wondering why you spent so long in the toilet at his flat.

"Anyway, needless to say that the busies aren't happy with us. They are threatening to hang us out to dry at our court case."

"So, what can we do, boss?" McMillan asked. "We pulled his flat and workplace apart. He could have hidden that tape up his arse for all we know."

"Exactly," said Hastie as he scanned the pub for unwanted listeners. "Our only option is to pick him up and see if there is something stuck up his arse or to get him to tell us where the tape is. I can get my hands on a van and we can head down the next time the three of us have a furlough. There is a three-day lookout patrol being planned for this weekend. Put your names down for that and I'll talk to the captain about a couple of days off next week."

"Not some fuckin trench in a farmer's front garden, I hope," said Burr. "I did one of those last year. You have to shit and piss into a bag and take it with you when you leave. After two days, the stink would knock you out. We thought it was our little bags of shit, but it turned out that the farmer had run a hose from his slurry tank down to our trench. The bastard. We poisoned his dog before we left. Teach him, the Paddy scum."

"Just sign up for it, Burr," the sergeant said. "This is South Armagh, not fuckin Butlins. We'll pick him up in the van on his way home from work. The Polis man has given me the keys to a shed just outside Banbridge. We'll take him there and get him to tell us where he put that fuckin tape."

Burr could hardly contain his excitement. "Fuckin brilliant. Can we rig him up to a table with his legs spread and then set up a circular saw that slowly works its way towards his nuts?"

"He's not James Bond, ya numpy," McMillan interrupted. "He's an insurance clerk. We could give him a slap and he'd tell us where the tape is and the whereabouts of Shergar if we pushed him. We don't need any fancy stuff."

"I wouldn't be so certain, big man," Hastie said. "We tried to grab this little fucker three times over the weekend, but he managed to slip away every time. I reckon we're not being told the full truth about this guy. It wouldn't surprise me if he's some sort of secret agent. Next time we're not taking any chances."

"There's just one other thing," Hastie said. "The busies want us to close out this business so to speak."

"Do you mean what I think you mean?" McMillan asked.

Hastie nodded. "They want us to top the little Mick bastard after he tells us where the tape is and bury him in a place where he'll never be found."

Burr had brightened. "Inside your wallet would be a good place then, Sarg. That hasn't seen daylight in years. The notes you're carrying still have the king's head on them."

Hastie took the hint and went to the bar to get a round in and left the others to contemplate the magnitude of what he had just suggested.

When he returned, he found the two deep in conversation.

"So, what do you think? I don't want to force you into anything you're uncomfortable with." He looked first at McMillan.

"I'm a soldier, Sarg" he said. "I do whatever I'm ordered to do. It's easier than having to think."

"What about you, Burr?"

Burr laughed. "I joined this fuckin army to kill Micks. Count me in."

Hastie nodded and they chinked glasses.

"Right, I'll talk to you when you get back from that trench. And bring your shit home, Burr. I don't want any trouble until this operation is finished and put to bed. Now let's get some shots in, because I don't know about you two but I'm getting rat arsed."

The following Monday, Hastie picked up Burr and McMillan in their best civvies and pointed the van south. British soldiers were warned to avoid the Republic on their off days (and even more so when they were on duty), but curiosity got the better of most of them. As a result, many urban myths developed and could be heard in the army canteens across Northern Ireland. The tale of Captain Nairac was embellished with each telling as were the stories of soldiers who had let their accent or occupation slip. There were several tales of troopers being chased out of Dundalk pubs by angry mobs and hair-raising car chases back to the border.

Hastie ensured that the van had enough diesel to get them to Dublin and back and resolved to speak to nobody en route.

"What about grub?" Burr barked from the back of the van.

"I pinched some field rations. That will have to do," Hastie replied.

"Fuckin dried chicken powder again. You're kidding, man. That's what we ate all week in that stinking trench. We dug our trench in somebody's garden on a hill above Camlough. We were right under the farmhouse kitchen window and the fucker baked all weekend and deliberately left the window open to wind us up. I was all set to break in one night and steal some cakes, but then I remembered what you said about keeping our noses clean."

McMillan laughed. "One night when you were sleeping, we sneaked down to Crossmaglen and got fish and chips."

"Ya bastards, why didn't you wake me?"

"You are an idiot, Burr. How do you think seven soldiers with blackened faces would have gotten on in a chipper in Crossmaglen? But the farmer's daughter did come down one night and asked if any of us wanted a blow job for twenty quid."

"You're taking the piss now, Mac. Anyway, I sneaked a look at her in the shower and she's a minger."

———

They reached Dublin around 4 pm and parked outside Morgan's office. As expected, he emerged just after 5 pm and they saw him adjust the headphones on his Walkman and pull up the hood on his parka jacket as a chill northerly wind swept across the city.

They waited until he turned onto Leeson Park before

pulling the van alongside. They jumped out, leaving the side door open. Burr grabbed Morgan from behind and McMillan grabbed his legs. Hastie was ready with some masking tape and he quickly applied it to Morgan's mouth to stifle his high-pitched screams.

"Right, let's get him into the van and get out of here," Hastie shouted.

McMillan and Burr bundled Morgan into the back while Hastie jumped into the driver's seat. He reached for the ignition key but it wasn't there.

"What the fuck!" he squeaked and started desperately searching his pockets.

"Is this what you're looking for?" Hastie turned to his right and met the steely gaze of Tina, resplendent in her Garda uniform. She held the ignition key aloft.

"I've radioed for back-up. They'll be here in about two minutes so don't try anything stupid."

Hastie assessed his options. His training taught him that discretion was often the better part of valour.

He turned to the others in the back. "Right, we're legging it. Leave him there and let's get the fuck out of here."

The others didn't need a second invitation. Hastie jumped across and exited by the passenger door and the three of them raced off towards the city.

Tina walked around to find Morgan sitting up in the rear of the van, his mouth taped and his hands bound with cable ties behind is back. His Walkman headphones lay smashed on the van floor and his parka jacket had been pulled over his head.

She reached forward and gently removed the tape from his mouth. He was shaking and she held him closely until he settled down.

"You're my guardian angel," he said.

Tina smiled. "Maybe. Now, do you want to tell me what's on that tape?"

———

Morgan let Tina into his flat and put the kettle on. When they'd finished tea, and dressed the various scrapes and bruises that adorned his body, Morgan got up and went to the extractor fan outlet and peeled it back. Then he reached inside and extracted a dust-covered tape.

Forty minutes later the tape came to an abrupt end as the voice of McGuinness could be heard, berating the referee in Glentoran's most recent match as being a blind, Fenian bastard.

Tina closed her notebook and stared at Morgan.

"Do you realise the importance of this tape?"

"No," replied Morgan. "They mention a few people but I've never heard of them. Who is that 'Oriel' chap they kept referring to?"

Tina stood and walked to the window and took a cautious look outside. "Maybe it's best you don't know. I recognised the name when they said who 'Oriel' is. But, like I say, I think it's best that you don't know. The key thing is that it's not safe for you to stay here. Do you have somewhere you could stay tonight? I'll go into the office tomorrow and see if I can get the keys to one of the Gardai's safe houses and I'll take you there."

"The Gardai have safe houses?" Morgan replied. "I thought that only happened in FBI-type movies."

"There are a lot of things about the Gardai that the public doesn't know about. But the less you know the better. So, what about somewhere to stay tonight?"

Morgan sat back and thought. His parents lived three hours away at the other end of the country and most of his friends lived in that part of the country too. Dublin had always been his escape from that life, and he lived a lonely existence with few people around him that he could truly call a friend.

"What about Orla?"

The words hit Morgan like a thunderbolt. How had Orla described their relationship when she spoke to Tina? Did she describe it as the sort of relationship where either of them could drop round and stay the night at a moment's notice? He was intrigued.

"She lives with her parents," he eventually muttered. "I don't think they'd be too impressed."

"Rubbish," said Tina. "I know Frank and Anne. They'd take in a blind beggar if he knocked on their front door. Let's drive to the pub and you can call her from there. You look like you could do with a drink. Oh, and you might want to write up a letter for your parents. Tell them you've been sent to England for a couple of weeks on a training course by your company. That you'll be busy in a centre somewhere in rural Surrey and you won't be able to contact them. You should expect to be away for a couple of weeks and you won't be able to call anybody. There is no phone in the house I'll take you to and I'll bring you food once a week, so I don't want you wandering down to the nearest village looking for a chipper. There's a telly and a VHS player with a box of videos that we confiscated from a smuggler. So, that should keep you busy.

"This business will take a couple of weeks to play out. I'll speak to my boss and we'll try to make overtures to the police up north. Hopefully, we can clear this up without any more nastiness."

"Who do you think those guys were?"

"From their accents and haircuts, I'd say they are British soldiers. But not particularly clever ones. I don't think they are SAS or anything like that."

"Why do you say that?" Morgan asked. He was increasingly impressed by Tina's calmness and obvious knowledge.

"The SAS would have just shot you and not risked a kidnapping," she said calmly. Morgan suddenly realised that Orla's bluntness was a family trait.

They settled into Smyth's Bar and Morgan enjoyed a pint of Guinness before ringing Orla.

"Hi, it's James here. I'm with Tina, your cousin, in Smyth's."

"Oh, my God, that bitch. I knew she'd hit on you if she thought I was interested. She's been doing that to me since we used to go to the Lansdowne Rugby Club discos."

"So, are you interested in me, Orla?" Morgan asked.

"What? Well, no, not in that kind of way. But anyway, I asked her to help you, not drag you to the pub so she can jump on you."

"She is helping, Orla. Three guys tried to bundle me into a van tonight and she was right there to save me. It was amazing. Anyway, she reckons I need somewhere safe to stay tonight and she suggested calling you."

"Oh, well, why didn't you say? I want to hear all the gory details. Can Tina drop you off? I'll talk to Mum and Dad and get the spare room set up. This is so exciting, Morgan! I want to hear all the details when you get here."

"It doesn't feel very exciting when you're in the back of a Toyota Hiace with duct tape over your mouth and two smelly Scotsmen sitting on you. But thanks for the offer, Orla. I'll see you soon."

He returned to the table to find Tina intently studying her notebook.

"How did it go?" she asked.

"Fine, she's setting up the spare room. She thought you were taking me here to get me drunk so that you could take advantage of me."

Tina caught his eye. "I don't think I'd have to get you drunk to do that, would I?"

Morgan smiled. Women were like buses, he thought. You wait ages and then two come along at the same time. But while you might enjoy the ride, eventually they'll dump you in the middle of nowhere.

———

Frank was Tina's uncle, so she came in for some tea and a half hour of family gossip when she dropped Morgan off. Orla and Tina embraced and spent some time together in the kitchen, slandering other cousins and outdoing each other with tales of boyfriends and career progression.

Morgan saw Tina to the door. She kissed him gently on the cheek and held his gaze.

"I'll pick you up tomorrow when I've sorted the safe house out with work. I'll call into your office and tell your boss that you've been called up for emergency jury service due to an outbreak of food poisoning among the reserve jurors in a high-profile case. He'll believe it if he hears it from a uniformed Garda."

She let herself out and Morgan turned to find Orla standing at the top of the stairs.

"You really are the international man of mystery, aren't you? Let me show you to your room, Mr Bond."

Morgan followed her up the stairs. He had often dreamed of this scenario. Orla in her night clothes, luring him to her boudoir. But his mind was not on Orla. He was thinking about Tina and her dark stockings and plain but polished shoes.

"I'm in here," Orla said and Morgan followed her voice to what was clearly the spare room. An ironing board stood against the wall and a sewing machine rested on a small table. A single bed had been made up and Orla was perched on it, resplendent in her red cotton pyjamas and with her blonde hair untied and requiring constant flick backs.

Morgan stood in the doorway wondering where to sit. There were no chairs available apart from a small and uncomfortable stool beneath the sewing machine.

Orla patted the bed beside her. "You can sit here but no funny business."

Morgan did as requested. "I don't know what you mean. I've never found dealing with girls to be the least bit funny."

"How come you never seem to have a girlfriend, Morgan? You're not completely hideous and you can be quite funny, particularly when you're not trying to be."

Morgan threw her a mournful look. I would have had a girlfriend years ago, if I hadn't wasted my time pursuing you, he thought.

"I'm waiting on Miss Perfect, I suppose," he said.

"And is that Tina?"

Morgan blushed and tried to change the subject. "Those soldiers seem to have it in for me. I don't know what I did to offend them."

"You're as red as a beetroot, Morgan. I think my little cousin has won you over, you dark horse." She tickled him and as he fell laughing on the bed, Orla fell on top of him. He suddenly froze. He could feel her warm breath and her hair fell gently on his face. He raised his head and brought his lips to hers. But before they could touch, she had rolled away and was at the door.

"Sleep tight, Morgan. And don't spend too long thinking of Tina and if you do, try not to make a mess of the sheets."

She was walking along the landing towards her room when Morgan called after her.

"Orla, sorry. Can we just talk for a while?"

She turned and smiled and walked back to his room. Morgan was sitting on the uncomfortable stool and Orla retook her place on the bed.

"So, what's happening in your life, Orla? It's all been about me so far tonight."

"Well, funny you say that. I was picking up my kid sister from the Wesley Disco last Friday and I met this guy outside who was also waiting for his kid sister. Turns out that he was the first guy I snogged at Wesley when I was fifteen. Me and my friend Mary had been dropped off by my parents. We were still wearing our school uniforms, I think. Anyway, we had a couple of miniskirts in our handbags. We changed in an alleyway in Donnybrook and then drank a bottle of vodka that I'd stolen from my dad's drinks cabinet. Paul, the guy I met last Friday, said he shifted me out on the rugby pitch, although I don't remember it. The only thing I remember about that night was the hiding my dad gave me when I got home."

Morgan noticed that Orla's mood always seemed to change when she mentioned her dad.

There was a pause and then she brightened. "Anyway, I'm going to meet Paul for a drink tomorrow and, you never know, we might recreate that scene on the Wesley rugby pitch."

"You said I never seem to have a girlfriend, and you seem to have lots of boyfriends but none of them ever last for long."

It was Orla's turn to change the subject. "So, what have you got against the English?"

"Nothing," he said. "I love the English. I think every house should have one. Preferably as a butler. They make great butlers."

Orla stared at him blankly. Yet again she hadn't gotten the joke.

"Anyway, they were Scottish," he said. "Not English. But I've nothing against the Scots either. But they seem to have a problem with me."

"So, what's on that tape you were hiding in your flat?"

"I don't honestly know," he answered. "Just some names. Tina seems to think they are important and she's going to speak to her boss. But they are just names to me."

Orla wasn't listening. That was normal when Morgan was talking. Quite often he would be in mid-sentence and he would notice that she was gazing over his shoulder at nothing in particular and nodding every few seconds. Morgan would sometimes start speaking in German to see if she noticed and would be answered with the same gentle nodding.

It wasn't that she lived in a world of her own. It was more that she lived in a world where Morgan was a sometimes welcome but often irritating visitor from outer space.

"You haven't answered my question about long-term boyfriends. You are a beautiful girl and I'm sure most guys would eat chips out of your knickers. So how come you don't want to settle down?"

Mention of the word 'knickers' had catapulted Orla back into Morgan's universe.

"Sorry, did you say knickers?"

They giggled for a second and then Orla got up and looked at a family photo on the wall. It was from her youngest sister's First Communion and showed a fourteen-year-old Orla beside her mother and three siblings. Morgan noticed that her father was not in the shot.

"Daddy wasn't always around when I was growing up." Orla's voice had dropped to a whisper. "Mam caught him cheating and she kicked him out. It was a few years before she let him back."

"They seem okay now," Morgan said. "I mean I'm no expert on

relationships, but they were holding hands downstairs and that's usually a good sign."

"I think they got old and tired and just can't be bothered fighting any more. And this is Ireland in the 1980s, Morgan. There are a lot of twitching curtains on our street and it's not easy to get your daughter into Mount Anville if she comes from a broken home. Dad was living in a flat in Rathmines and they couldn't afford the rent and to pay my sister's school fees. So, they are back together and to the outside world it's all lovey-dovey. There are a lot of unhappy people in Ireland, Morgan, who are only bound together by the clip on a wallet."

"They are talking about having a referendum to allow divorce," Morgan said. "I was thinking of campaigning for it. You could join me if you want."

Orla's face darkened. "Are you mad?" I don't want my parents to get divorced. I'd rather they were miserable than for me to have to explain that to my friends. Daddy would just run off and get a twenty-year-old bimbo for himself and I'd be left helping Mum get through three bottles of Blue Nun a night.

"Anyway, you wondered why I don't keep a boyfriend for long. I don't trust them, to be honest. I like to get out before they do. I can't face the prospect of ever being dumped by a man."

"Not all men are like your father, Orla."

"Aren't they?" Orla asked. "What are you like, Morgan?"

He thought for a second. Orla's confession had made him feel that he should also share some of his past.

"I thought I was in love when I was eighteen. I met a girl in my last year in school and became obsessed with her. I used to write to her every day. I'd pen a couple of heartfelt poems each week that were basically plagiarised from Patrick Kavanagh. She must have wondered why I made so many references to Monaghan when we were both from Tipperary. She wrote back about once a week, which at the time I put down to her putting more thought into her missives.

"I thought she was obsessed with me too. Turns out she was only mildly interested. We lasted for a few years, but she had gone off to university in Galway and a whole new exciting world opened to her. It was a world I didn't live in. I lived on the boring old planet she had left.

"She sent me a letter to say that she had met a guy and didn't want to be cruel and two-time me. I was so smitten by her that I actually thought that meeting another guy while she was still going out with me, but telling me about it, was actually a decent thing to do. In a strange way, it made me love her even more.

"I went to my local pub that weekend and noticed that most of my mates had girlfriends and were talking about houses and kids. It was like I'd been on a merry-go-round for a long time and when it stopped and I'd climbed off, I discovered that the fairground was closed and that everyone had gone home.

"So, that's where I am now, Orla. Wandering around an abandoned fairground."

Orla came over to him and kissed him gently on the forehead. "My tunnel of love is still open. You just have to find the correct tokens."

With that she was off, and Morgan climbed into bed. He wouldn't sleep.

McGuinness invited Anderson to lunch at Shandon Park Golf Club in the safe leafy suburbs of South East Belfast, a world away from the barricades and incessant threat of the city centre. In addition to an excellent and challenging course, the club offered a discreet book-lined members-only bar, where the more entitled members of the security services could confer in dark and uninterrupted shadows.

"I'll meet you there at 1 pm. Don't drive directly from the station and make sure you wear civvies. You know the routine."

Anderson arrived and found McGuinness in the dimly lit lounge bar overlooking the verdant 18th green.

By instinct, McGuinness always sat with his back to the wall so that he could observe all the comings and goings without being surprised.

He was greedily tucking into an Ulster Fry when Anderson got there. Butter and tomato juice trickled down his chin and he raced through his food as though eating was a distraction from the important things in life, best to be dealt with speedily.

"That looks like a good feed," Anderson said.

"Yeah, the only question is whether the fried bread or the IRA will kill me first."

Anderson ordered some stew and a glass of milk and sat opposite his boss. He was expecting a bolloxing, and it didn't take long coming.

"Those knuckle heads you hired from Rent an Idiot have really fucked up. Could you have made a bigger shit mess of this?"

"Look, boss, they've been looking for a needle in a haystack. We don't even know if he still has the original of that tape and if he did, he could have buried it in a hole up in the Dublin Mountains."

McGuinness cut off a large slice of bacon and chewed it slowly while keeping a fixed stare on Anderson.

"Don't you worry, Anderson. He had the tape and he had it in his flat. Those Jock soldiers missed it."

"How do you know?" asked Anderson, although he suspected that he already knew the answer.

"Oriel contacted me. He doesn't know about the tape and I wasn't going to tell him. But he said some female cop from Garda Head Office is taking a close interest in this Morgan fellow. I'll wager she's the one who spooked your soldiers when they were trying to lift him. Oriel said that she has moved the young fella to a safe house down the country. I asked him to make some discreet enquiries as to where that house is and then I need you to go down there and finish this job off."

Anderson gulped his milk. He had slapped a few suspects around interrogation rooms and got his baton out once or twice during Republican parades. But his police-issued gun had always rested quietly inside his holster. Killing a person was not something he ever imagined doing, particularly an innocent soul like Morgan who had stumbled into a mess that was not of his doing.

"Boss, are you sure we're doing the right thing here? I get that we take out terrorists. Live by the sword and you die by the sword. But this guy isn't a terrorist. He's an innocent bloke that was in the wrong place at the wrong time. Shouldn't we send the soldiers again? Get them to maybe rough him up a bit. I mean if it's a simple question of being heavy handed, then I'm sure they are capable of it. We've been asking them to find a tiny tape or to extract information from a suspect. That's not really specialist soldier work. But beating up an innocent victim is."

McGuinness stopped eating and raised his fork in Anderson's direction.

"Are you going soft? Nobody is fucking innocent, Anderson. We need Oriel. He's our most important asset. He gives us intelligence about the IRA that the Guards in their 'fucked up sense of independence and deep-down hatred of all we stand for' refuse to give. That helps us to intercept terrorists and save lives. Do you want to fuck that up by feeling sorry for a dumb Mick like this? And remember when the trial of these soldiers comes up in Belfast, they'll play that tape and it will demonstrate that we stood by and watched the soldiers beat this guy up. That's not going to be good for my career or yours, Anderson."

"I get that, boss, but how do we know he hasn't given the Irish cops the tape already? Then we're talking about killing a young fella for no real gain. The Dublin media will go crazy if the Gardai announce that they have outed an RUC spy and that the guy who gave them the tape has been found dead in a ditch in Tipperary. Even those clowns down south would be able to link it back to us."

McGuinness sat back and chewed on a sausage. "Then let's make sure he isn't found in a ditch. Let's make sure he isn't found at all. Dig a deep hole in the middle of a dark forest. Isn't that what our friends in the IRA do? Anyway, if he had given the Gardai the tape then Oriel would already be in a cell somewhere and not chatting to me like he was this morning.

"I wanted to do this the easy way, just get the tape and move on. But I gave you the chance to do that and you screwed up. So, it's time to cut to the chase. It's a dog-eat-dog world out there, Anderson. And it's no fun being a fuckin poodle."

"Okay," Anderson said. "But let's get the Scottish lads to do it then. That way we're not directly connected. If it all goes tits up, then it will look as though the soldiers did it to stop Morgan testifying against them in their upcoming court case. If they try to implicate us, we can deny ever speaking to them. I've only dealt with them by phone, so I can easily say that never happened."

McGuinness sat back with his pint and smiled. "Now you're starting to talk like a true RUC Special Branch officer."

———

Tina picked Morgan up at 9 am and they drove south for two hours. The journey was largely silent. Morgan hadn't slept well and his head was full of intrigue and confusion about the tape and the mess it had gotten him into. Why hadn't he just bought a pad and a ballpoint pen and recorded his family history that way? Why hadn't he kept his mouth shut when he got to that army checkpoint and why had he made a copy of that tape? He fell into a fitful slumber, waking every five minutes as the car braked or the engine revved. In the end, he gave up and spent the journey staring at the unkempt hedgerows they drove past.

They passed through a sleepy village in County Wexford. Tina stopped the car at the entrance to a shadowy and overgrown laneway. She checked her mirrors and when she was sure they weren't being tailed she pulled off the road and drove up to a remote farmhouse with whitewash that looked that it had been applied to welcome President Kennedy in 1963.

It had a red tin roof that was rusted and overhung with oak branches that creaked in the wind.

"It's pretty spooky," Morgan said as he took his bag out of the car. "Does it come with its own ghost?"

Tina opened the front door and waited a moment to allow some of the trapped, stagnant air to escape.

"There's a reason we don't have safe houses in the middle of O'Connell Street," she said. "Nobody will notice you here. There is a Superser heater if you're cold. But don't light the fire. We don't have Apaches living around here, but they can still read smoke signals."

Tina moved through the house, opening all the windows. Cobwebs colonised the corners and she brushed away mice droppings and leaves that had found their way down the chimney.

"It's pretty musty in here. I think the last time it was used was during the hunger strikes when we hosted a couple of 'off the record' meetings between local priests and the IRA. As priests were involved, that probably means that the drinks cabinet is empty, but I'd suggest you stay off the booze while you're here anyway. It's best to be alert."

Morgan carried in the small sports bag that contained all the clothes he could pack in the five minutes that Tina had allotted, and he placed it on the worn and dusty settee. The house looked dark and unloved. Mould surrounded the windows and dampness crept up the wallpaper in the kitchen like a slow incoming tide. An old television dominated the living room with a top-loader VHS player beneath.

"We do get somebody to come in every now and again and give it a quick clean, but it's not the Ritz." Tina was at the fridge. "I've brought you some cheese, sausages, eggs and bread. And lots of cornflakes. I'm afraid you're going to be eating lots of cereal. I know the milkman around here and he's going to drop off a pint each morning. But don't talk to him or anyone else. If you need some air, go for a walk in the back fields. If you meet anyone, say that you are one of the Furlongs and you're down here doing family history research. If you threw a stone down here, you'd hit a Furlong. Everyone here goes by that name.

"That's the best excuse because you can rest assured that no one will stop to talk to you then. They are sick of Americans coming here trying to find dead relatives."

"Yeah," said Morgan. "I'm looking into my own family's history. That's how this whole mess started. I went to the local presbytery to start with. Told him I was looking to trace my ancestors who lived in that parish in the nineteenth century. The parish priest met me at the door and said, 'Sorry to break the news to you son, but they all died years ago.' Then he closed the door on me. So, I was planning to talk to some old relatives. That's why I bought the recording device."

"Well, you might have a few days to catch up on that," Tina said as she put on her coat. "Look, stay low and don't be tempted to head into the nearest village for a few pints. Locals will be curious about you, and you'd be amazed how quickly word gets around in these places. Under no circumstances let the local Gardai know you're here. We're all trained to look out for strangers staying in remote cottages. It will smell of an IRA safe house and before you can say boo, that information will be passed up to headquarters in Dublin. And as your tape has proven, we don't know who to trust up there. I haven't even told my own boss that you're staying here. That's how paranoid I am."

"You look pretty cool to me," Morgan said as Tina tied her hair into a bun. She came over and took his hands in hers. "Mind yourself, James. I'll come down next Tuesday and check in with you and bring you some food. Maybe I'll pick up a takeaway and we can watch one of those pirate videos I've left for you. There are a couple of raunchy ones if you fancied that."

Morgan wanted desperately to say something cool and romantic but could only manage a toothy grin.

"Sounds great," he said. "I just hope I don't have the tapes worn out by then."

She kissed him, slowly and deliberately on the lips. Morgan was desperate to open his mouth and thrust his tongue into her mouth. But years of rejection hung round his neck like a slave's chain.

Tina withdrew and smiled. "See you on Tuesday," she said and was gone into the spring drizzle before he could reply.

He brought his sports bag into the bedroom and placed it on the saggy queen-sized bed that filled the small room. It had two moth-eaten woollen blankets and a bed cover that looked like a remnant from a Second World War bombsite. Morgan jumped on and heard the bedsprings creak. His mind raced forward to Tuesday night. Could he talk Tina into staying and if he did would these bedsprings get any action? He nodded off now and again as the rain fell softly on the Wexford fields outside his bedroom window.

In the meantime, Tina drove back to Dublin for an appointment with her boss. She had told him nothing so far but realised she had to at least fill him in on some parts of the story. She was a professional, but she cared about Morgan too, and this was the first time in her career that this had happened. She smiled as she thought about his small overnight bag and his goofy grin. It might be possible to mix business with pleasure she thought, as she turned on to the N11 and pointed her car towards Dublin.

She arrived early for her appointment and sat in her boss's office waiting for him to return from the gents. His desk was covered in string-bound cardboard files stuffed with photocopied paper straining to escape. In the centre of the desk was a small toy car. A Model T Ford. Tina picked it up and caressed it gently between her fingers.

"A marriage guidance counsellor gave me that. Anne and meself were having a few problems. Stress of the job and all that. He said that all relationships are a journey. But if you sit back and relax you might occasionally enjoy the ride."

Inspector Joyce, her boss, stood behind with his hand on Tina's shoulder.

"And are you enjoying the ride?" Tina asked.

"That's none of your business, young lady," Joyce said as he smiled and sat behind the desk. "Now, you said you have an urgent case to discuss with me. What is it?"

"You know we've always suspected that the RUC have a spy in our camp. That somebody here at Head Office has been feeding Belfast with information for years."

"We don't suspect it, we know it. We've lost some of our best touts because the RUC gets to know about them and grab them as soon as they cross the border. We had information about a building firm in Newry that was sourcing explosives and feeding them to a bomb-making factory in Dundalk. We sent round an internal memo that mentioned the building firm's name and within twenty-four hours, the RUC had raided the place. The bomb-making factory upped sticks and was gone before we could get round there. We lost our lead and two years of good work went down the drain. So, you don't need to tell me that we might have a spy."

"Well, I think I know who it is," Tina ventured. "I've heard a taped conversation between two senior RUC officers where they talk about their spy in Dublin. They call him 'Oriel' and then they mention his real name."

Joyce stared at her for a few seconds. "Write the name on this sheet of paper. Show me and then take the paper and swallow it. I run security here and even I don't trust that the walls aren't bugged by some spook or other."

Tina took the paper and wrote out the name and pushed it across the desk.

"Holy fuck, the old bastard," he said. "I know where they got his codename. He's a season ticket holder at Dundalk FC. He probably meets his handlers up there in Oriel Park." Joyce chuckled. "Imagine what the locals up there would do if they realised that RUC handlers were regular attendees of Dundalk games. I probably don't want to know, but how did you happen upon this information?"

Tina told him about Morgan, the court case, the break-ins, the attempted kidnapping.

"I've moved him to a safe house. I'd rather not say where. You always trained me that the fewer people who know about an operation the better."

"But I'm your boss."

"I know that, boss. I'd just like to run this myself for a few days. But I would like help staking out his Dublin flat. I'm sure they'll come after him again and if we can nab them, it will give us a bargaining tool with Belfast. Of course, we could also just call the RUC and say, 'We know who Oriel is so you can call off the dogs.'"

Joyce leaned across the desk. "Have you forgotten everything I taught you Tina? When you achieve a breakthrough in a case you don't scream it from the rooftops. You think how best you can use that knowledge. Now, the first thing we'll do is test out your information. I'll put out a memo saying that we've recruited an IRA informer in Dundalk and that he goes across the border every Thursday to collect his dole in Newry. I'll put in the usual shite about keeping an eye out for this fella and so on. I'll make sure that

'Oriel' is the only officer to receive the memo. And if your theory is true, then our little tout will be in handcuffs on Thursday before the back wheels of his car cross the border."

"And then what?" Asked Tina.

"We'll see, we'll see. But let me worry about that. You look after this Morgan chap till it all dies over."

"Look, this guy is an innocent victim in all this. I feel sorry for him; he's stuck in a damp safe house waiting for three Scottish soldiers to come and kill him. I'd rather that he didn't have to sit around for a few weeks while we play spy games."

"This isn't a game, Tina. The RUC are quick-kill agents. If they get a sniff of a suspect, they jump on him straight away and before we know where we are, the courts in Belfast throw out the case for lack of evidence and our suspect disappears into the ether. We want to beat the Provos as much as they do, but if we are playing a game, it's a long one we're playing. We don't want to arrest individual suspects, Tina, we want to arrest all of them. And do you think that the RUC ever give us any information? Do they bugger. They knew about the UVF coming down to Dublin 1974. Did they tell us? Yet they expect us to share all our intelligence with them. We have a vast network of informers, Tina. That gives us a window into the entire Provo structure. If we shared that information, the RUC would just arrest whatever touts were dumb enough to do their shopping in Newry."

"Okay, boss, message received and understood. Can I have some resources to watch his flat?"

"Talk to O'Brien, he's allocating resources this week. Ask for whatever you need. And let me know how things go with Morgan. If I didn't know better, I'd say you're a little smitten, Tina. Remember, we're professionals. We don't shit on our own doorstep."

Tina rose and walked to the door. "Message received and understood, boss."

———

Morgan woke around 5 pm and turned on the TV. He flicked through RTE 1 and RTE 2 and then met a world of snowy static. He'd forgotten that the British channels were unavailable this far south. Neither Irish channel offered anything vaguely interesting, so he lifted the box of videos that Tina had left onto the sofa.

The pirates who put them together made little effort to hide the fact that they were counterfeit. The covers were all photocopied in black and white and the tapes themselves had a handwritten sticker with the film's title attached. Many of them were misspelled and Morgan chuckled to himself as he pondered whether to watch *Porkies* or *Witnes*.

He spent the evening watching videos before heading back to bed at 1 am. He had thought of Tina a lot that day but as the evening wore on, his mind returned to Orla. Tina seemed available. With a small surge in self-confidence, he felt that he could storm her barricades and plunder the treasure within. Orla, on the other hand, seemed to have several levels of fortification. And for some reason that he couldn't quite explain to himself that made her more attractive. That old Groucho Marx line about 'not wanting to be a member of a club that would have him as a member' kept repeating in his head.

He woke late the next morning and while the safe house was as cold as his own flat, the itchiness of the blankets was enough to spur him out of bed. He made some tea and poured out some cornflakes and wondered what to do with the day. He remembered his holidays at home on the family farm when his days would be kept busy mending fences and bringing hay in. He wasn't used to having time that needed to be imaginatively filled.

Mind-numbing boredom was starting to set in. He tried watching one of the videos, but in his head, that was a nighttime activity. So, after another bowl of cornflakes for fortitude, he donned his coat and set off through the fields. As a farm boy in his early life, he felt at home among the hedgerows and the freshly ploughed fields waiting with open mouths for that season's planting.

The thick aroma of slurry filled his nostrils, but this didn't bother him. Smell is the strongest memory sense and Morgan's head was filled with happy thoughts of sitting on his father's knee as his tractor pulled a muck spreader around their Tipperary farm.

The land was generally flat, but he noticed a small hill with a single tree on top and, with a sense of adventure, he set off to climb it. When he got there, he saw that the tree was a magnificent oak with a thick and rugged trunk. The winter had not been kind to its outlying branches and many lay broken and bare, while those safe in the inner sanctums were already sprouting their new-season leaves.

Morgan sat by the base of the tree and removed his jacket. As he sat there, he noticed a small village about a kilometre away, which he guessed was the one that Tina had asked him to avoid. A large GAA ground stood at the entrance to the village with a rickety old wooden stand and the same green-topped whitewashed walls that adorned every other ground in the country. The village itself wasn't much more than a crossroads with a church in the Gothic nineteenth-century style on one corner, a pub on another, a corner shop on the third and an old and formerly magnificent country house on the last corner. This was probably the occasional summer home of whatever absentee English landlord had previously owned the land around here. But now it was only a skeleton with no roof and tenanted by a family of crows.

Curiosity, boredom and thirst drove him to ignore Tina's warnings, and he set off down the hill. The sun was already drifting into the west and the bright lights of the corner shop were calling him. He passed the sign for 'Best Village in Wexford, Tidy Towns 1983' just as an empty crisp packet whistled past on the wind. The thought struck him that the village had either let itself go or the competition had been weak.

The shop was the only colour on what was otherwise a drab grey street. It was painted a shiny mustard colour with red trimming and had a large door with a well-worn ornate handle. A spiked railing ran under the window as an obvious deterrent to the youth of the locality from planting their posteriors there.

A brown cellophane sheet covered the front of the shop but that had failed miserably in protecting the window display from fading.

As Morgan got closer, he noticed a wasp, no doubt teased out of hibernation by the first flush of spring, now trapped between the cellophane and the window.

He opened the door and an old and rusty bell heralded his entrance. A faint whiff of paraffin greeted his nostrils as he slalomed past piles of peat briquettes and old newspapers to get to the counter.

"What can I do you for?" the shopkeeper asked as he looked up from the crossword he was working on.

"A can of Club Orange," Morgan replied.

The shopkeeper was wearing a dark woollen suit with a collarless shirt that looked like it had been last washed around the time the window display was being created. He moved slowly to a back shelf and took down a can.

"Do you have any cold ones?" Morgan asked.

The shopkeeper eyed him suspiciously. "You're not a feckin Yank, are you? I had one of them in last week looking for garlic or something like that. I said I could stretch to an onion, maybe. And do you know what he said? 'Do you have any red ones?' Red ones. Did you ever hear the likes of it?"

He pushed the can across the counter. "You're not in Spain, you know? This is Wexford in April. We don't turn the fridge on until July."

Morgan handed over a pound note and pocketed the change and turned to go.

"Are you passing through or staying for a few days?"

Morgan froze. Tina's warnings jumped into his mind. "Ah, I'm doing a bit of family history stuff. Tramping through old graveyards and so on."

The shopkeeper nodded sagely. "That's what brings all the Yanks over. They all want to see if they are related to JFK. I tell them to leave the dead at peace. They would be better off showing more concern for the living. But it keeps the place going, I suppose. You'd be a Furlong then, I'm guessing. They are as common as rats in this part of world."

"That's right," said Morgan. "I'm a Furlong, but on my mother's side. I heard that this was the place to look for them."

The shopkeeper pressed the button on his antique till and placed the pound note under a spring. "Yeah, well if everybody marries their cousins, that's what will happen. Families of amadáns, all with the same name."

Morgan took the cue to leave. The bell tinkled again as he opened the shop door. He turned and looked up. 'Furlong's Groceries and Hardware' was painted in vibrant red paint above the doorway.

That explained a lot, Morgan thought, and opened the can and drank its warm elixir in one gulp.

The sun was starting to sink below the western hills and a chill started to wrap itself around the village. Morgan wrapped the coat around his shoulders and as he did, he heard the change jingle in his pocket. A green telephone box stood across the street outside the pub. Orla would be home from work by now, he thought, and he knew her number off by heart. Tina had warned him not to speak to anyone, but surely it would be no harm if he called Orla. She already knew about the tape and the break-ins. If he brought up his secret hideaway, it could only add to the intrigue and nourish her interest in him.

He dialled the number and Orla answered. Before he could say anything, he had to listen to a ten-minute summary of her weekend. The meeting with Paul at Wesley. How he had called her three times since, but she didn't answer. Treat them mean and keep them keen was her motto.

Eventually they got around to Morgan's situation. "I'm staying in the middle of nowhere down in Wexford. It's a draughty old house. I could do with some company. Someone to cuddle to stay warm."

"Have you asked Tina?" Orla said pointedly.

"I was hoping you might come and visit me," he ventured. His heart was pounding but he felt a new confidence born out of desperation.

"I was hoping I might get to see those pyjamas again. They were rather fetching."

He heard a sharp exhale of breath on the other end of the line. His heart sank. Yet again he had peaked his head over the parapet only to receive a sharp sniper's bullet to the skull.

"Look, I'm sorry," he said. "I don't mean to be pushy, but if you ever fancied a day trip, there are some really nice walks around here. It's just that I'm going out of my mind with boredom."

"Alright," she said. "I'll think about it, but I've got a lot on this week. But maybe we'll catch up when you're back. Keep in touch anyway."

He gave her the address and they spent five more minutes discussing south Dublin gossip before he hung up. A few cars had pulled up and thick-cut country men made their way into the pub. A handwritten poster in the window advertised that 'Deep Throat featuring Dinny Dempsey' would be playing that night.

Morgan was tempted to enter but he remembered Tina's warning about alcohol and loose tongues. He turned the collar of his coat up and headed back towards the lonely cottage through the chilly air. Did he overstep the mark with Orla, he wondered? In a way, he didn't care. He could be dead by the end of the week. That thought kept him morbid company as he slowly walked home through the fields.

———

Orla had just been to receive communion. St Patrick's was full for 11 am Mass and nobody noticed that she headed straight for the back door, rather than returning to her pew.

"Are you trying to beat the traffic?"

Tina was standing in the vestibule beside the holy water fountain.

"Maybe, it's just admin after communion and I get enough of that at work. Are you on a stake-out, Tina?" Orla asked as she embraced her cousin and they exchanged air kisses.

"No, I got here late. I was working last night and I didn't want to march up the central aisle in the middle of Mass. Mammy and Daddy are here and I thought I'd surprise them and take them out for lunch. There is a new Italian restaurant in Blackrock. Apparently, pasta is the new spud. Although now that I think of it, I'll have to check that they have something with potatoes or else Dad won't touch it."

"I wouldn't touch that pasta stuff, Tina, I've heard that it's very fattening. You don't want to be putting on any more weight."

Tina subconsciously pulled her stomach in and opened her jacket button. "Inside every fat woman, there's a thin woman trying to get out," she ventured nervously.

Orla leaned across and whispered, "In my experience, outside every thin woman, there is a fat man trying to get in!"

Tina pulled away in mock horror. "Orla Reynolds. You're still inside a church you know."

"I'm only joking. You're looking well, Tina. And I hope you are looking after Morgan. He called me during the week. He seemed quite lonely."

"James called you?" Tina's voice had changed back into police mode. "I told him not to call anyone. I don't think he realises how much danger he's in."

"Sounds to me like you're trying to keep him all to yourself. Squirrel him away to some love nest down in Wexford. But surely Tina, you could have found somewhere more romantic?"

"Orla, this is serious. He's not down there for a holiday. He's caught up in the middle of something big and not of his own making. I'm just trying to protect him."

"It sounds terribly exciting. Maybe I could help. Do you need me to do any legal work? Maybe investigate extradition and that sort of thing."

"Thanks Orla, but I think we can get by without any civilian help. I know you have a low opinion of the Gardai, but we do understand the law."

Orla raised her eyebrows. The Gardai knew the right time to

kick people out of pubs (apart from the ones that other Gardai drank in), they would stop you if you didn't have a light on your bike and they could crack you over the head with a truncheon if you dared to protest at the visit of a murderous US president. But she doubted if they could even spell extradition.

"No problem, Tina. I'm just trying to help. Morgan is a good friend of mine and I want to look after him as much as you. But I'll stay out of things and leave it to the Guards. I'm sure he's in safe hands. Enjoy the lunch and say hello to your folks for me."

They exchanged two more air kisses and Orla headed off down Donnybrook Road. I'll show her, she thought. Orla had found Morgan first and was annoyed that somebody else was moving into her territory. She had always seen him as a welcome diversion from the brain-dead rugby types who normally orbited her social circle. And she liked the fact that he never seemed to have a girlfriend and was always available when she needed a sponge to soak up her emotional residue. Now she could feel him slipping away and, to make matters worse, it was her cousin who was doing it.

She could drive down to Wexford in two hours and if she got bored, she could be back in Dublin that evening. It was time to show Morgan which side his bread was buttered on. And maybe she thought, I'd better pack those pyjamas after all.

———

Morgan didn't go to Mass that Sunday. Or any other Sunday for that matter. He had stopped when he moved to Dublin. Not deliberately, but without a mother to worry him out of bed, Sunday mornings seemed to offer more tempting alternatives, like sleep.

But sleep evaded him today. The coarse blankets seemed to

itch at his skin. The mattress was as lumpy as badly stirred porridge and the house felt like the inside of a fridge on this chilly spring morning.

So, he donned his coat again and took off for the village. He had no intention of speaking to anybody but wanted to at least see people in order to validate that he was still part of the human race.

The church car park was full and mud-splattered diesel cars were double parked along the road. From inside the church, Morgan could hear the massed responses to the prayers and the priest's microphoned sermon. The back of the church was filled with farmers in their Sunday best with one eye on the altar and the other on the pub which was due to open once the service was complete.

One foot in heaven and the other in hell, Morgan thought, as he entered Furlongs in search of the Sunday papers. He picked up a *Sunday World* and a *Sunday Independent* and brought them to the counter.

"Soft day, thank God," said the shopkeeper. "The Hurlers have a big league match today. Are you going?"

"No, I'm more of a football man myself," Morgan answered. "I think I'll spend the day with the papers."

"Are you staying in that cottage out by Stonehouse?"

Morgan froze. Tina had warned him that the village would be curious about him.

"Yeah, I've rented it for a few days while I do the family history stuff."

The shopkeeper leaned across the counter. "A couple of Scottish lads were in earlier looking for directions to that cottage. And they didn't strike me as the sort who were looking for dead relatives."

"Right," said Morgan. "I'll keep an eye out for them I suppose."

Suddenly the door opened and Morgan's heart leapt. But Mass had just finished and the congregation were chasing papers, milk and ice cream for Sunday dessert. Morgan pushed his way past the on-rushing crowd. The car park was emptying quickly and the double-parked cars had moved on.

He turned left and headed back towards the cottage but suddenly stopped. Further down the road a white Hiace van was parked with distinctive yellow Northern Ireland registration plates. Morgan could just about make out the silhouette of at least two figures in the front of the van.

He turned on his heels and ducked behind the shop where a small laneway led down to a stream. He had walked this route earlier in the week and was confident he could find his way back to the cottage through the fields. The grass was waterlogged after the morning rain and his shoes proved less robust than he thought. The cottage was cold and unwelcoming and Morgan's socks played a squelching symphony as he approached. He thought about lighting a fire to dry things out but realised that would send smoke signals and make it clear that he was home. He stuffed the property pages from the Sunday papers into his shoes and put them in the hot press beside the boiler with his squeezed-out socks.

Then he sat on the floor with his knees tucked under his chin. He was too scared to turn on the TV or any lights and he realised that staying in the house was probably the most dangerous thing he could do. But he didn't know where else to go. The weather was deteriorating and he now realised that he had brought little rain protection, not least a spare pair of waterproof shoes.

Eventually his bladder forced him into movement. He inched along the floor towards the toilet when suddenly the beam from a vehicle's headlights danced across his face. He was blinded by the light but ducked quickly behind the sofa. A vehicle slowly pulled up outside and Morgan could hear a door opening and closing and then the slow deliberate sound of footsteps on gravel.

He searched the room for a weapon and the best he could find was a metal poker beside the fireplace. Morgan wriggled towards it as the front door opened. Why hadn't he locked it, he thought? Not that this would have made much difference. But it might have slowed them up for a few seconds. Morgan grabbed the poker and then turned to face his foes.

"What were you planning to do with that, Morgan? Start a fire or smack me with it?" Orla stood in the doorway, her hair sparkling with spring mist. "I brought you some Mikado biscuits. I figured you could do with some sweetness in your life at the moment."

Morgan sat back against the fireplace and expelled some pent-up air.

"You've no idea how pleased I am to see you, Orla."

Orla walked into the kitchen to put the kettle on. "I bet you say that to all the girls."

She brought the tea back to the sitting room where they sat in darkness while Morgan brought her up to date on that day's events.

"So, you think the soldiers are here in this village and they are coming for you?"

"Yeah, they've been asking for directions to the cottage. They are probably just waiting for it to get completely dark."

"Then I don't think we should stay here," said Orla. "Let's drive back to Dublin. You can stay in my place."

"But Tina told me to stay here," Morgan muttered meekly. "She'll be annoyed if I end up back in Dublin."

Orla shook her head in disbelief. "Do you do everything that Tina tells you to do? If she asked you to stick your hand in the fire, would you do that? She's not always right, you know. She's a cop. They always have ulterior motives. Having said that, she'll be even more annoyed if you're dead. Look, we can stop at the call box in the village and let her know that we're coming back. She'll understand. Operations are always at risk of being compromised. I read that somewhere in one of those spy books you gave me."

"Orla, I'm really grateful you came here today. What made you change your mind?"

Orla tilted her head to the side and smiled. "I bumped into Tina at Mass and she said you needed cheering up. And you know me, I'm always a sucker for a puppy in distress."

Morgan nodded. He was rather hoping that his new role as an action hero had brought her to Wexford, but he wasn't going to complain.

"Look, I'd like to give you the full tour but things are a little awkward at the moment. There's not much to see. It's a one-bedroom fridge in the arsehole of nowhere."

Orla shuffled across the living room floor to where Morgan was sitting. She rested her head on his shoulder and her blonde strands caressed his face.

"It's a crying shame that there are a bunch of soldiers out there in the fields waiting to get you. I was kind of looking forward to cuddling in front of that fire and talking about World War Two or whatever else came up. And I brought my pyjamas in case something else came up."

Morgan gulped. He was tempted to ignore the world outside, with all its menace and threat and surrender to the warm charms snuggling into his shoulder.

He met her lips and they kissed passionately. Then he took her hand in his and gazed into eyes. It felt like the first time he ever had her full attention.

"I think we should go."

Morgan packed a light overnight bag and threw it in the back of Orla's Land Rover. "Do you drive this to your lawyer's office in town?" he asked.

"Don't be silly, Morgan. This is for pulling my horsebox. You know I have a couple of ponies."

Morgan smiled. He had often fantasied about Orla in a fetching pair of jodhpurs, but he wasn't going to admit that now.

They climbed in and Orla headed down the driveway. Suddenly a white van blocked their progress and two hooded men carrying automatic rifles jumped out. Morgan squealed and buried his head in his hands. Orla instinctively pushed the Land Rover into reverse and the wheels spun on the loose gravel until they found a grip. The car raced back towards the cottage before she spun it ninety degrees and headed straight through a hedge into the neighbouring field. The Land Rover bumped over stones while bullets rattled against the vehicle's exterior.

"Shit, shit, shit," Morgan kept repeating.

"Can you shut up?" Orla said. "I'm trying to concentrate here."

The Land Rover lurched suddenly to the left as it hit a ditch that Orla had missed in the dark. She tried to maintain control, but it careered wildly from one side to another before finally flipping onto its right-hand side. Neither of them had buckled their seatbelts so Morgan was flung into the driver's seat where he landed on top of Orla, who was pinned to the driver's door.

It was eerily silent. The gunfire had stopped and the Land Rover's engine had cut out. Then they heard shouting and the sound of a van being revved and driven away at high speed. A blue flashing light illuminated the interior of the Land Rover and Morgan noticed that his face was inches from Orla's. She had never looked more beautiful.

"I love you," he said.

"I love you too," said Orla. "Now, can you get the fuck off me?"

8

MORGAN DRAGGED HIMSELF UP AND WITH ALL THE STRENGTH
he could muster, he managed to open the Land Rover's passenger
door and clamber out. As he did, a torch illuminated his face and
behind it he could just make out the silhouetted figure of Tina.

"Are you two okay?" she asked. "I was worried that I might
have got here too late."

"We're fine, I think. I might need some help getting Orla out. I
landed on top of her and I think that might have done more
damage than the crash."

As he said this, Orla's head popped out from the open door.
"Hello cousin," she said. "Fancy you turning up in the nick of
time."

She clambered out and started assessing the damage to her
beloved vehicle. "Just as well I insured this with your company,
Morgan. You can help me with the claim."

"Let's head inside the house," said Tina. "You two look like
you could do with a cup of tea, and we need to make sure there are
no bloodstains or broken bones that you've missed. Adrenalin will
be masking all that at the moment."

They trudged slowly back to the cottage. Morgan's arm was aching but he could move his fingers, so he figured that nothing was broken. Orla marched in front with her head held high like a matador who had just slain an angry bull.

They went off to separate rooms to inspect themselves for blood and bruises and then reconvened in the kitchen where Tina had set out three cups and a pot of tea.

"So, Orla, I should ask what you're doing here but I could probably guess the answer."

Orla cradled her tea and glanced at Morgan. "I guess I'm here for the same reason you are. Looking out for our International Man of Mystery. Nice of you to turn up when you did, though. I guess you scared them off."

"I had a roof siren in my car. I put it on when I saw the white van parked at the front of the driveway. They must have thought it was an Armed Response Unit. Anyway, they panicked and had taken off by the time I arrived. I thought about chasing them, but one unarmed policewoman chasing three heavily armed soldiers is not a good idea. And, of course, I wanted to make sure that James and my darling cousin were okay."

Morgan had been quiet. The ordeal had really shaken him and he was shocked but not surprised that Orla was taking things so calmly.

"But how come you arrived today?" Morgan asked. "I thought you weren't coming until Tuesday."

"Well, I wasn't planning to come today. But then I bumped into Orla here at Mass this morning and she told me about your phone chat. I did warn you not to speak to anyone, James. It got me worried that you'd been talking to other people like your family or friends. The people we're dealing with have lots of resources and they will be monitoring people you know to try and find out where you're staying."

Morgan suddenly felt a wave of paranoia. Was somebody watching his mother's house? Had they bugged the phones at his office?

"I swear that Orla was the only person I called. I've been down to the shop a couple of times, but they think I'm just a family history researcher. Maybe it was somebody in the Guards who told them I was here. You say that it is riddled with spies."

"I don't say that," Tina indignantly replied. "There is one bad apple. And I didn't tell anyone that you were staying here. Not even my boss. And I took precautions to make sure we weren't being followed when I dropped you here."

Tina rose and walked to the window. The night was quiet and darkness enveloped the cottage. She appeared deep in thought, her eyes darting from side to side as she bit tightly on her bottom lip.

"A penny for your thoughts, cousin?" Orla ventured from the kitchen.

Tina turned and placed her palms firmly on the kitchen table. She stared at Orla and held the gaze for what seemed an eternity. "Orla, you seem to be the connecting key to all of this. Did you tell anyone else that you'd spoken to James? Maybe your parents or a shared acquaintance?"

It was Orla's turn to be indignant. "What sort of lawyer do you take me for? I know when to respect client confidentiality and to use my discretion. There are no spies in my line of work, Tina."

Tina smiled. "Okay Orla, I'm just doing my job. James, how many people know about your friendship with Orla? Does your family know, or people at work, for example?"

Morgan's face reddened at the thought of having to publicly discuss his almost but never quite there relationship with Orla.

"I've never mentioned Orla to anyone. Certainly not to my family or work. If I mention a woman to my mother, she's off buying a new hat and booking a church before I can get out the girl's second name. And the guys at work always want to know the gory details if you mention a girl. And that can be an embarrassing conversation if you don't have any gory details to share. So, I haven't shouted it from the rooftops. Orla has been my dark and unspoken secret."

Orla squirmed in her seat. She had never wasted a moment wondering how Morgan viewed her or publicised their relationship. But having its guts displayed to the public like this was uncomfortable nonetheless.

"How do you usually contact Orla?" Tina asked. "I notice you don't have a phone in your flat."

"I usually call her from work. From my work phone."

"And how often do you phone her? What I'm trying to get at is if I looked at your work phone records, would Orla's number stand out or would it get lost in the thousands of phone calls you make to customers?"

"I don't call customers. That's not my job. I deal with national brokers. So, I probably only call two or three numbers regularly and my work is usually done by letter. I don't like the phone, so I try not to use it."

He sneaked a furtive look at Orla. She threw him a smile back. "So, yes, Orla is probably the only person I call regularly. I usually call her at her home when I'm working late and the boss has left for the evening. They don't like you making personal calls at my place."

"Okay, I think we need to head back to Dublin." Tina said. "James, you can stay in my spare room for the time being until I sort out another safe house. And Orla, I think I need to make a visit to Uncle Frank's house and have a look at your phone. I just need to stop at the nearest village and phone in this incident to the local station. Somebody will have heard the shooting, and I don't want the local Guards coming across a bullet-riddled Land

Rover in a local field and coming up with wild conclusions. Although I doubt if they could come up with a wilder conclusion than the actual truth. This is a crazy situation. I also noted the registration of that van, so I'll get the local guys to get it into the system and start doing some checks. They won't have reached the border yet, so I'll get a few checkpoints set up. Although I doubt if they'll be dumb enough to drive that particular van back to the North."

———

The trip back to Dublin took almost three hours. Tina took a lot of back roads to ensure that they weren't being followed. They hardly spoke. Tina was in work mode, constantly checking her mirrors and writing furtive notes in a pad attached to the windscreen. Orla sat up front beside her cousin, her eyes focused on the road ahead.

Morgan sat alone in the back seat, nursing his sore arm and trying desperately to sleep. But in front sat the two women who occupied most of his waking thought and this kept sleep at bay. He stared at the back of their heads. Tina's hair was tightly bound in a stern bun while Orla's flew freely across the car head rest. But he could clearly see Tina's neck, freckled and covered in wispy auburn hair. He had a sudden urge to kiss it and he leaned forward almost without thinking. Just as his lips were about to reach Tina's neck, Orla turned around and smiled at him.

"When this is all over Morgan, we'll head out to Kehoes and get hammered. We might even invite Tina along if she's not too busy saving the world from itself."

Tina ignored her and continued checking her mirrors. They rounded a bend in Kilmacanoge and the soft orange glow of the Dublin skyline appeared before them. It was almost 1 am when they arrived at Orla's house. Morgan got out to give her a hug and a kiss that was at least three times longer than any previous kiss he had managed to secure from her before their kiss at the cottage.

"Mind yourself, Morgan, and be careful with my cousin. Once she gets her claws into you, she won't let go. And we wouldn't want that, would we?"

"Wouldn't we?" he said. "I thought you'd be happy to have me off your hands. You must be tired of my pathetic jokes and desperate attempts to impress you?"

Orla smiled and tilted her head gently to the side. "I could never get tired of somebody trying to impress me. Sleep well and despite what Tina says, do stay in touch."

Tina's house was nearby and soon Morgan had his bag on the spare-room bed and was busy unpacking his meagre belongings. He turned and Tina was standing in the doorway. She had changed out of her work clothes and her hair had escaped from the prison of its bun. Thick auburn locks flowed over the shoulder of the red silk nightdress she had changed into.

"The central heating has been off all day and it will take ages to get these radiators to warm up." She was holding two tumblers with a generous serving of whiskey in each.

"It might be warmer if we both snuggled up in my room." Tina's eyes smiled at him.

"You had me at central heating," said Morgan as he took her hand and they walked together down the hallway to her bedroom.

Morgan smiled as she lifted the covers and slid into bed. I wonder if I could talk her into putting her police uniform back on, he thought.

———

Eighty kilometres further north in the Cooley Mountains, the three British soldiers parked the Hiace van in a forest clearing, 500 metres south of the border. They unpacked their weapons and then spread the contents of a petrol canister around the van's interior. Hastie took out a box of matches, lit a rag stuffed inside a milk bottle full of fuel and then flung the bottle into the van's front seat.

The soldiers stood back and watched as the fire took hold and eventually consumed the van's fuel tank. It exploded, momentarily illuminating the forest in a brilliant blue and orange light.

"Right, it's about six miles to Forkhill army barracks. Let's start walking before the Irish busies get here. Somebody will have reported that explosion." Hastie was already forty metres ahead of the others and marching up a small rise towards the border.

"Does this remind you of the overnight march into Port Stanley, boss?" McMillan asked as he caught up with his sergeant.

"No," replied Hastie. "It reminds me of Napoleon's retreat from Moscow. Except Napoleon didn't have to face a pissed-off policeman when he got home."

"Fuck them if they can't take a joke, boss," ventured McMillan as he lifted a piece of broken barbed wire and they squeezed through. Hastie took out a small torch and examined his map.

"Right lads. I reckon we're back in the United Kingdom. And if I never have to set foot in that fuckin Fenian Free State again it will be too soon. We need to avoid the roads lads, so it will be a cross-country slog I'm afraid. But we should get back to the barracks in time for breakfast. I'll then ring the busies in Belfast and break the bad news to them."

It was a cold clear night. Frost crackled beneath their boots as they climbed over farm gates and trudged through fields. A weak sun rose above Dundalk Bay as they finally made it to Forkhill army barracks. As they approached, they raised their rifles above their heads to signify to the watching guards that they were friendly. Heavily armed men approaching a British army base in civilian dress would normally be met with a hostile response, so a protocol was developed to allow undercover operations to happen and plainclothes soldiers to sneak back to base.

Hastie approached the reinforced slit beside the barracks gate. "Edinburgh Castle," Hastie said. A voice came from behind the slit. "That was last week's password, ya numpty. You look a wee bit rough there, big man. I'll open up for you."

The main door slid open and the three soldiers walked inside.

———

McGuinness stormed through the office of the Knock Road police station and barged into his room, almost taking the door off the hinges.

"Get in here, Anderson," McGuinness screamed. The guys around Anderson's desk didn't even bother to play the mood guessing game that morning. McGuinness had been in foul form for weeks.

Anderson entered and closed the door carefully behind him.

"I know you want to shout and scream, boss. But I think it's time for calm heads. I can sort this out."

"Can you, Anderson? And how do you intend to do that? Have you got the combined forces of the UDR and the Gurkhas on hand to invade Dublin? I spoke to Oriel this morning. He's getting worried. That woman who's looking after the Fenian is keeping things close to her chest. She's not submitting any paperwork or sharing information with the wider team. That makes him think that the Guards know that they have a spy in the camp. I had to spend an hour talking him off the ledge. I told him that the Guards are still leaking plenty of information that is making its way back to us. If they knew there was a spy, that information channel would dry up."

"Okay, boss. I think we need to act quickly. Why don't you sign me off for a few days and I'll slip south and clean things up?"

"Do you have the stomach for it, Anderson? This needs to be clean and clinical. We need this Morgan guy to be out of the picture as soon as possible. Every day that passes increases the risk that he'll hand the tape over to the Irish cops. I'm amazed that he hasn't already, to be honest. But we have to assume that as Oriel is still sitting at his desk, that hasn't happened yet. I'll give you a week to sort things out. I'll tell the team you've taken stress leave. That's the most common cause of absenteeism around here, so nobody will bat an eyelid.

"And needless to say, don't take your own weapon. We don't need any traceability. Talk to McKinney down in stores. Tell him I sent you. Ask for a couple of guns from D consignment. He'll sort you out."

"What's that, boss? A couple of old shotguns we found in IRA arms dumps?"

McGuinness laughed. "We have other means of obtaining untraceable weapons, Anderson. Our friends in MI5 are always keen to ensure that we're well stocked when it comes to the war on terrorism. Mr McKinney will sort you out with something much more powerful than a shotgun. Just make sure that your aim is a bit more accurate than those Scottish buffoons that you hired."

———

Morgan woke with sunshine streaming onto his face. For a moment, he was confused. The sheets were smooth and the duvet warm and comforting. So subconsciously he knew that he wasn't in the safe house in Wexford. But where was he? He looked around the room and his gaze stopped at a framed picture on the wall. It was Tina in her full uniform on the day she graduated from Templemore College.

Then it all came back to him, the silk pyjamas, the whiskey guiltily gulped down, the embarrassed fumbling, the socks that wouldn't come off, the thick-thumbed grappling with bra straps and then the best sex Morgan had experienced in years. Although, in truth, he thought, there wasn't a lot of competition.

The house was quiet. Where was she? Had she grabbed her clothes and fled in shame? Morgan's self-doubt kicked in until he remembered that it was her house and she'd have to come back eventually. Then he noticed a note in vibrant green writing on the bedside table.

Had to go to the office early. You know how to tire a girl out before work!!!! I'll be back around 6pm. Please, please, please stay in the house all day and don't call anyone (especially Orla). There is plenty of food in the fridge. I'm going to speak to my boss to try and sort this mess out. Then we can have more fun!

Tina xxxxx

Morgan smiled. It seemed so long since he'd received a letter from a girl that wasn't effectively telling him to cease and desist. He pulled on his Y-fronts and headed downstairs to investigate the fridge. Tina's house was typical of a relatively well-paid female who wasn't at home much. Everything was where it should be. The microwave had no tomato-encrusted stains. There were only glasses in the glass drawer and only cups in the cup drawers.

Morgan settled for a bowl of cornflakes and headed for the living room. It was spotless apart from two magazines sprawled across the coffee table. *Magill* was open on a story about the rise of The Workers Party. Morgan recognised the same green pen in the notes that Tina had scrawled in the margins. *Cosmopolitan* sat beside it, pristine and seemingly unopened. His eye fell on a headline on the front: "Who is he thinking about when he's making love to you?"

Was he thinking about Orla when he was making love to Tina? He honestly couldn't remember; the previous night's activities were all a blur of sweat and panting. But he was certainly thinking about her now. The way everybody stopped talking when she entered a room. The way her head nestled in the crook of his neck when they hugged. The way her hair could catch sunlight on the cloudiest day.

He thought about calling her but remembered Tina's warnings. It was 10 am. He had eight hours to kill, so he picked up *Magill*. If nothing else, he could spend the day trying to understand why Tina was so fascinated with The Workers Party.

———

Meanwhile, Tina was at work. She cleared her backlog of paperwork and then headed out for an early lunch. She drove directly to her uncle's house and rang the bell. Uncle Frank answered the door with a smile. "Ah, my favourite niece, to what do we owe the pleasure?"

"Orla might have mentioned that she had a few problems with her car over the weekend. She needs to make an insurance claim and I said I'd stamp it from a Garda perspective. But she left the insurance paperwork in her bedroom and she can't get out of work today, so I said I'd pick it up and I can lodge the claim for her."

"That's very nice of you, Tina. You two always were very close. Did she have some sort of accident? She got home late last night and I didn't really get a chance to speak to her."

"It was nothing serious. Just a small prang. I won't trouble you for long; she told me exactly where it is."

"Take your time, Tina love. I'm just out the back doing a bit of gardening. I'm afraid I neglected the weeds over winter. Help yourself to a cup a tea."

Frank trotted out the back door and disappeared into the wilds of the back garden. The phone was on a small table in the hallway. Tina took a screwdriver from her inside pocket and set about dismantling the headset. It didn't take her long to find her quarry. The small listening device fell into her palm. She recognised it immediately as the sort used by the Gardai to bug subversives and journalists.

"Got it," she called to Uncle Frank. "I'll see you at Mass on Sunday."

––––––––

Tina drove back to work and waited for her boss to return from his weekly meeting with the commissioner. She cornered him as he came through the double doors.

"Boss, I really need to speak to you about the Morgan case. Things are getting a bit out of hand."

"Keep your voice down, Tina, and meet me in my office in ten minutes."

She bided her time before marching in. "I presume you heard about the fireworks down in Wexford at the weekend. My cousin was in that vehicle with Morgan when they opened fire on him. These guys are getting ruthless. God knows how many civilians are at risk. We need to do something to stop it."

"Of course I heard about it, Tina. What do you think I've been doing for the last two hours? I've been dreaming up bullshit on the spot to stop the commissioner from launching a full-scale enquiry.

If that happened, then you and your off-radar activities would be out in the open. I told you to leave this with me, but you couldn't help yourself, could you?

"The local cops put in a report about a Northern Ireland Hiace van being seen in the village and the boys in Dundalk sent in a report yesterday about a van found burnt out in the Cooley Mountains. Now the commissioner may not be Kojak but even he is starting to join the dots. So, if we want to keep this little adventure between us, Tina, then you're going to have to start being straight with me. What exactly happened down there and where is this little prick now?"

"I need your help, boss."

Joyce sat silently with his hands together below his chin. "What do you want me to do, Tina? Drive up to Belfast and ask them to please stop their Shoot to Kill campaign?"

Tina put her hand in her pocket and took out the bugging device. She placed it on Joyce's desk.

"I found this in the phone at my cousin's place. Oriel must have put it there because it's one of our devices."

Joyce picked up the device and smiled. "Ah, we used to have a lot of fun with these in the old days before that Doherty head case went rogue on late-night TV. So, you reckon Oriel found out where your young fella was staying and he tipped off the soldiers? He wouldn't be authorised to get his hands on one of these."

Tina leaned across the desk. "He's been spying for the RUC for God knows how many years while sitting at a desk a few feet from your office. You think he wouldn't be capable of breaking into the storeroom if he needed to?"

Joyce bristled. He wasn't used to subordinates, particularly female ones, standing up to him. He threw the bug back at Tina.

"And anyway, even if Oriel was bugging the phone, you don't know that he told the Brits."

Tina snorted and shook her head. "Of course he fucking told them. Morgan called my cousin and told her where he was staying and those goons turned up a few days later. It's not fucking rocket science."

"If Oriel was able to bug your cousin with that piece of pre-World War Two technology, what makes you think the Brits weren't able to do their own surveillance?"

He looked around the room. "They are probably listening to this as we speak. And you've just disclosed more information than Oriel could manage in a lifetime."

"Of course he told them. Why else would he bug that phone?"

She folded her arms and leaned back in the chair.

"How did you ever become a senior detective, boss? You have the investigative skills of Inspector Clouseau."

Joyce stood and looked out the window. The rain was sweeping across the park and young deer were huddling under trees for cover.

"I'm sorry, Tina. This is becoming too big a case for a woman to handle. I'm going to have to take over myself."

Tina was too shocked to speak. Joyce stood at his desk but leaned towards her. "Look, you're a good cop, Tina. But I was dead against having women on the squad from the start. I had to give in because the commissioner was barking on about diversity the whole time until he was giving me a pain in me hole. There are dark arts here in Special Branch. A bigger picture that you couldn't even begin to comprehend. So, I think it's time you went back to your desk job. Now, be a good girl and write down where I can find this Morgan chap."

He passed a notepad across the desk. Tina pushed it back. "I don't care what little games you're playing. We need to out Oriel as soon as possible so that those bastards in the North know that there is no point going after Morgan, because he has already given us the tape. If you're not willing to do it, I'll go over your head and go straight to the commissioner. I don't give a shit any more. This is more important than playing spy games."

Joyce sat down and chuckled. "You think this is a little game, Tina? Have you been to any Garda funerals? Have you ever had to tell a young mother with three kids that her husband has been gunned down outside a post office? Well, I have Tina, and I never want to do it again. I realised years ago that the only way to beat these subversive fuckers was to play them at their own game. I wouldn't expect a girl with a head full of airy-fairy ideas to understand, but if I am playing a game, it's a big-boys' game."

Tina wasn't buying it. Her face tightened and she drew her arms closer to her chest.

"I used to be all holier than thou as well you know," he continued.

"Years ago, I was a young cop up at one of the border barracks. We'd pick up all these hard-nosed Provos who had been well schooled in the art of avoiding interrogation. They could stare at the wall for hours like a Tibetan monk. The older lads used to beat the shite out of them but when they'd turn up in court with black eyes and a bandaged head, the Provo lawyers would have the case thrown for police brutality.

"I thought I could crack them with intelligent questioning. Use good cop, bad cop and that sort of thing. But it wasn't working. So, I went off and bought myself a rider's whip, the sort a jockey would use. Then I'd whip their shirt off and tie them to a chair. I'd start working on their backs. The soft ones would start squealing after two or three lashes. The hard cases could hold out for an hour, but if you got your shoulder into it, you'd break them down eventually.

"The blood would be pouring from them and if they weren't

cooperating, I'd stand over them with a cut lemon and ask them if they wanted some juice on their steak.

"The best part was we'd turn up in court and there wouldn't be a mark on their face or hands. They'd scream at the judge to be allowed to take their shirts off and show the marks, but the beaks were on to it and they'd whip them downstairs to the cells if they made too much noise."

Tina wasn't impressed. "I couldn't give two shits about your heroics in the seventies, boss. I'm talking about an innocent civilian caught up in a web that he didn't create. Isn't it our job as Gardai to protect the innocent?"

"Don't you fucking dare tell me what my job is, Tina," Joyce snarled as he stood up and with knuckles firmly planted on the desk, leaned across and faced Tina.

She could smell his cheap aftershave and stale breath, and she braced herself for an expected assault.

"Solving burglaries and helping little old ladies across the road is the job of the ordinary Gardai. We're Special Branch, we're different and you need to get that into that pretty little head of yours," Joyce told her, as his face reddened and his eyebrow twitched like an out-of-control Morse code machine.

Tina maintained eye contact, but she wasn't really listening. She knew her boss fancied himself as a modern-day Napoleon, but she was political enough to recognise authority and to play along with his tantrums.

Joyce turned and faced the window that overlooked the unkempt grasses of Phoenix Park. He stood for a moment in silence with his hands clasped behind his back.

"Our job is to stop this banana republic from slipping round the U-bend and into the great sewer beyond," he continued in a softer voice.

"This country is ten minutes away from falling off a cliff and the only people with their hands out trying to stop it is us in Special Branch."

He walked over to Tina's chair and bent down so that their faces almost touched. She could feel the anger trembling in his body like a bubbling volcano threatening to explode.

"Do you know how many signed-up communists are sitting in the Dail?" his voice quivering as he asked.

"Do you know how many bomb attacks and post office robberies are planned in this very city by fucking Provos treating this place like the Yanks treated Saigon back in the day? Do you know how may trade unionists are planning to use the thousands of unemployed to bring the whole country to a standstill?

"This is a war we're fighting, Tina. If a civilian or two gets caught in the crossfire, then tough shit. If that stops the Soviet flag from being flown above the GPO or the Brits pouring over the border in tanks, then I'll take it."

Tina let the dust settle for a moment and then got up to leave. She stopped at the door and turned towards Joyce.

"I feel sorry for you, boss. I really do. That's a sad way to go through life. I don't care what you say. I'm going to do my job and go above your head."

Joyce leaned over and took an envelope out of his top drawer. He pushed it across the desk in Tina's direction. "I'm sorry it has come to this; I was planning to use this as a last resort. I only got these developed this morning. Had to call in a few favours with the boys in the surveillance team to get them done so quickly."

Tina emptied the contents of the envelope onto the desk. Five grainy photos popped out. The first showed Tina and Morgan hand in hand outside her front door. The rest were shots in her bedroom that captured her red silk pyjamas in full colour.

Tina felt as though the air had been sucked from the room and she froze momentarily as she tried to process this new development. Her mind was a medley of confusing thoughts. Part shame and embarrassment, part anger and part grudging admiration for the sheer cunningness of her boss.

"I told you not to shit on your own doorstep, Tina. But if you want to take this story to the commissioner, go right ahead. I'm just not sure that he'll take kindly to finding out that you are fucking the main protagonist and that this is the man you want us to sacrifice our entire security network to protect. The commissioner is a bit of a family man. He likes to think that sex only happens overseas."

Joyce leaned back with the expression of a Cheshire cat who had just discovered a hidden consignment of cream.

"So, if I was you, I'd hand over the file and leave this to me. I told you to trust me and you obviously didn't. So, is it any wonder I don't trust you? Now, get back to your desk like a good little girl. Oh, and if you ever raise your voice to me like that again, you'll be directing traffic in Ballina from now on."

Tina slunk back to her desk and buried herself in a file. She didn't like being beaten. And she wasn't about to let that change.

———

She got home at 6 pm as promised and met Morgan in the living room. He rose awkwardly, not knowing whether to kiss Tina or wave a friendly hello. She helped him to avoid having to make a decision by walking straight past him and shutting the blinds on the patio door. She then marched around the house shutting all the other curtains.

Eventually, she returned to the living room and beckoned Morgan to sit beside her on the settee. "James, I really enjoyed last night and I want to get to know you better. But things have escalated. So, we have to go back to being professional. I've lined up another safe house. This one is in the city and you can move in tomorrow. I'm afraid tonight you'll have to stay in the spare room. I'll make sure the central heating is on this time though."

"What's happened, Tina? Are they still trying to kill me?"

Tina welled up as she fought hard to keep her emotions in check. She wanted desperately to protect Morgan from the knowledge that the world he had innocently dropped into had just become more complicated. And she felt a little guilty that her emotions had contributed to that complication.

"Things are just a little difficult, James. People I thought were friendly have turned out not to be."

"That could be the title of my teenage memoirs," Morgan said and squeezed her hand. "I trust you, Tina. You'll sort it out."

———

Tina rose early the next morning. She could hear Morgan snoring soundly from the spare room as she made her way downstairs. She drove to work and headed straight for the canteen to grab some breakfast. It was busy, a mixture of bleary-eyed early risers and jaded plain-clothes cops coming off monotonous night surveillance jobs.

She found a spare seat beside a uniformed female Garda, who turned to her and spoke.

"Hi Tina, you probably don't remember me, but I'm Grainne. I was in the class behind you in Templemore. We always looked up to you. The way you wouldn't take any shit from the lads. I hear you have a big job these days with Special Branch."

"Hi Grainne. I think I do remember you. Did you play Ladies Football for the college in 83? What are you up to these days?"

"Yeah, I was on the team in 83. I wasn't much good though."

Grainne fiddled with a ring on her right hand and stared into her coffee.

"After we graduated, I worked down the country for a couple of years. Then I met a fella and asked for a transfer to Dublin. He was a journalist working for one of the music magazines. The only posting I could get was here in headquarters in the storeroom. Six months after I moved here, he buggered off to London. Said he was taking his career to new places and he wasn't taking me with him."

"Sorry to hear that, Grainne. Men can be bastards."

"It wasn't all bad. He got pulled in by Customs at Heathrow with two ounces of cannabis in his bag. Got six months in Wormwood Scrubs. That's the best thing about being a Guard, Tina. You can always make a discreet phone call and get your revenge."

"I'm happy to hear that you've learned to work the system, Grainne. You certainly take your life in your hands if you dump a Guard. So, are you still in stores?"

"Yeah, stuck in a windowless basement for another year or so before I can put in for another transfer. I don't suppose you guys are looking for a devious young detective upstairs?"

"If I hear anything, I'll let you know, Grainne." Tina reached into her pocket and took out the phone bugging device. "Do you guys keep these down in stores?"

Grainne picked up the small device and examined it. "Oh yeah, they don't go out much though. Not since that journalist scandal. I think you need a court order to get one. Or maybe an inspector can sign one out. Yeah, that must be the case because the last one we signed out was to an inspector. He didn't have a court order but said he had the authority to sign it out anyway. He was pretty stroppy about it actually, now that I think about it."

"When was this, Grainne? Was it recently?"

"Earlier this week. One of your guys from Special Branch actually. Inspector Joyce. Do you know him?"

"Oh, I know him alright," Tina said as she stood to leave. "And like I said, some men are bastards."

———

Morgan rose at 9 am and showered. Then he neatly folded his meagre belongings and packed them into his sports bag. He carried it downstairs to the hallway and then sat on the settee.

He had spent most of the night pondering his predicament and what his next move should be. He was useless at making decisions. Life had more or less just happened to him. His childhood sweetheart had drifted casually into his orbit with little or no effort on his part and she had drifted out again with a similar lack of action by him. The job in Dublin had come about after a conversation with an uncle at a family funeral, and even his relationship with Orla was founded on chance and not design.

They met when he literally bumped into her in the upstairs section of Kehoes and spilled the contents of his pint over the snow-white summer dress she was wearing. Instead of admonishing him and demanding dry-cleaning compensation, she had laughed and talked about the vagaries of fate. She then proceeded to talk for ten minutes without drawing breath and ended by giving Morgan her phone number without him having to ask for it.

He would later discover that she was trying to escape the lecherous attention of a testosterone-overloaded jock at the time and James was her escape ticket. But he didn't care. Life had always worked for him that way. He was a passenger, rather than a driver, on life's journey. So far, it had worked out well enough. He had enough money for takeaways, beer and rent. A small car, insured by his mother, where he was a named driver and the pretence at least that he had a girlfriend in Orla.

But as he sat in Tina's sitting room, staring at the happy family photos on the wall, the certificates of achievement for marathons run and the smiling faces of girls on holiday together, he had the sudden feeling that life could be better if he took some sort of control. He had sat in the back seat of the car for too long and it had taken him to a destination he wasn't overly comfortable with. It was time he climbed into the driver's seat.

He found a pad of paper and Tina's green pen and he sat down to write her a note:

Hi Tina,

I'm really sorry, but I need to get away for a couple of days to get my head around everything. I'll get some cash out of the bank and stay in a B&B somewhere. You've been a huge help but I'm feeling a bit paranoid and I need to figure out who I can trust and what direction I should take. I'm thinking of contacting the media because if the story goes public then those soldiers will be scared to come after me. I don't know. I just need time to think. I've taken down your number and I'll call you in a couple of days.

James xx.

He picked up his bag from the hallway and quietly let himself out the front door.

Tina arrived home just before 6 pm and opened the front door. She called out James's name but there was no answer and a small ball of panic developed in her stomach. The house was in darkness as she had left all the blinds closed when she went to work that morning. She flicked on the light in the living room and saw the handwritten note on the coffee table.

"Shit, shit, shit," she said and then grabbed her car keys and raced back out into the driveway. Twenty minutes later she was at Orla's house. Uncle Frank answered the door and smiled. "Tina, every time I open the front door you're standing there. Are you looking for Orla? She's upstairs in her room."

"Thanks, Uncle Frank, I won't be long."

Orla was sitting on her bed, reading a legal document with a red pen clenched between her teeth. She looked up at the stern face of her cousin in the doorway.

"Everything alright, cous? You look like you've seen a ghost."

"James has disappeared. He left me a note saying he needs to sort his head out. I'm just worried that he's going to do something stupid. Did he call you?"

"No, I haven't heard from him since we got back from Wexford. But look, if he lies low and doesn't contact anyone, then those baddies from Northern Ireland won't be able to find him either, will they? You're not upset because he dumped you, are you Tina?"

Tina marched over and stood beside the bed. "I haven't got time for this shit, Orla. We're not sixteen and at school any more. He's talking about contacting the media and if that happens, I can't control what the outcome will be. I need to find him before he does that. Now, you know him better than me. He doesn't have his car. It's still parked outside his flat and I checked that he's not hiding under the bed there. So, my guess is that he's booked into a B&B or a small hotel in Dublin. Does he have somewhere special? Somewhere you think he'd go if he needed to clear his head?"

Orla sucked on the pen for a second until a thought came to her. "He's always trying to get me to go for a hike with him on Howth Head. He used to go there regularly, particularly in summer. I think walking in a circle is the height of madness, myself. And why would you bother walking in the countryside when you could just as easily ride a horse across it. Anyway, he seemed to think it was the hidden jewel of greater Dublin or some such nonsense."

But Tina was already gone. The front door slammed shut and Orla could hear the sound of a car being reversed at speed over gravel and then the screech of tyres as it sped away.

Tina pointed her car northwards and headed for Howth. As she did so, a rental car pulled out and started following her at a discreet distance. Anderson sat at its wheel with a map of Dublin laid out on the passenger seat. He had never been to this city before, even though it was only a two-hour drive away. But he knew how to follow a car and not to be noticed. He had no idea where they were going but was confident that Tina would lead him to his prey. Tina checked her mirrors regularly but didn't notice the hire car as they sailed through the city centre and took the coast road northwards.

9

Tina tried five B&Bs around Howth Village before she walked up to the Harbour View House. A large lady in a floral pinny met her at the door.

"I take it you are the landlady," Tina said.

"I am dear, but if you're looking for a room, I'm afraid we're full. A bus load of Yanks turned up this evening and we had to scramble round all the B&Bs here to get them rooms. And they are already complaining."

The landlady leaned closer and dropped her voice to a whisper. "Would you believe one of them asked for a room with an en-suite toilet, whatever that is. I told him this isn't the Gresham, but sure I might as well have been talking to the wall. Anyway, if you want a room, you might have to head into Sutton."

Tina produced her Garda badge. "I'm not looking for a room. I want to know if a young man, by the name of James Morgan, checked in today."

"Oh, yes, James. A lovely young fella. Is he in trouble?"

"No, he's not in trouble. I'm just looking for him. He's helping with our enquiries."

"Right, well he did take a room. One of the small ones. He wasn't fussy. But he went out about an hour ago."

Tina took out her notepad and pen. "Did he say where?"

The landlady pulled the door behind her and stepped outside. "Actually, he said he was going for a walk around the summit. I thought that was odd because it was already pitch dark. But he said he needed some air and that he was trying to clear his head. You don't think he was planning to...."

Tina looked up from her notepad with a worried look on her face.

"Planning to do what?"

"Well, you know, the cliffs are a popular place for, how would I put it, doing away with yourself. We have a bad history of suicides round these parts. Ever since they put in that new DART train, we've had people coming out here and just throwing themselves off the cliffs. But James paid for his bed and breakfast. That would be very unusual now, wouldn't it?"

"Unfortunately, not," said Tina. The worst part of a Garda's job she thought was dealing with suicide. They were the ones who had to break the news to relatives and, as a policewoman, Tina was asked to do it more often than her male colleagues. It was tougher even than telling a mother that her son had been killed in a car accident. In those cases, there was very little blame that could be placed on those left behind. While, in the case of suicide, friends and relatives always blamed themselves. And in a lot of cases, people would book themselves in somewhere away from home before committing the act.

She closed her notebook and put her pen away. "Let's assume he just went for a walk. Do you know which direction he went in? I'm guessing he'll do the loop so I'll head the other way and meet him on the way back."

"He went down by the pier, so if you head off to the left there along Church Street, you might meet him. Oh, and if for any reason he's not coming back, can you let me know? It's just that there are still a lot of Americans in town looking for a room."

Tina drove as far as she could go before the road ran out at the summit. She grabbed a torch and a high-visibility vest and set out along the clifftop walk. Her instincts told her to rush but the path was boggy, uneven and covered in sheep excrement. Her nostrils were filled with a rush of sea mist that crept up the cliffside like a pungent ghost and all around was silent apart from the distant hum of a jet liner approaching Dublin airport.

She walked gingerly while calling out Morgan's name regularly. It was a clear moonlit night and the Irish Sea glimmered below. Every time she looked down, though, her heart filled with dread that Morgan might be among the rocks below with the merciless waves sucking his lifeless body into the tide. She forced herself to stay focused, however, and to remember her training.

Then a figure appeared before her in the gloom. She was momentarily excited until she saw that it was a heavy-set man accompanied by a large dog. The dog reached Tina first, circling her with its snout perched like a suspicious customs officer.

"Don't worry. He's a friendly little fella. He won't bite."

"That's grand," said Tina. "I don't suppose you met a young fella on your walk tonight? About six-foot-high and probably wearing a green snorkel jacket."

"Jaysus, if it's a young fella you're looking for, you've come to a strange place. You'd be better off in one of those discos in town."

Tina took out her Garda badge. "This is a serious matter, sir. Did you see anyone or not?"

"Ah, sorry Guard. Yeah, there was a young fella sitting on a rock about 300 yards back that way. I nearly missed him, but Charlie here ran up to him for a sniff and was told to fuck off! Can you believe that, Guard? There is no civility any more."

"Thanks, mister. Have a good night."

She took off at pace and after rounding a bend, she saw the figure of Morgan sitting on the same rock that the dog walker had described. His jacket was hanging loosely off his shoulders and she noticed this his laces were untied. A wave of panic overcame her as she suddenly realised that he might be preparing himself to jump into the sea.

She approached quietly and Morgan didn't notice her coming.

"If I sniff you, will you tell me to fuck off?"

Morgan jumped off the rock in fright. "Tina, how did you find me?"

"I am a detective, James, it's my job to find people in situations like this. And, to be honest, you didn't make it too hard. If you're trying to avoid the massed ranks of the RUC and the British Army, then you might have to be a bit cleverer about it."

She sat beside him on the rock. "I know this is stressful, James, and you are wondering who to trust, but I've gone out on a limb to help you and you have to believe me. And this media stuff. Do you honestly think they'll believe you?"

Tina studied Morgan's face, anxiously checking to see if her words were sinking in. But Morgan's face was a blank canvas as he stared out at the rolling waves.

Tina took his hand and squeezed it tightly. "The Garda have a lot of influence with the media and things are delicate politically at the moment. Nobody will want to hear that there is an RUC spy sitting in the middle of Garda headquarters. And if you do tell the media, I guarantee that news of that will get to the people we are fighting before it ever gets on air."

Morgan nodded slowly. "Okay Tina. I believe you. I'm just struggling to deal with all this. All I ever wanted was a quiet life. I'm not cut out for car chases and leaping across rooftops. I just want to be able to go to the pub again. To watch a football match. To sleep in my own untidy and dust-covered flat."

"I know, James. I want the same too." She gripped his hand tighter and wiped away a tear that had suddenly appeared. She turned Morgan's face towards her and held his gaze for a moment.

"Unfortunately, we can't always choose the cards we're dealt. We still have to play them. Let's get back to the village and we can try to relax and calm down. We'll go for a couple of pints and a takeaway and then you can come back to my place."

Morgan smiled and they began walking hand in hand back along the clifftop path. Tina had her torch focused at their feet to spot the nooks and crannies that would trip them up. The light caught the lace from Morgan's Adidas trainers flowing freely.

"Your laces are undone. That spooked me when I saw you on the rock. If you're not careful, you'll trip and fall down that cliff and then all my efforts to get here will have been in vain."

Morgan bent down to tie his lace and as he did, he felt a whoosh of air above his head followed by a sharp cracking sound. Suddenly Tina jumped on top of him and pushed him to the ground.

"What the hell was that?" he asked.

"A gunshot. High velocity, and it came from over there," she said, pointing towards the south. As she spoke, she silently removed her high-visibility jacket and slipped it into her pocket.

"Okay James. Follow me; we're going to crawl to that rock to my left. Then I'll reassess the situation."

They crawled on their belly to the rock, which gave them sufficient cover to sit up. Tina searched the landscape carefully.

"Okay, there is a gully down there to the left. If we head for that it will give us enough cover to get around the next bend. Then I suggest we run like the clappers downhill and to hell with the amount of sheep shit we'll tread in."

"Can't we just wait here?" Morgan asked. "I mean they might get fed up and leave."

Tina stared at him with a look of exasperation. "James, I know you're not a man of adventure. But trust me. You don't stand still on a lonely hillside when there are men with high-powered rifles trying to find you. Now follow me and you'll be grand. Just keep your head down until we get around that bend and then run like you've left the immersion on."

Tina headed off, crouched like a cat stalking a mouse in a hedge. Morgan followed closely behind, conscious that his arse was stuck up in the air and feeling like it had three circles and a bullseye painted on it. They made the bend safely and Morgan raced ahead, snorkel jacket flowing in the wind. He waited for Tina at the bottom and they stepped behind a gable wall and kissed passionately until the adrenalin had ebbed.

"Let's get that pint I promised you," she said, and they locked hands and headed for the village.

———

Back on the mountain, Anderson packed away his Lee Enfield rifle and night sight. A wave of relief had passed over him when he saw Morgan duck and the bullet pass over him. He had spent the day battling his conscience and finally forced himself to pull the trigger by picturing all the dead comrades whose funerals he had attended. He didn't buy McGuinness's bullshit about saving lives and this all being part of a bigger struggle. But he had joined the RUC and he realised that this meant that he would sometimes have to act outside his conscience.

Nevertheless, when the bullet missed, his instinctive feeling was that this was meant to be. That God or some other power was looking after him. McGuinness of course wouldn't see it that way.

But, for tonight, Anderson was going to let fate dictate his course. He set off down the mountain and decided a beer was called for before he headed back to the small hotel he had booked in the city. He stopped at the first pub in the village and ordered a pint of Guinness at the bar. A country and western group were in the middle of murdering a Dolly Parton ballad and the clientele were huddled around small circular tables, engaged in furious conversation and doing their best to ignore the band.

Anderson found a high stool at the corner of the bar and tried to block out the wailing coming from the small stage. He heard a guttural laugh and looked to his right. Tina and Morgan were sat at a small table, hands clenched tightly together and noses inches apart. Morgan's snorkel jacket was stuffed under the table and Anderson could see the corner of Tina's high-visibility vest sticking out from the corner of her coat.

He smiled to himself. He had decided to trust himself to fate and now it had delivered this gift to him. His quarry and his police guardian. And it turned out that she was taking 'to serve and protect' to whole new levels. That made things interesting. Perhaps blackmail was now on the cards? That was much more palatable to Anderson than the sordid business of guns and blood. Years of turning IRA suspects into touts had taught him that a little scandal provided enough leverage to get what you wanted, without the need for violence.

Anderson remembered that he had a camera in his car. He instinctively knew that this information was valuable and he needed to record it. So, he finished his pint quickly and left by the back door. He returned seconds later with his camera. He needed to use the flash so he positioned himself behind the band and waited for one of the regular flashes from their garish stage lights. He timed his picture accordingly and managed to grab a few snaps without being noticed.

Tina and Morgan were certainly too busy gazing into each other's eyes to notice an extra flashing light. The excitement of the night had brought them closer together. Morgan hadn't thought about Orla all evening.

"I wouldn't have thought that you liked this sort of stuff," he said. "I thought I was the only person in Ireland under the age of fifty who was into country music," he said.

"This isn't country music," she said. "This is country and western. It's different. Our forefathers took this music to America and it got put in a washing machine with lots of other stuff. Then groups like this brought it back to Ireland and changed it again. It's like the bastard child of two mutant Neanderthals."

"You're not like a normal policewoman, are you?"

"I don't know, what's your experience of normal policewomen? Do you think we're only interested in crime? That's like saying you are only interested in insurance. And I think there is a lot more to you than that, James."

"How about we pick up that takeaway and take it back to your place," he said. "Then I can maybe invite you back to my place in the spare room to continue this discussion. You can sit on my knee and we can talk about the first thing that comes up!" He winked at her as he drained his drink.

They rescued their coats from beneath the table and headed for the door. Anderson finished his drink too and followed them at a discreet distance.

Tina and Morgan spent the night at her house behind tightly closed curtains and drove together to Garda Head Office the next morning. Anderson stopped tailing them when they got to the security barriers and then drove back to the car rental shop to drop his car off.

———

It was a dull March morning and Dublin was busy with shoppers and American tourists who had arrived for St Patrick's Day and decided to hang around the land of their ancestors for a couple of weeks. The Americans huddled in noisy small groups on street corners, clutching oversized cameras and bags filled with Aran sweaters and toy leprechauns.

They were taking photographs of the statues and historical buildings, oblivious to the litter that swirled around at street level, the boarded-up shops and the general misery that was etched on the faces of the Irish, who hurried along the street as though shocked that the weather had turned out much wetter than expected.

The Americans, on the other hand, had dressed appropriately for the Irish weather with garish green and yellow rain jackets that contrasted with the grey Dunnes Stores-attired locals.

Anderson was carrying his rifle in a long case and had a small backpack perched on his shoulder. He weaved his way down a busy Talbot Street as he headed for the train station.

"What ya got in the case, buddy?" the American asked.

Anderson was perplexed. He wasn't expecting to engage in conversation on his journey across the city and he only now realised how odd it was to be carrying a high-powered rifle through a built-up area.

"Is it a fiddle or a mandolin? Somethin like that? We're looking for a place that is doing some traditional music. You look like a player so I thought I'd ask."

"It's a machine gun actually," said Anderson as he flashed a toothy grin at the Americans. "But don't tell anyone. I'm playing this lunchtime in Brogans, just down the street there. You should come along."

The American laughed. "Just like Bugsy Malone, huh? We'll see you in Brogans. Slan leat."

"Same to you, sir," Anderson replied as the traffic lights changed and he made his way into Connolly Station.

The two-hour trip to Belfast was pleasant. A weak low sun lit up the carriage and Anderson slept most of the way while his brain tried to reformulate the new information it had received. He resolved to approach McGuinness this time, rather than wait to be summoned and to present a new plan. He had watched Morgan in the pub in Howth and he remembered the scared and timid boy being kicked around the army checkpoint outside Newry. This wasn't his fault, he thought. He had seen plenty of truly evil people in his time as a police officer. The sort who would gun down an unarmed person in front of his kids. The ones who would tie somebody to the wheel of a truck and force them to drive a bomb into a checkpoint. They were the sort of people he would happily shoot on a lonely hillside.

But Morgan wasn't one of those. He was an innocent civilian caught up in the games that security services play. There must be a better way of solving this, he thought, while the train trundled over the Craigmore Viaduct and he fell into a deep sleep.

He called McGuinness when he reached Belfast and arranged to meet him in a park in the east of the city. The park was deserted. Even the trees seemed determined to ignore the arrival of spring for as long as possible. Anderson slipped through the park gate. The imposing hulk of the Harland & Wolff cranes stood before him blanketed in the smoke from a thousand choking chimneys.

McGuinness was waiting for him when he arrived, huddled beneath an overcoat on a park bench that gave him a clear view of all approaching paths.

"This better be good, Anderson. I'm freezing my gonads off here. Why couldn't we meet in a fucking pub or a café?"

"I'm still on stress leave, remember. I don't want to bump into anyone from the team and I reckon the last place those lazy bastards would be is the park. Anyway, I wanted to present a new plan to you and I thought I'd do it in a place where you can shout your head off to your heart's content."

"A new plan, huh? What's this one going to be, Anderson? Get a couple of lads from the boy's brigade to sell him poisoned biscuits? Or maybe post a couple of really sharp letters to his office and hope that he dies from paper cuts? What's wrong with just shooting the fucker, like I asked?"

"I'm a policeman, boss. I'm trained to gather as much information as possible and to use that to draw out more information. I'm not a cold assassin. If that's what you want, then there are plenty of brain-dead lunatics in the force who'll do that for you. I want to figure this out logically."

McGuinness retreated inside his overcoat. Anderson was a lily-livered liberal but he was also the smartest cop on his team, so he was willing to give him the opportunity to pitch his case.

Anderson paced around trying to collect his thoughts. "This policewoman is the key I reckon. Her name is Reynolds. I did a bit of digging when I was down in Dublin. She lives beside an old biddy, who was more than happy to share all the local gossip. Morgan has been staying there a lot recently. I also spoke to Oriel about her. She works in Special Branch in Head Office. A high-flyer apparently, but also one who likes going on solo runs. The word around the office is that she's had a couple of run-ins with her boss recently and they are not talking. That could be good news for us."

"Good for us how, are you trying to recruit her?"

"No. But one thing we're expert at is interrogation. Think

about it, we've been making assumptions to date. It's time we got some hard and fast information. We've assumed for example that he has made a copy of the tape and that he hasn't handed it over yet. We could try and lift him and extract that information, but even if he says he handed the tape over, we don't know what the Guards have done with it. Anyway, she's got him under wraps, so I don't think we could get near him.

"So, I was thinking, we go straight for the head of the snake. Our problem is not with this Morgan guy, it's with the Free State Police. They are the ones refusing to share information with us. So, let's try and draw her out. Get her to come to a place where we can lift her and start squeezing her for information."

McGuinness rose and stood at Anderson's shoulder. "Follow that through to its logical conclusion, Anderson. If she gives us the information we want, which for example might be that she's never heard of a fucking tape, what do we do with her afterwards? We can't let her go back to Garda Head Office and say she just had a friendly conversation with a couple of RUC guys about a mysterious tape. We'd be playing our hand."

Anderson felt the uncomfortable, brooding presence of McGuinness standing directly behind. He could hear his shallow breath and could feel McGuinness's eyes drilling into the back of his head. Anderson knew where this conversation was going and his stomach was telling him that he didn't like it.

"And if she tells us she does know about the tape," McGuinness continued. "And the Guards are watching Oriel, then she'll know that we'll tip him off. Either way, we can't just shake her hand at the end of this interrogation and say thanks for all your help."

"I know that, boss. I've thought about it and I have to admit it troubles me but I agree, we'd have to take care of her afterwards.

But if I do the interrogation, maybe you could find somebody else to do that? I don't think I have the bottle for it."

"That's disappointing, Anderson. This is a game where you need to give full commitment. There are bigger things at stake here than your sensibilities."

A crow landed and perched itself on the bench beside Anderson and cast a conspiratorial eye on the proceedings. McGuinness placed a hand on Anderson's shoulder and began to speak when they were interrupted by a pensioner with a Jack Russell on a lead.

He greeted them with cheery "'hello" as he passed and this single word seemed to drag them back into the real world. They both muttered a polite reply and waited until he was out of earshot before diving back into the world of subterfuge.

McGuinness sat back down beside Anderson, dismissing the crow with a contemptuous wave of his hand.

"Look, you're a smart guy," he said. "I'll give you one last chance to pull this off. You get the information and I'll sort out the rest. Maybe we need to go outside the force on this one. We're owed a few favours from our friends in the Loyalist fraternity. They should have a gunman for hire. But how are you planning to draw her out? We can't risk another of those broad daylight, snatch-off-the-street jobs."

"Yeah, I think it's time that we got a little more sophisticated on this. I got a few interesting snaps of her in Dublin, being all lovey-dovey with Morgan. As I see it, there are two possibilities."

McGuinness sat deadly still, staring at the Harland & Wolff cranes. Anderson watched him intently. He was trying to work out a compromise strategy on the hoof and he needed to read his boss, to see what was working and what wasn't.

"One possibility is that there is no second tape and the Free State cops don't know about Oriel. Alternatively, Morgan has given her the tape and she hasn't passed the information up the chain. So, I plan to send her a letter with a few of those romantic pictures and a cover note from Oriel saying 'I know the little games you're up to. Meet me at such and such a place and I'll give you the negatives in return for some information.' If she's never heard of Oriel, she'll probably turn up for the meeting out of curiosity; if she has heard of him, she'll definitely turn up for the meeting out of fear."

"I like your thinking, Anderson. Set it up. I'll talk to our friends on the Shankill Road and see if I can source a shooter. I'd recommend that you take her to our place outside Banbridge. We can finally put all of this to bed. I'll sign you off for another few days on stress leave."

Anderson let out a deep sigh. He felt like his stress leave might actually be justified.

McGuinness laughed and squeezed Anderson's knee playfully. "The boys will be curious," he said. "So, I'll tell them you're having a few marital issues. That'll stop them asking any questions when you get back. You know nobody on the force wants to talk about that; it's too fucking close to the bone. Let me know when you have her and when you're ready for the shooter."

They went their separate ways: McGuinness back to the station and Anderson to a photo development shop he knew on Malone Road. He was busy rehearsing the letter from Oriel that he would send in his head.

———

The gymnasium at Garda Head Office smelled of stale sweat and rubber but was empty when Tina smuggled Morgan into the changing rooms from her car. They had stopped off at Dunnes Stores on their way to her work and bought some new clothes that were radically different from the jeans and Pringle jumpers he normally wore. Tina was anxious that he should avoid looking like an insurance clerk and should blend in better with the youth of the city.

The changing rooms had a full-length mirror and Morgan stood in front of it resplendent in his new outfit. Tina had chosen baggy cotton pants with an elasticated bottom and a tie-dyed T-shirt, finished off with an ostentatious purple waistcoat. She had also insisted on some hair gel to create a fringe and mop in the style of Duran Duran.

I look like an idiot, he thought, as he shifted uncomfortably from side to side, trying desperately to feel normal. Tina had told him that he could go out each day but had to avoid any of the places he used to visit. She said that he could ring his family and the occasional friend (she avoided using Orla's name, but he knew who she was talking about) provided he used a different pay phone each time and spread it around the city. Under threat of a severe spanking, he wasn't to tell anyone where he was staying. Tina explained in detail how the Wexford incident had happened, and he didn't need to be told twice.

She was sure that the Northern security forces would have people out looking for him, armed with photos of him in his traditional attire and hairstyle. He could drift around the city each day dressed as he was now, with little fear that he would stand out from the thousands of other Dubliners who were attired in that manner.

Tina wanted him back at the apartment at 6 pm each evening. "I'm not afraid of the dark," she said. "But I am afraid of what some people do with it." She promised to come around most evenings, so long as she could be sure that she wasn't being followed. The apartment wasn't going to be ready until the next day, so she gave him clear instructions on how to get back to her house through back streets and to enter by the back alleyway. Then she kissed him underneath a basketball hoop and led him to the back gate on Blackhorse Avenue.

Morgan gathered as many coins as he could and set out into the chill morning air with Orla's work number in the back pocket of his new baggy pants.

He passed three vandalised phone boxes until he found one that worked. He kicked away a half-empty snack box and took out the number from his pocket. A receptionist answered and when he asked for Orla, the receptionist asked what it was in connection with. Morgan had to think quickly. He looked around for inspiration and all he could see was the snack box on the ground.

"I'm looking to get planning permission for a fast-food restaurant."

It seemed to suffice because after two rings, Orla's dulcet tones came across the line.

"How are you doing, Morgan? Where do the cops have you holed up now?"

"Can't say, I'm afraid. You know what happened last time."

"Yeah, I've just received the bill for the repair to my Land Rover. Your insurance company is going to have a fit. But you can tell Tina that I got the garage to avoid mentioning the bullet holes on the estimate. So, what you up to?"

"Just trying to keep my head down and work on some family history. I was thinking of spending some time in the National Library; see if I can track down some of these dead Morgans that are responsible for all the dodgy genetic traits I seem to exhibit."

"You can't blame everything that's wrong in your life on your relatives. We're all responsible for our own destinies."

Morgan remembered their conversation about relationships, and why she blamed her inability to last more than five minutes in one, on her parents' break-up. But he thought better than to mention it. His limited experience with women had taught him that when a man thinks he had the last word in an argument, he was in fact only having the first word in the next argument.

"So how are you Orla, have you been up to anything?" he asked.

"Well, I have been seeing this guy from work. Big mistake. I mean what will I do when we eventually break up? I'll still see him every day. It will be mortifying. I'll probably have to get a new job."

"So, let me get this straight, Orla. You've only just started going out with this guy and you're already planning the break-up?"

"Yeah, well he's married. So, there is no future anyway. We went out last Friday after work and I got a bit pissed. We ended up in a car park in the Dublin Mountains at 2 am but I'll spare you the details. Anyway, I opened the curtains on Sunday morning and who was standing in the driveway? Only your man. I'm not just going to have to change job, I'm going to have to move feckin' country as well."

"What sort of man are you looking for, Orla? Maybe while I'm doing some research I could see if that sort of man ever existed."

Morgan was being facetious but sometimes Orla was so shallow that you could paddle in her. She took his question seriously.

"I guess I'm looking for a guy who will get home from work before me and have a gourmet meal ready each night. A guy who is good at housework, cries at the end of *It's a Wonderful Life*, but is good at DIY and who earns a fortune."

"And what are you offering this bloke in return?"

There was a slight pause on the line and Morgan was worried that he'd lost the connection. Then Orla spoke in a soft sultry voice.

"The best sex he's ever had."

Morgan gulped and then replied. "Would you give me a couple of months to learn how to cook?"

Orla laughed. "Anyway, how are you, Morgan? Has anyone tried to kill you lately?"

"Yeah, there was an incident on Howth Head, but luckily Tina turned up to save me."

"Ah yes, my intrepid cousin. Does she have her claws into you yet, Morgan? I saw those little glances you were throwing each other when we were in Wexford."

Morgan didn't know how to reply. Part of him wanted to tell Orla all about his bedroom antics with Tina. To make her jealous perhaps or to simply celebrate the sheer fun he was having. But part of him wanted to hold back, to make Orla think he was still available.

"Yeah, we eh, we're kind of close now. She seems to be there for me when I most need help. And I think she's kind of special, don't you agree?"

"Even when she was a kid, Morgan, she wanted everything I wanted. If I wanted a pony, she had to go out and get one first. If I mentioned that I was going on a school trip to France, I'd arrive in Paris to find her standing on the train platform like bloody Paddington Bear."

"What are you saying Orla. Do you want me?" His heart was racing and he wondered if he was finally getting through.

"I want you as a friend, Morgan. She'll do her best to stop you seeing me." The words pierced his enthusiasm like a pin pierces a balloon.

"I want to go back to the old days," she continued. "When we could just go for a beer and a chat. I don't think I ever said it enough. But I really liked those conversations we used to have. If you start going out with Tina, she'll make sure we never meet. She's pretty jealous and possessive, Morgan. In fact, I'd say she's already been round to your flat to go through your wardrobe and has chucked out all the shirts she doesn't like. Has she taken you clothes shopping yet, by any chance?"

Morgan looked down at his New Romantic attire. "I didn't get to pack much from my flat, so she did help me buy a few new threads. But I had the final say."

"I bet you did, Morgan. I bet you did." Orla laughed in that high-pitched giggling way that always reduced him to butter.

___

Tina parked outside Garda headquarters and sat in her car for a few minutes gathering her thoughts. She wanted to avoid Joyce if possible. She wasn't convinced that she could control her emotions. He was a complete bastard, but she couldn't bring herself to believe that he was happy to go along with all this. To put Morgan's life as well as her own at risk. She needed more time to figure things out. She sensed that there was a piece of the jigsaw missing and she was determined to find it. And it might even be a corner piece.

She took the stairs to the second floor and breathed a deep sigh of relief when she noticed that Joyce's office was empty. A few of her colleagues nodded hello as she passed but she wasn't in the mood for chit-chat. She hung her coat and handbag on the hook at the back wall and slid into her desk.

She had been out of the office for three days and a mountain of mail had built up. Inter-office memos concerning criminals on the run, feedback from Garda stations around the country on suspicious movements in their area and letters from retired army officers concerning possible sightings of Shergar.

She skimmed through them quickly until all that was left was an A4 brown envelope with her name scrawled in green handwriting across the front. As was her habit, she held the envelope in her hands to judge the weight while she inspected the postmark. 'Dun Dealgan' was etched in smudged writing around the stamp. Her curiosity was tickled. Special Branch officers learned to pay particular attention to mail coming from Dundalk.

She tore the edges carefully and a white typed letter and five photographs fell out. She picked up the first snap. It was her and Morgan holding hands over a bar-room table and gazing into each other's eyes like teenagers at a school dance. The others were similar, including one taken outside her house.

Tina exhaled sharply as she picked up the letter. It was typed in a small font and had enough mistakes to make her think that it was the work of a police officer.

To: Tina Reynolds

I hope you like the romantic picturs I've enclosed. You look lovely. But I don't think the boss would be best plesed to see one of his officers connudling with somebody in the witness protection program.

Anyway, I know what you're up to. And I know what Morgans up to too. You think you might know all about me but you don't know the full truth. You've got something I want and if you give it to me, I can let you in on the full truth and you'll be amazed by what I can tell you.

If youre up for it, meet me at the Wellington Memorial at 7pm on Tuesday. Come on your own or I'll scarper. I'm a cop too remember, so I know all the tricks.

Oriel

Tina sat back and gazed around the office. She had the sense of being watched. She gathered up the photos and letters quickly and stuffed them back into the envelope and then put that into her handbag. She went back to her desk and got out a blank sheet of paper and then wrote Morgan's name in the middle with Oriel's at the top and Joyce's name at the bottom. She wrote Orla's name in small writing beside Morgan's and the name of the two Northern policemen beside Oriel's.

She sat back and stared at the picture, trying desperately to connect the dots in her head. What was Joyce's game? Was Oriel really a double agent, feeding shit to the Northerners while they thought he was their key asset? Maybe Joyce was also working for the RUC? Was Orla a Mata Hari figure sent by the North to seduce Morgan? She discounted that theory straight away. If Orla was sent to seduce Morgan, she was going about it in a funny way.

She walked to the window and stared out at the early-morning fog that blanketed Phoenix Park. The Wellington Memorial rose majestically from the mist. Was Oriel setting a trap? She didn't care. She would go and meet him anyway. Her gut told her to do it and her gut was usually right.

Tina got back to her house just after 6 pm to find Morgan huddled on the sofa with the curtains pulled and the front door bolted, as he had been instructed.

They kissed briefly before she headed upstairs to the shower.

"If the door-bell rings, come and get me. Don't let anyone in under any circumstances. I won't be long. There is some stew in the freezer. You could defrost it in the microwave, and I'll be down in a jiffy."

Morgan padded into the kitchen and opened the freezer with the enthusiasm of a condemned man facing his last meal. He had been brought up on stew for dinner three times a week and vowed when he left home that he would never face it again. Part of the attraction of moving to the city was the abundance of takeaways, none of which offered the traditional Irish fare of vegetables and cheap beef boiled within an inch of their lives.

He levered the frozen blob of stew onto a plate and set about trying to work out the microwave controls. He'd only ever seen a microwave on television before and the control panel may as well have been the dashboard of a spaceship. He pressed a few random buttons and the light came on and the internal plate started turning. So, he turned away in triumph and retreated to the sofa. The news was covering another explosion in Northern Ireland and the sight of black-faced British soldiers on screen sent a shiver up his spine.

Suddenly, the doorbell rang and he almost jumped out of his skin. He froze momentarily, before he remembered Tina's instructions. He ran upstairs and raced into the bathroom without knocking. "Someone's, someone's here," he spluttered, pointing haphazardly towards the front door.

"Calm down, James. It's probably Mormons or somebody selling encyclopaedias. You stay up here and stay quiet and I'll deal with it."

She slipped on some tracksuit pants and a Garda sweatshirt and headed downstairs. Morgan peeked through the banisters and watched as Tina stooped and looked through the spy hole in the door.

"I don't believe it," she said as she undid the bolt and opened the door. The next thing Morgan heard was the familiar high-pitched laugh of Orla and the sound of fake air kisses.

"Hiya, cous. I was just dropping off some legal documents in this part of town, so I thought I'd drop in and say hello. I believe you've been looking after Morgan and I imagine that can be quite trying, so I thought I'd invite you out for a quick drink. I know this is a rough end of town, but there must be at least one bar around here that you don't need tattoos as a condition of entry."

Tina hustled Orla into the hallway and closed the door quickly before redoing the bolt locks.

"Look Orla, it's not a good time. I can't really leave the house at the moment. Things are a little delicate."

Morgan had crept out of the bedroom and was standing at the top of the stairs straining to hear the conversation. He leaned across the landing to rest his hand across the far wall and to gain more leverage. In the process he accidently hit the light switch and suddenly the stairs and landing were illuminated. The two girls looked up to see Morgan in an acrobatic pose at the top of stairs.

"Em, how are you doing, Orla? It's nice to see you," he said.

Tina shook her head. "I have a bottle of wine in the fridge. Why don't we all head into the sitting room." Orla smiled and winked at Morgan as she followed her cousin out of the hallway.

They ate the stew while Tina brought Orla up to date on as many of the details as she thought she needed to know. She finished by explaining that Morgan was staying with her temporarily while she sorted out another safe house.

"Sounds very exciting," Orla said. "This is yummy, by the way, cous. Is it Beef Bourguignonne or Goulash?"

Tina eyed her with the suspicion of somebody who thought they were the victim of a piss take. "It's Irish stew, Orla. I've eaten this loads of times at your house. Your mother makes a great stew, even though most of the spices in her spice rack look like they were brought back by Marco Polo."

"My mother makes a nice goulash," Orla answered. "And if she makes stew, she uses lamb, not beef that you'd need an angle grinder to chew." As she said this, she picked up a piece of meat and viewed it with undisguised contempt.

Tina sat back with her arms folded. "So, when you thought it was Beef Bourguignonne, you thought it was delicious, but when you find out it is stew you turn your nose up at it and have the cheek to tell me that I'm not even using the correct ingredients."

Morgan watched all of this with amusement. He had rarely

stood up to Orla when she let loose with her strongly held but lightly thought-out opinions. He admired the way that Tina was not cowed in Orla's presence and was able to give as good as she got.

"Ladies, if I might interrupt. My mother was of the opinion that the key ingredient in stew was any meat that could take five hours of boiling in a large pot and still be chewable. As to the type of meat, well from my experience, there wasn't a donkey, goat or ram in Tipperary that was safe from my mum's pot. And when you mention all those foreign foods, it just makes me think that the Irish weren't the only ones to come up with the lazy solution of throwing everything into a pot and boiling the shite out of it. The foreigners just came up with fancier names."

The two cousins looked at each other and shook their heads. The best way to end a family argument was to find a common adversary and Morgan's attempts at humour provided that.

"What will we do now?" Orla asked. "I guess you two don't want to leave the house and go for a drink. So, it feels like Christmas Day, when you're stuck inside with nobody but your boring family to keep you company."

Tina got up to look for the newspaper. "I could see what's on TV, perhaps. Or maybe we could play cards or something."

Orla jumped up enthusiastically. "I know. Remember we came to your parents place last St Stephen's Day? It was so boring. Your mother wouldn't let us turn on the TV and we had to listen to your father droning on about his allotment for hours. Then you saved the day by bringing out that board game that you bought in New York. What was it called? Trivial Something?"

"Trivial Pursuit," Tina answered. "And St Stephen's Day wasn't nearly as awful as Christmas Day at your house. I've had better dinners out of a snack box at 3 am on a stakeout."

Orla crossed her arms defiantly. "Well, you might have

enjoyed dinner more if you hadn't wolfed it down in ten minutes so that you could head into the sitting room to watch *Top of the Pops*."

"That was as long as I could spend staring at the pool of mush your mother called 'Brussels sprouts'. And my only surprise when I got to the living room was that your family weren't there already, watching the Queen's speech and channelling your west Brit tendencies. Coming as you do from the Fine Gael side of the family."

"I pick the blue pie holder," Morgan interjected. "I've never played Trivial Pursuit. But I've been to a lot of pub quizzes."

Tina stood up. "I think I have it somewhere. But it takes a few hours to play. James and myself have a few things to organise."

Orla let out a low guttural laugh. "I'm sure you do. But we'll be quick. I'm brilliant at quizzes and I'll whip your butts."

Tina searched under the TV and emerged with the box. While she was doing this Orla picked up the plates and took them to the kitchen. As they passed each other, Morgan realised he was in the same room as the two women who had dominated his recent erotic thoughts. His eyes followed Orla as she glided into the kitchen. She was wearing a sleeveless off-white dress with a zip that ran the length of her spine. He pictured himself slowly undoing the zip while he nuzzled the back of Orla's neck.

"Penny for your thoughts?" He looked up suddenly to see Tina standing above him with the board game in her hands.

"Err, I was just thinking about strategy. Do I, em, try and go for Sport first, but that would be a mistake cause it's the American version and it would all be baseball and NFL. Or go for geography cause I used to know all the capital cities in the world."

Tina sat down beside him and put her hand on his knee. "James, you're babbling. Is my cousin casting her spell on you?"

Morgan was suddenly wracked with guilt. Tina had welcomed

him into her life with no demands or expectations and he had totally taken it for granted. He had spent most of his adult years aimlessly wandering life's highway looking for love and affection, circling the airport without ever landing. And here it was right in front of him and he didn't even see it. But at the same time, he felt like a small boy who had been taken to a toy shop by a kindly aunt but told that he could only choose one present.

"No, Tina, you are the one who has me spellbound. I know you're smarter than Orla. I want to sit back and enjoy watching you kick her butt."

The game started and Orla raced ahead. She had an amazing memory and could instantly recognise questions she had heard before in the three times she previously played the game. So, when Morgan asked, "What is the longest river...?" she would quickly reply, "The Amazon" without needing to hear the rest of the question.

But Tina wore her down in the end. Her police training meant that she had a deductive mind and could figure out answers from clues in the question. Morgan trailed along in last place and was happy to sit back and enjoy the sarcastic volleys that the cousins hurled at each other. He found that he could conjure up answers to obscure Art and Literature questions but fell down on anything that involved knowledge of the real world.

Tina answered the last question correctly and allowed herself a short smile before tidying up the game and returning the box to its home under the TV.

"I don't want to be pushy, Orla. But James and I have to discuss the next few days and he has to pack. I'm looking for a safe place for him to stay."

"I don't want to be the gooseberry," Orla replied as she picked up her coat. "I'll leave you to it. I'm sure it will be a busy last night in the love nest."

Morgan rose and offered to see Orla to the front door. "It was nice to see you, Orla. I'm not sure if you came around to see Tina or me, but it was good to catch up anyway."

She kissed him lightly on the lips. "Who do you think I came to see? Mind yourself, Morgan. And call me if you need me. Don't mind what my cousin says. We can be clever and talk in code. For example, if you wanted to meet in Kehoes at 9 pm on Saturday, just say I'll meet in the place where I threw a pint of beer over you. And we'll meet at the time I normally meet you, but on the day of the week that Tina washes her hair. I know she only does that on Saturdays. If there are spooks listening in, they'll never crack that."

"I've never met you on a Saturday," he said. "I always saw that as premium Orla night. I never saw myself in the premium seats."

"You never know, Morgan. Play your cards right and you might qualify for an upgrade."

With that she turned on her heels and was off. Morgan suddenly realised he was alone in open sight. He shut the door quickly and set the bolt lock. Tina was waiting on the sofa with an open bottle of wine and two glasses in front of her.

10

Hastie sat at a window seat in Kinneys bakery and watched the April afternoon melt into an evening of sleet and wind. Belfast was a strange and forbidding city to him, full of security barriers and road blocks and with an air of upcoming menace that seemed to ooze from the footpaths. It was a world away from the partying he had witnessed in Dublin on St Patrick's weekend and while that wasn't the best fun he'd ever had, he knew which city he preferred. His tours of duty had been spent in South Armagh where everyone outside the barrack gate was the enemy. At least you knew where you stood.

Here on the damp streets of Belfast, he didn't know who was friend and who was foe. His army crew cut was a bit of a giveaway, so he kept the hood of his parka up most of the day and not just because of the weather. Anderson had called him the day before and asked to meet in Kinneys and said it was on the safe eastern side of town. But nowhere felt safe to a Glaswegian in Northern Ireland.

The officers told the rank and file that they were there to protect the civil authority. But it didn't feel like that when you were manning a midnight checkpoint in South Armagh. Like most British soldiers, Hastie hated all Northern Irish people equally. At least in the Falklands, you could see the joy and relief on the faces of the locals when they liberated Port Stanley. In Northern Ireland you had two communities. One would treat you with open hostility. The other side would sneer at you and ask why you hadn't got there sooner and gone in harder.

He was on his second pot of tea and fruit scone when Anderson arrived and slid into the seat beside him.

"Good to meet you again, Hastie. You look smaller out of uniform."

The soldier looked at him suspiciously. "I don't think I've ever met you, big man. How do you know what I look like in uniform?"

"We're Special Branch, Hastie. We don't deal with anyone unless we've done a bit of background research. I called your CO and asked him to send up your file. It had a nice wee picture of you pinned to the front. Made me think you were bigger. Plus, I was there the day you and your mates kicked seven colours of shite out of our friend from the South."

"Ach, well that's the poor diet on the west coast of Scotland's fault. We're all wee fuckers over there."

"The diet isn't much better here," said Anderson. "Have you tried our fried bread? Sorry I'm late by the way, there is a security alert in the city centre. I had to take a bit of a detour to get here."

Hastie's professional instincts were pricked. "Anything serious, is the army involved?"

Anderson shrugged. "I don't think so; probably just an unattended handbag in a shop in town. Left there by accident or containing an incendiary device that will kick off a chain of ten explosions across town. That's the roulette wheel we spin every weekend, Hastie. We don't know where it will land. It makes going to work interesting. Don't you know that we're all adrenalin junkies in the RUC?"

"This placed is fucked up," said Hastie as he drowned his tea.

"Yeah, I agree, but unlike you, it's the only fucked-up place I know. So, I need to protect it and that's why I called you."

Hastie looked like he had just swallowed a wasp. "I thought we had messed up enough times that you were happy to see the back of us."

The waitress interrupted them, and Anderson ordered tea and some madeira cake.

When she had left, he turned to Hastie and whispered. "Just like this being the only fucked-up place I know, you and your friends are the only fucked-up henchman I know. I have one more job and I can't ask anyone inside the police service. This has to be completely off record."

"I'm not going after that little Fenian again, Anderson. He's bad luck. And that female cop has him in her pocket. If she sat down, she'd break him."

"I'm not going after the little Fenian this time Hastie. We're shifting up a gear and we're going after the cop herself."

Hastie spluttered the tea he was in the process of drinking. "You're telling me that you want us to help you to knock off a serving police officer? That's raising the stakes a wee bit, isn't it?

"She's a serving Free State police officer, Hastie. We don't consider them to be proper police. They refuse to send terrorists back across the border to face justice. They turn a blind eye to the boyos who make bombs in Dundalk and then drive up to Crossmaglen to try and kill you and your friends.

"Anyway, I'm not asking you to knock her off. We want to talk to her, so we've arranged a meeting in Dublin. I'll do the complicated stuff. I just need you and your two buddies to be in the background when I need some heavy lifting done. Then we'll drive her to our place in Banbridge and set up an interrogation. Once things are set up you guys can go."

Hastie nodded. "If we do this, we're quits. You guys back up our story at the court case and we never have to hear about this fucking business again?"

Anderson offered his hand. "You have my word. You can trust me. I'll call your barracks on Monday and we'll agree on logistics."

Hastie shook his hand and stood to put his coat on. He pulled the hood tight around his head. "No offence Anderson. You seem like a nice bloke. But you're still an Irishman and I wouldn't trust you as far as I could fucking throw you."

———

Tina brought a takeaway around to Morgan's safe house on Monday and they settled down afterwards on the sofa to watch a video. She rested her head on his shoulder and he stroked her hair gently. She turned her head to his and they started kissing passionately. In no time he started unbuttoning her jeans.

"Should we move to the bedroom?" she whispered as she nibbled his earlobe.

"That will take about thirty seconds; I don't think I've enough time."

She laughed and slipped her jeans and underwear off. Anderson fumbled with his belt with one hand while searching for a condom in his pocket with the other.

"Where do you buy those, by the way? Do you have a prescription?" she asked while Morgan unrolled the condom and put it on.

"I have a supplier up the North," he said. "Is it safe to tell a Garda that I'm illegally importing contraceptives?

"It's fine as long as you don't inhale," Tina said with a smile as she gently pulled Morgan into her.

They made love on the sofa and then lay in silence for a few minutes. The TV blared in the background but neither of them noticed.

Morgan raised himself and rested on his elbow. "It's a big day tomorrow," he said.

Tina instantly thought of her planned meeting with Oriel. She sat up with a start. "How do you know about that?"

"Know about what?"

From the confused look on his face, she could see that she had jumped too quickly to a conclusion.

"Sorry, what's so big about tomorrow?"

"It's my birthday, I'm twenty-seven tomorrow. That's when you hit your peak apparently."

"Really?" said Tina. "I think I hit my peak at twenty-one. That's when I was fittest and at my best weight."

"I don't mean physical peak. I mean maturity, intelligence. That sort of stuff. They say that the music you are listening to when you are twenty-seven is the music you'll listen to for the rest of your life. The clothes you wear will be the same. Do you ever wonder why ould ones and ould fellows go around in tweed overcoats and three-piece suits with collarless shirts? That's because those clothes were trendy when they were twenty-seven."

She looked at him suspiciously. "You mean you'll still be listening to Wham! in forty years' time?"

He tickled her and they fell off the sofa giggling. "I don't even listen to Wham! now, so I doubt that. I'm more a Christy Moore fan. Anyway, the reason I brought it up is because I was wondering if we could go out somewhere to celebrate my birthday. I've been cooped up in this place for the last few days and I'm gumming for a pint."

Tina was conflicted. She wanted so much to have a normal relationship with Morgan. To do things like getting drunk on birthdays. But she had that meeting with Oriel planned for tomorrow evening.

"How about this," she said. "I have to meet somebody as part of my work tomorrow at 7 pm in Phoenix Park. I'll park my car just inside the main gate on Chesterfield Avenue and leave the key behind the back wheel. If you get there just after seven, you can wait for me in the car and then we'll go somewhere and we can do something fun? That way, you'll want to do it every birthday for the rest of your life, because it will be what you did when you were twenty-seven."

Morgan smiled. "My supplier just told me that a shipment of those illegally imported prophylactics has just arrived. Could I interest you in moving to the bedroom?

———

Morgan spent Tuesday in the National Library, searching through microfilm records of birth and death registers. His family came from an area of Cork that had so many people with his name that people had to take blood tests before they got married to make sure they weren't marrying their cousin. He rested his chin on his hand and turned the wheel slowly, all the time thinking that he was hunting a very small pin in a very big haystack.

"Who you searching for, man?" asked the middle-aged American at the next desk.

"Morgans. They come from County Cork. I'm checking the parish my dad came from and then working outwards."

"You can search by parish?"

"Yeah, what way are you doing it?"

"Well, I'm looking for a Patrick O'Brien who left Dublin for

Boston in 1846 or 1847. I got a bit excited when I spotted one. But then I spotted about fifty more. Seems that Patrick O'Brien was a pretty popular name back then."

"Yeah, might have helped if they were a bit more imaginative about first names during the famine. But I suppose if you are starving, you're not going to give a lot of thought to family history researchers a century later."

"Shoot, I flew over from the States to do this. I didn't realise it was going to be this hard."

Morgan was at a loss to offer any advice. He was a half-hearted researcher himself and hadn't progressed beyond his grandparents in his own work.

"On the plus side," he said. "The pubs are now open."

Morgan grabbed his backpack and said his goodbyes. He wasn't planning to head to the pub. It was tempting, but he wanted to save his thirst and ammunition for his birthday date. He spent the day circumnavigating the city, stopping every now and again to make a phone call. He called his mother first and told her that he was still in England on a training course. He had been lying to his mother from an early age, so he found this easy. She warned him about the evils of drinking too much and asked when he was next going to deign to honour his family with a visit.

Morgan was non-committal. He had never given much thought to leaving his home place. It had just happened. But when it did, it felt like the elastic band that had been tied to his back had snapped. His home was in Dublin now and his family felt like the past.

After speaking to his mother, Morgan walked back to his own flat in Rathmines. He didn't have the key and Tina had warned him that the security forces were probably still watching it. But he stood across the road and looked at his faded curtains and the

'Vote No to SPUC' poster he had bravely taped to his window and then forgot to take down after the abortion referendum had been lost.

A wave of nostalgia for his old boring life washed over him. He longed for the routine of getting up for work every day. The Chicken Kiev that he treated himself to in the Waterloo Bar for lunch every Thursday and his regular meetings with Orla that went nowhere but offered at least an interesting journey.

He wanted that life back so much, to feel ordinary again. He set off to find a city centre phone box so that he could call Orla and listen to ten minutes of disappointing boyfriends and successful pony regattas. It was a slice of his old life and he would enjoy it like a piece of cake.

Orla didn't keep him on the phone for long. She was busy at work, a feeling Morgan himself longed for. He couldn't face the cold and characterless apartment, so he wandered around town until it was time to meet Tina. He walked slowly up the quays to the main gate of Phoenix Park past the sludge of the Liffey at low tide. The evenings were starting to stretch and the low sun was slipping down over the park as he approached. A few curious deer had wandered down to the main gate as though they were there to welcome the incoming traffic. A mist was settling over the grass as thousands of Dublin fires were lit and expelled their noxious fumes over the city.

He spotted Tina's car neatly parked on the left-hand side of the main drag through the park and the key was where she had said it would be. The evening had cooled considerably since the disappearance of the sun and he snuggled into the driver's seat and turned the heating on.

After he had warmed the car up, he turned the engine off, tuned into Radio 2 and wound the seat back. The park was quiet and the only cars parked along the road belonged to dog walkers and those who chose the solitude of the park for the sort of romantic encounters that were illegal in Ireland in 1986.

Morgan drifted off to sleep and was awoken by the humming of a diesel engine beside the car. A white van had pulled up beside Tina's car and was reversing into the space behind. Morgan glanced up from the reclined driver's seat and was shocked to see one of the Scottish soldiers sitting in the passenger seat.

He slunk deeper and deeper into his coat and scanned the mirrors. He saw the three soldiers alight from the van and walk towards the Wellington Memorial. They clearly hadn't noticed him, but then he remembered that Tina said she was meeting somebody and he suddenly realised that it was probably in connection with the case. As he sank deeper into the seat, it dawned on him that the soldiers were probably looking for Tina and not him.

He was at a loss as to what to do. So, he decided to follow them while he tried to work out his options. They stopped at a clump of trees and took up position behind them. It was only now that Morgan noticed that they were dressed entirely in black with dark lines across their faces. They were almost invisible in the darkness that had fallen on the park. Morgan looked at his garish New Romantic outfit and regretted leaving his navy snorkel jacket at home. He hung back and found a bulbous oak tree to stand behind.

Then he heard a shout and saw the three soldiers race forward. A moment later, they returned. They were carrying a lifeless body while a fourth man followed closely behind. Morgan stared at this man. He seemed vaguely familiar. As the party grew closer to him, he hugged the tree and tried to make himself as small as possible. They passed within a metre or two of the tree and crossed a spot where a streetlight cast a weak spot of light into a muddy puddle.

It was just enough light to allow Morgan to see the cold face on the body they carried. It was Tina and his heart sank to a depth he didn't even know existed. In a flash he realised how much she meant to him. He feared that they had killed her, but as they reached the white van, he saw her twitch and the soldiers moved quickly to apply cable ties and bundle her into the back. The soldiers then climbed in and the fourth man raced ahead and jumped into a separate car. The vehicles pulled out and headed for the park gate. Morgan raced to Tina's car and jumped in. He turned the key and pulled out behind them. He desperately tried to remember Tina's instructions about avoiding detection when you are following somebody. But it had all gone over his head, to be honest, so he decided to trust his instincts.

After all, that had never gotten him in trouble before.

———

The convoy soon joined the main road north, following the same route to Newry that Morgan had embarked upon on his faithful trip in February. The road was busy and Morgan was able to stay two or three cars back. But when they crossed the border, the traffic thinned out and he found it more difficult to avoid being noticed. Luckily, the soldiers were trained in many things, but avoiding being followed wasn't one of them.

Morgan spent the trip wondering what he would do when the vehicles eventually stopped. He had no grand plan or experience to call upon. In the end, he decided to take a 'cross that bridge when we come to it' approach. It was easier than letting on how little he knew about this sort of activity.

The identity of the fourth man was bothering him. Then he suddenly remembered the court case in Belfast. A picture in his mind appeared of the two RUC officers who had shown so much interest in the tape. Detective Anderson, that was his name. The jigsaw was starting to come together. Anderson was one of the voices on the tape. He wanted it back and these soldiers were just his henchman.

Just before Banbridge, the van turned right off the main road. Morgan waited a few seconds before doing the same. The road rose to a peak and when he reached the crest, he could see the red lights from the two vehicles turning into a farmyard. He drove past and glanced across to see the four men bundling a kicking Tina into the house. He parked at a farm gate further up the road and then walked slowly back.

The lights were on in the farmhouse and Morgan made his way to the front yard and hid behind a rusting tractor. He could see the soldiers roughly position Tina at a kitchen chair and then tie her hands and feet with cable ties. Her mouth was covered in masking tape, which he imagined had been applied en route to avoid her screaming. He was only just getting to know Tina, but he knew that she would not go meekly into the dark night.

The four men spoke for a moment in the doorway and then after cursory handshakes the soldiers left, leaving Anderson alone in the house with Tina. Morgan hid under the tractor while the soldiers jumped into the van and drove away. Then he crept to the kitchen window and wondered what to do next.

Anderson waited in the hallway of the house trying to gather his thoughts. He'd been to this house many times before. It was Special Branch's favourite haunt for when they wanted to scare the life out of terrorists who they didn't want to process through the normal channels. Loyalists were the most regular visitors because if they were interrogated in a police station, word with get back to the Loyalist leadership within minutes.

He had participated in many a gruesome interview in these rooms. But he was always able to justify it to himself on the grounds that the people he was torturing had done much worse things to their victims. This was different. For all McGuinness's talk of national emergencies and us against them, he knew in his heart that Tina was just a cop like him. Nevertheless, he straightened his tie, tried to clear his head of doubt and opened the door into the kitchen.

He sat at the table opposite Tina and slowly removed his gloves. He looked into Tina's eyes and saw no fear, just unadulterated defiance. He knew this was going to be tougher than the average teenage bomber that he usually dealt with.

"Miss Reynolds, you're a cop, just like me. So, you know how these things work. I've taken you to this place because it's remote. You can scream as much as you like. Nobody will hear. I've forced IRA suspects to tell me their life story in the holding cells at Castlereagh, so I've a high tolerance for screaming."

He removed the tape and handed Tina a glass of water that she consumed greedily. As he tried to pull the glass back Tina held onto it tightly and met his gaze. He was suddenly filled with self-doubt but fell back on his years of training which had taught him that the first rule of interrogation was to portray absolute certainty at all times.

Tina gradually released the glass and he moved back to his seat. She did a quick scan of the room. There was no clock and no sign of cooking equipment in what otherwise looked like a kitchen. And the windows would not have looked out of place in a prison.

"Sorry about the chloroform back in Dublin," he said. "But you do understand that we are keen to talk to you and the normal police method of turning up at your house at 6.30 am and asking you to drop down to the station for a chat wouldn't really work in this situation."

Tina threw him a filthy look. "Particularly as you don't have any fucking jurisdiction to call to my house at 6.30 am."

Anderson smiled. "Ah yes. Jurisdiction. Your IRA friends

don't have to worry about that. They can float back and forth across the border at will. And you guys just wave them through."

"What makes you think the IRA are friends of ours?" Tina asked. "We spend most of our time keeping tabs on them. They rob banks and post offices down south as well. And they have killed a few of my colleagues too."

Anderson leaned forward. "I'm sure you do a marvellous job. You just don't share any information with us. And that's what I wanted to talk to you about. We notice that you've become very friendly with this Morgan fellow. I have these pretty pictures we took down in Dublin."

He spread the pictures he had taken in Howth in front of Tina.

"Nice to see young love in full bloom. I'm sure your pillow talk has been enlightening. No doubt, the subject of a little tape would have come up. So, tell me, how much do you know about Oriel?"

"Nothing," Tina replied.

Anderson walked to the sink and filled a large bowl of water and opened a drawer and took out a screwdriver and a pair of pliers.

"The great thing about interrogating other police officers is that they understand the depraved lengths we'll go to in order to extract information. If I put these tools down in front of a terrorist, he might think I'm bluffing. But you will have been in enough interview rooms to know that if anything, I'll use these before I even need to."

He nodded to the bowl in front of Tina. "The water thing is a new trick. Learned it from our chums in MI5. Apparently, if you have your head dunked in a bowl of water, you think you are drowning long before you actually are. We'll give that a go later if the questioning doesn't work. Now I'll ask you again. What do you know about Oriel?"

Morgan watched all this through the window. He knew he had to do something but for the life of him he couldn't think what. Then Anderson lifted the pliers and moved towards Tina. Morgan ran around the side of the building to the front door and hammered his fist against it. Anderson stopped and turned. A moment of panic raced across his face while he worked out the possibilities.

"Most likely our soldier friends, I imagine," he said to Tina. "Probably looking for directions back to Belfast. Those army boys couldn't find their arsehole with a torch and a map."

He moved to the door and undid the bolt lock before opening it. The night was dark and quiet outside.

"Who is it?" he called but there was no reply. He walked further out into the farmyard in order to see around the gable wall towards the road. As he did so, Morgan stepped out from behind the front door where he had been hiding and raced into the house. He quickly closed the front door and applied the bolt.

Anderson came running back and tried the handle. "Open up, you bastard. I can burn this place down you know."

After a minute the banging stopped and Tina and Morgan heard the sound of footsteps running on gravel. Morgan used the pliers to undo the cable ties and then hugged Tina tightly.

"Now, you are my hero," she said. "But we need to move quickly." She pushed him towards the back of the kitchen, turning the lights off as she did so.

"Where do you think he's gone?" Morgan asked.

"To his car I imagine. RUC officers all carry guns, so I'd guess he's gone to get that. But I noticed this was a specialist interrogation centre when they were carrying me in. The door is reinforced and the windows all look strengthened and have locks on them. It's designed to stop people from getting out. But luckily for us, that also means it stops people from getting in."

"But what about his threat to burn it down?"

"They went to a lot of trouble to get me here. Once they had me in that van, they could have put a bullet in my head and dumped me in a shallow grave in the Cooley Mountains. They clearly want information from me. So, I don't think he's going to jeopardise all that that by setting a match to the place. Also, you probably don't appreciate how petty police forces can be. This is obviously a prized interrogation centre for the RUC Special Branch. This guy is going to have to do a lot of explaining to his boss if he burns the place down. I imagine he's out there trying to figure out a smarter way of getting us out."

"His name is Anderson," Morgan said. "He's one of the two RUC officers on the tape."

"That makes sense. Things must be getting critical. They are dispensing with the rough and ready soldiers and doing things themselves. He also mentioned Oriel, so they must know that we have the tape."

Tina and Morgan were huddled on the floor at the back of kitchen. The house was in darkness, but they wanted to avoid being seen through the windows.

In the meantime, Anderson had raced back to his car before realising that he had left his keys in his jacket pocket. The jacket that was now on the back of a kitchen chair inside his house. He cursed the police training that made him automatically lock a vehicle when he got out. His police revolver was under the driver's seat and he mentally ran through his options.

He knew his would have to break a window to get into the car and he was reluctant to give away his location to Tina and Morgan. He figured that if they knew he was at his car, which was a good seventy yards from the front door, then they would likely make a run for it in the opposite direction and he'd have little chance to find them in the dark. But he found a large rock anyway and took off his jumper to muffle the sound. Then he thought about what he would do when he did get his gun. He was still a virgin when it came to firing it in anger and there was the small matter of having to explain the missing bullets at the regular weekly count. But he figured he could get around that. There were enough colleagues in the locker room with contacts in the underground to source a few spares if he needed them. And if the worst came to the worst, he could make up a story that he was ambushed and fired off a couple of shots in defence. That story had been used by many officers who had gotten drunk on Saturday nights and fired at the moon or whatever else was troubling their addled mind.

In any event, using his weapon was preferable to his threat to burn the house down. While that would undoubtedly flush them out, it would leave him with the small matter of having to explain to McGuinness why he had destroyed the RUC's prized off-site interrogation cottage and the flames would likely rouse the curiosity of the neighbours, and he wasn't really in the mood for making up stories for the benefit of the local fire brigade.

Then he noticed that he was still carrying the screwdriver and vice. He used both to lever the car door open and retrieved the gun. He walked slowly back towards the house. He needed a way of getting in without letting them escape in the process. The gun was cold and unfamiliar in his hand. He hadn't gone to all this trouble to get Tina into that chair just to shoot her. It was a conversation he wasn't finished with. But when he thought of Morgan, he felt nothing. Up to now, he was willing to give Morgan the benefit of the doubt. To accept that he was a civilian caught up in a military conflict. But the longer it went on, the more he realised that Morgan had spurned lots of opportunities to escape from this process. To go public about the tape. To walk into an RUC barracks and come clean. But he was clearly working with the Guards now and that made him a player and he was a player who had nothing to offer to Anderson.

He paced around outside the dark and silent house, trying to avoid the gravel and its crunching noise. He regretted the security that McGuinness had insisted they install. But every facility had a flaw and Anderson suddenly felt his memory sweep back to a storm a couple of winters back. The roof had almost been ripped off and the skylight had been temporarily repaired with heartfelt but unfulfilled ambitions to bring it up to the security standards that the rest of the building enjoyed.

Anderson found a ladder and began silently climbing towards the roof.

Tina was also thinking through the possibilities. "There are two of us and one of him. We have to use that to our advantage. He's going to assume that we're going to try and leave by the front door as that's the only exit we can unlock. So, I'm guessing he's sitting right outside the door waiting for that to happen. So, we need to see if we can open one of the windows at the other end of the house. They have tools in that drawer over there. I imagine they are designed for more evil purposes than forcing open a locked window. But they might do the trick."

"There are two of us and only one of him," Morgan said. "But he's the only one with a gun."

Tina moved silently to the kitchen. She searched the drawer that the screwdriver and pliers had come from. She found a vice and a hammer and took them back to where Morgan was sitting.

"You stay here and shout if he tries to get in from this side of the house," she said. "I'll start checking out the windows at the back."

Tina slid away, keeping her head as low as possible. Morgan suddenly froze. It was a moonless night and the room was pitch dark. Tina was working quietly in the next room and in the silence, he could hear the creaks of the trees outside. He felt trapped, with dark forces circling around him. He flinched at every shadow that passed across the kitchen window and tensed up each time the wind caused the trees to shake.

He felt a hand on his shoulder and had to stifle a scream. It was Tina, returned from her handiwork.

"I've found a window that might work. There is a lock but I think I can break it with the vice. It will create some noise and probably make Anderson run around to that side of the house. So here is my plan. I'll snap the lock and open the window. You wait by the front door. There is gravel outside, so if he is where I think he is, you should hear him running to the other side of the house. If you do, open the front door and run like the wind until you hit the hedge at the other side of the farmyard."

Morgan was shaking now and little of Tina's instructions had registered, apart from 'run'. His legs felt like jelly and running was the last thing he felt like doing. He wanted to crawl into a ball and hope it all went away.

"Leave the front door open," she continued. "Because I won't leave by the window. I'll double back and run out the front door. He'll chase me but I'll have a head start and he looks a bit pudgy. So, I'm confident I'll outpace him."

She pointed through the kitchen window. "Do you see that house at the top of the hill? They have a light on. Make your way there and I'll meet you there as soon as I can. Tell them your car has broken down and you need to ring the AA. But make sure you walk along the hedgerows and don't use the road. And get away from this place as fast you can."

Morgan nodded. He felt much more comfortable being told what to do.

"Good luck, Tina," he whispered. "I'll see you on other side."

They kissed and then Morgan crawled towards the front door while Tina moved towards the back window.

Suddenly Morgan heard a floorboard creak and was filled with the sensation that another body was inside the house. He curled up on a seat with his back to the front door and his knees under his chin. He could hear footsteps slowly approaching. Then a shadow appeared in the kitchen doorway and Morgan could just make out the outline of a gun.

"Right, you little fucker. I don't suppose you knew there was an attic with an unlocked skylight?"

Anderson moved towards the seat and put the gun to the back of Morgan's snorkel jacket hood. "I didn't want to do this. But you've pushed me over the edge, Morgan. Say a quick prayer to that Pope of yours before I despatch you."

But as he pressed the gun against the hood, he felt no resistance. He pulled the hood backwards and exposed the head of a broom and a cushion that Tina had placed there when Morgan came into the house. He almost felt like smiling at her ingenuity. Suddenly Anderson heard footsteps behind him and turned to see Morgan darting through the front door. He raced after him but as he did, a foot appeared and he tripped and smashed his head against the door frame. He slunk to the ground with blood oozing from his forehead.

Tina stood over him and gently picked up his gun. "It's an old Gaelic football trick," she said. "If you're going to trip someone, make sure they've got somewhere awkward to fall."

She met Morgan at the hedge at the far side of the farmyard.

"Let's get out of here," said Tina as she placed Anderson's revolver in her coat pocket. "I presume you came in my car. Is it parked nearby?"

Morgan nodded and they set off at fast pace. It was unlikely that Anderson was going to recover quickly from that fall, but they weren't going to take any chances. Neither of them looked back at the house of horrors. They got to the car and headed south and didn't even speak until they had crossed the border.

————

McGuinness was waiting at home by the telephone, nursing a large Bushmills whiskey. Anderson had promised to call at 10 pm with an update. It was now 11.15 pm and McGuinness was getting worried. Anderson was a professional and understood that communication was key to a successful operation.

He was an inpatient man, so he threw back the whiskey, picked up his service revolver and car keys and headed for Banbridge. As he approached, he saw Anderson's car in the driveway and the front door ajar. His suspicions were heightened by the fact that the house was in darkness, so he drew his revolver as he slowly approached the door.

He saw the lifeless body of Anderson on the hallway floor and checked for a pulse. It was weak, but there nonetheless. The body was cold, however, and he knew he had to act quickly. He hastily checked out the rest of the house and confirmed that it was empty and then raced back to his car. He radioed Head Office and explained that an officer was injured and needed help urgently.

Twenty minutes later a helicopter landed in the farmyard. Two paramedics jumped out and quickly had Anderson on a stretcher and bundled him away. The helicopter took off in a whirr of noise and dust and left McGuinness alone on the ground. He stood there in the darkness listening to the trees as they whistled a ghostly tune. He muttered slowly to himself. This had just been business up till now. But now he could feel anger, raw visceral hatred for those fuckers from the South and their bog Irishman ways. He wasn't going to let the Southern police get the better of him.

He went back into the cottage and inspected the tools that were scattered on the floor and the cut cable ties. He concluded that Anderson had managed to get Tina here, but she must have somehow overwhelmed him. This case was getting murkier and murkier. He guessed he would have to wait for Anderson to wake up to find out the truth. In the meantime, he would have to take control of things. It was time to head to Dublin to have a face to face with Oriel.

——

Tina called in sick the next day and spent it in bed with Morgan. Neither of them was interested in sex, but they spent a lot of time hugging each other as though their lives depended on it.

Morgan lay rigid on the bed, twitching every time a car passed or footsteps rang out on the street outside. Tina sat bolt upright beside him. She doodled in a notebook and drew diagrams and names connected by broken or solid lines. Every now and again she would stare into the distance while tapping gently on her chin with a pencil.

"I don't know who to trust any more," she said. "My boss is not supporting me and these Northerners look like they will stop at nothing. I think we might have to take things into our own hands."

Morgan was staring at the rose-patterned wallpaper, counting the petals. He got to 140 before his mind forced in a thought about the previous day's events.

"What do you mean, Tina?"

"Well, I know who Oriel is. I think it's time that I confronted him and told him that we know that he's a spy. If that information gets back to Belfast, then they might call the dogs off. There is no need to get the tape back if the information contained in it is already in the public domain."

"But I thought your boss didn't want you to do that?"

"Yeah, well fuck him. He wasn't the one tied up in an RUC safe house staring at a pair of pliers. If you hadn't come in at that point, James, I'd be looking at a few missing fingernails now," she said as she examined her hands.

"And I'd be missing a few brain cells, if you hadn't come along when you did. Do you think you killed him when he fell?"

"I don't think so. He was still breathing when we left. But I don't know when he was found. That would make all the difference. But there has been nothing on the news today, which means he either hasn't been found or he's still alive.

"Either way, we can't just sit here and wait for them to find us; we have to take the initiative. I'm going to head into work tomorrow and confront Oriel."

"Is there anything I can do?" asked Morgan.

"I'll drop you back at the apartment tomorrow. I don't think they know about that yet. Keep your head down and wait for me to come back tomorrow evening."

They kissed and then turned the lights off and tried to rest. Both were exhausted from the events of the previous night, but neither could sleep. Tina was trying to map out all the possibilities and found herself running down rabbit holes and struggling to find her way out. Morgan was yearning for his old boring life. As he lay in bed, he thought about Orla and how he would like nothing better than to sit in Kehoes nursing a Guinness and running his hand through Orla's light blonde hair.

"I'd love to James, but not tonight. I'm exhausted," Tina said.

It was only then that Morgan realised that he was spooning her and that his manhood had got away on him a little.

He turned and they went back to back.

"A penny for your thoughts?" she asked.

Morgan opened his eyes and stared at the door. His urge was to run but his head held him back. A scary world of rogue policemen waited outside the front door and Tina was his only protection from it.

"I think my thoughts would cost a lot more than a penny," he said. "It would take hundreds of pounds to get a shrink to unravel them for a start."

She turned over and cuddled him. "When this is over, let's go away somewhere fun. Maybe down the West or over to Scotland."

"I think I've had enough of Scottish people," he said. "But a trip down the West sounds fun."

"Try and picture it in your head and it will help you sleep. Imagine the sand between our feet as we walk down Barna Strand and the sound of the wild Atlantic lapping on the shore."

Morgan closed his eyes and imagined the scene. Soon he was sound asleep, dreaming of a warm Connemara day, hand in hand with a beautiful lady. But in his dream, he wasn't sure who the hand belonged to.

11

ORIEL'S ACTUAL NAME WAS SEAMUS BELTON AND HIS DESK
was stationed on the floor directly above Tina's desk. She prepared
a speech in her head and then marched upstairs to confront him.
When she got there, however, the desk had been cleared of
paperwork and was more or less empty. A framed wedding picture
took pride of place. By the hairstyles and mini wedding dress, Tina
guessed it was from the mid-sixties. Beside it was a cutting from
the *Dundalk Democrat* from 1982 with the caption 'Supporter of
the year "Seamus Belton" with the League of Ireland trophy'.

Belton was paunchy and balding in the picture and Tina
noticed that despite his broad smile, his eyes hid a deep sadness
that wasn't evident in the wedding photograph.

She stood there for a moment at a loss as to what to do next.

"Are you looking for Seamus?" a voice from the next desk
asked. "He's gone on two weeks' leave. Quite sudden apparently.
Sick mother or something. Can I help you?"

"Ah, no, that's okay. I just wanted to catch up with him about
an old case."

She returned to her desk and pondered her next move. Her

only option was to approach her boss again. She hadn't spoken to him since she had discovered that he was the one who had planted the bug in Orla's phone. She tapped on his door and nervously asked if she could come in.

Joyce sat back in his chair and smiled.

"You've come to apologise, have you?"

"No, boss. I don't think I have anything to apologise for. But I wanted to bring you up to date on things. I need your help."

Joyce's eyebrows rose.

"Of course, Tina, as long as it doesn't interfere with the operational plans we discussed."

"There have been a couple more incidents and I think they have changed their focus away from Morgan and towards me. I was kidnapped on Tuesday night."

Joyce leaned forward. "Really, let's go for a walk. As I said so before, I don't trust this fucking place since this whole business started. We'll head out into the park. It's a lovely day."

They left the building without saying a word and found a bench in the park.

Tina sat down and took Joyce through the incidents at Howth Head and in Banbridge. Joyce said little but his face grew as dark as the Dublin sky.

When she had finished, he got up and walked to the roadside. He stood there for a moment shaking his head and muttering at the passing traffic. Then he turned to face her. His eyes were bulging and damp.

"I fucking told you to be careful, but you wouldn't listen to me. That Morgan guy is toxic. How many times have I told you to keep clear of him?

"I never wanted bloody women in the branch. You are too fucking emotional. Ask you to get close to a suspect and you can't wait to jump into bed with him. I suppose I'll have to fuckin clean up this mess."

Tina was indignant and she stood up and faced him eye to eye.

"I'm a serving officer of the Garda Siochana. I was kidnapped by the British Army and RUC and taken to an interrogation centre in another jurisdiction and all you can talk about is who I decide to sleep with. You're a prick of the highest order, who I normally wouldn't piss on if you were on fire. But you're my boss and I expect some fucking support. And, by the way, in what twisted world of yours is Morgan a suspect? He's a poor innocent bystander, caught up in something he can't control."

Joyce stared at her intensely. She couldn't figure out if he was about to hug her or slap her. He walked slowly back to the park bench and took out his notebook and pen.

"Alright, Tina. Keep your knickers on. I told you I'd sort this out, but this is not how I expected it would play out. You are one of my officers and while I might be a ruthless bastard, I look after my own. Even the bloody female ones. You're not a bad cop, Tina, that's the shame of this whole business. And I've had enough of those fucking Northerners dictating events. I think it's time we recalibrated this situation. The RUC are not the only ones who can play at being James Bond.

"You're a trained cop, so give me more observations. What was the registration of the vans you saw? Was there any writing on the side? Would you be able to find the farmhouse in Banbridge again?"

Tina picked up the pen and wrote down the registration number of the vans and the road that the farmhouse was on and its distance from the main road.

"What are you planning to do with this?" she asked.

Joyce bit his lip and looked around the park as though checking to ensure that no spooks were hiding behind trees with directional mikes pointing towards them. "I didn't want to tell you this, Tina, because obviously the less people who know the better. But listen up, I'm about to let you in on a secret that only a handful of hard-bastard, nutcase Guards are aware of."

Tina inched closer. She knew that if her boss trusted her with information, there was a chance he was still on her side.

"You are about to join a select group. The RUC are not the only ones who can plant a spy in another force's head office. We've had a spy in Belfast since the late seventies."

Joyce was enjoying himself now, as though a great burden had been taken off his chest. He lay back with his arms spread out across the bench top. He went on to explain how their spy sat in RUC Special Branch head office and did a bit of work for the Guards.

"Low-level stuff usually. He has access to their records, so he pulls a file out whenever we need to see it. We've long suspected that they had somebody in our office, so it makes sense that we have a spook up there too."

Joyce turned towards Tina and gripped her arm. He threw a few furtive glances around the park to ensure that nobody was in earshot.

"That's why I've been so keen to keep this Morgan business under wraps, Tina. If we out their spy, you can be damn sure they'll make every effort to try and find our one."

Tina pulled her arm away and stared with pursed lips into the distance. She was willing to take a lot of shit from her boss, but she drew the line at being patronised.

Joyce stood up again, hitched up his trousers and took on a Mussolini-like pose.

"See, it's been a nice status quo up till now," he bellowed to nobody in particular. "We both suspected we were spying on each other, but as long as nobody named the individuals involved, then both sides were happy to keep up the pretence. It's just a game, Tina. Like most of the fucking nonsense that goes on in this country."

Tina leaned back on the bench. "It doesn't feel like a game when you are tied to a chair in Banbridge looking at a pair of pliers and your fingernails."

"Like I said, Tina, I didn't want it to come to this. I'll call our man in Belfast and see if he can do a bit more snooping than just telling us about politicians who have been caught fiddling with kiddies. If we have a spy in Belfast, it's time he did some proper fucking spying. I'll run these details by him and see what he comes back with."

"Thanks, boss. I want to take a couple of days off. To lie low and try and get my head together."

Joyce smiled. "No problem. Check in with me each day and I'll let you know if Belfast comes back with anything. But if you want my advice, I'd cool things with that young Morgan fellow. Your own life is at risk now, Tina. It's time to put your police cap back on and start acting professionally again."

Tina nodded but said nothing. She took her leave and returned to her desk. The revelation that the Gardai had a spy in the RUC in Belfast did not sit easy with her. It was one more reason for Joyce to see Morgan as a nuisance who would be better off out of the way.

He seemed to show genuine concern for her, which she would expect within the collegial boundaries of a police force. But, if anything, that meant he would have less concern for somebody like Morgan, who sat outside those boundaries. Was that why he wanted Tina to move away from Morgan? To soften the blow that would eventually come?

She was determined to make her own mind up on that issue. She picked up her handbag and headed for the car park. She planned to pick up Morgan at her place and then head to the safe apartment in the city.

He wasn't there when she got home, however. A note was on the coffee table:

"Hi Babes, I've just gone out to make a few phone calls. I'll be back in the early afternoon. Don't worry, I'm in disguise and I'll be careful."

Tina flung the note back on the table and threw herself onto the sofa. Bloody men, she thought. They can never stay still.

———

Morgan had only made one phone call, however, and that was to Orla. He arranged to meet her for lunch in O'Neill's pub and he got there early and found a quiet corner seat. Orla arrived fashionably late as ever and howled with laughter when she saw Morgan's attire.

"Is that what she has you wearing these days?"

"It's to try and blend in with the locals. To look less like an insurance clerk than I do."

"The locals don't buy all their clothes in Dunnes Stores. You look like a 27-year-old, who is still being dressed by his granny. You want to go to Brown Thomas and get a decent jumper at least."

Morgan sighed. "I haven't been paid for a few weeks. I can barely afford Dunnes Stores, to be honest."

"Do you need a loan?"

"I'm okay. I'm staying with Tina and she's looking after me."

"I'd say she is. Are you two an item then?"

"I don't know, Orla. It's hard to fall in love when you have all this other stuff on your mind."

"You don't have to be in love to be in a relationship," Orla said ruefully as she picked up the menu.

"Is everything alright with you?" he asked.

Orla put the menu down and started fiddling with a beer mat.

"I don't know. All this stuff that is happening to you has been playing on my mind, Morgan. You mean a lot to me you know. And, like you, I want our old life back."

Morgan took a deep breath. He sensed that Orla had momentarily dropped her defences and if he could think of something smart to say he might finally be able to move their relationship to where he wanted it to be.

But, as ever, his mind was unable to convert thoughts into words.

"What takes your fancy?" was all that came out.

Orla looked at him momentarily as though he had found the secret key.

"What takes my fancy?

Their eyes locked across the bar table. The bar was filled with chatter from office workers munching sandwiches and old drunks who had rolled in at opening time. But in that moment, they were both oblivious to the sounds and smells around them. All they could sense was the energy between them.

"What do you fancy for lunch?" he muttered and the moment was gone as though somebody had shaken a bottle and then taken the cap off to let all the fizz out.

"Oh, em, I don't know, I'm not really hungry. I think I'll just have a salad."

They sat there awkwardly for a moment while Morgan pretended to read every word on the menu.

"Grand, I'll go up and order," he said.

When he returned Orla was smiling again and back to her ebullient self.

"So, Morgan, what are you going to do when all this is over? Go back to your old job and flat?"

"I hope I still have my old job. I'd say I'm pushing their patience at this stage. Tina told them I'm on jury duty on a secret fraud case that is being heard in private and could go on for months. But if they put somebody else into my role, I mightn't have a job to go back to. And jobs aren't easy to find these days. Most of my school friends have already emigrated."

"But this is your chance to go out and do something more exciting. After the last few weeks how are you going to go back and sit at a desk?"

Morgan shrugged. He didn't like being questioned about his lack of ambition. It was always a touchy point with him, because he yearned to do something more interesting but didn't have the nerve to try.

"I don't know. I kind of like my job. They are a bunch of idiots at my place, so it's kind of nice to sit back and know that you are cleverer than those around you."

Orla laughed. "Really, being the smartest in an office of idiots is the height of your ambition?"

Morgan shifted uncomfortably in his seat. "My father used to say that in a world of midgets, a small man can be king."

"But you're not a small man, Morgan. You shouldn't limit yourself to that. What does it say on that statue at the top of O'Connell Street? 'No man has the right to set a boundary to the march of a nation.' Well, the same goes for you Morgan. No man has a right to set a boundary to his own ambition."

"Doesn't that take away free will? Don't I have the right to be a feckless slob if I want to be?"

Orla leaned in and picked up the beer bottle that sat in front of her. She stroked it gently from bottom to top.

"Of course, you do Morgan. But it's not very attractive to the opposite sex. Tina might let you get away with it because she's one of those women who thinks she can change a man. But any proper woman wants the completed package, not a work in progress. You never know what you could be missing out on."

The food arrived at that point and provided Morgan with an escape from a conversation he wasn't exactly enjoying. Orla had a way of offering hope and dashing it in the same sentence.

"I have to head back to Tina's place soon. So, I'll have to wolf this down."

Orla raised an eyebrow but said nothing. She nibbled at her salad while regularly stealing chips from Morgan's plate. He smiled because those small acts of larceny were a window into his old life. Every time they shared a meal, she would under-order and then eat half of Morgan's food. In his wilder dreams, this made him feel like they were an old married couple, finishing each other's sentences and food.

They finished their lunch and Morgan walked Orla back to Grafton Street.

"I'll think about what you said, Orla. About ambition and stuff. But, to be honest, until these guys stop trying to kill me, it's hard to think about anything."

"I know, Morgan. Sorry if I give you a hard time. We all have to find our own place in the world. Mind yourself, and I've never thought of you as a small man."

She leaned into him and kissed him gently on the lips. So gently he hardly felt it, apart from the bulging it caused in his pants.

"I'll speak to you soon. Hopefully before you read about me in the papers."

She squeezed his hand and then turned and headed off down Grafton Street. He watched her disappear into the crowd of shoppers, tourists and buskers. She had left his brain in a fog of confusion again, but for a change he was happy to stand and let the fog embrace him. Then he turned up the collar of his coat and headed towards the apartment in Harold's Cross, to meet the other woman who occupied the dark and misty corners of his mind.

———

Tina was sitting on the couch when he got there.

"That was a pretty long phone call," she said. "Was it your mother listing everyone who died in your parish in the last six months?"

"No, I met somebody in town for lunch."

"Who was that?"

"A cousin of yours actually. It was Orla; she was asking after you."

Tina's forehead tightened and she rose from the sofa and walked towards him. "James, I hope you didn't tell her where we're staying. You know what happened last time."

"Don't worry," he said. "I was super careful. I even did that back-tracking stuff you taught me when I was walking there. I didn't say anything about this place and she was too smart to ask. You should trust her more, you know. She's really clever and she could help us."

Tina returned to the sofa and lifted a magazine. "So why did you meet her anyway?" she said without lifting her gaze.

"Ah, you know, I just want a bit of my old life back. Not to be cooped up in here all day like I'm in prison."

"You mean that old life where you chased after her like a puppy dog in heat? And she treated you like a dog at the same time."

Morgan sat in one of the armchairs. He could feel a tension in the room, but he couldn't understand how it had gotten there.

Women remained a mystery to him. They were like a warm summer's day in Ireland. You could enjoy them but at any minute a storm cloud could come marching over the horizon and soak you.

He figured that silence was his best option, so he sat there diligently inspecting his fingernails while Tina pretended to be fascinated by an article previewing the 1986 World Cup.

They maintained that silence for what seemed an eternity when their tension was ended by a loud knock at the front door. They looked at each other with questioning faces.

Tina said, "Nobody knows we're here. Who the hell could that be?"

The knocking was repeated. Tina ran to the kitchen and retrieved the largest knife she could find. "You answer the door," she said to Morgan. "It could just be the bloody Jehovah Witnesses, but in fairness they don't normally hammer the door down. If it's somebody more sinister, just call out my name and step backwards. I'll be waiting behind the door with this."

Morgan nodded and headed towards the front door. The knocking intensified. He undid the bolt lock and slowly opened the door. A large and angry-looking man stood there.

"Tina," Morgan croaked in a barely discernibly voice as he instinctively stepped backwards. She stepped out and raced past Morgan with the knife held out before her. She just about stopped herself from plunging it into the heart of her boss.

"Joyce," she said, "what the hell are you doing here?"

Joyce glared at the knife. "I might ask the same about you, Detective Reynolds. I take it that's lover boy who just answered the door. Are you going to let me in or not?"

She stepped to the side and Joyce walked past her. Morgan was pasted to the hallway wall but Joyce hardly even acknowledged him. He walked into the living room and marched straight to the window and slid back the curtains. He scanned the street but it was quiet, apart from some school kids ambling their way home.

"Tina, I have some operational stuff to discuss with you. Do you think you could send the young fella down to the shops for some sweets or something? He shouldn't hear this."

Tina pulled Morgan into the hallway and whispered. "This is my boss. Go down to the café on the corner and I'll meet you there when I get rid of him. I won't be long."

Morgan nodded, grabbed his coat and left without saying goodbye. He was used to not having control over his life any more.

Joyce sat on the sofa and motioned for Tina to sit on an armchair.

"You have to move out of here today," he said. "And you can't use any of the other Garda safe houses."

"You bastard, you're pulling the rug out from underneath me, aren't you? You want Morgan dead as much as the Northerners do. You just want them to do your dirty work for you. You're afraid he'll upset this little mutual-masturbation project you have with your spies in Belfast and Dublin."

Joyce smiled. "I thought I trained you not to jump to conclusions. I'm not kicking you out of here. You need to leave for your own safety."

He let that comment hang for a second to see if Tina would react. She was still angry and was doing her best not to explode.

Joyce leaned towards her. "Two weeks ago, a detective on the drugs team asked for a safe house because they are hoping to turn some heroin warlord in North Dublin. The facilities guy sent him a list of all the Dublin safe houses and copied in the whole fucking department. I only noticed this when I was clearing paperwork this morning. That means that Oriel will have that information, and it won't take the Northerners long to get here through a process of elimination."

Joyce walked to the window again and edged back the curtains to peer outside.

"I figured out where you were after visiting two houses and if I could figure it out, you can be sure that those Northern boys will too. So, stop treating me like the bad guy, Tina. Just get out of here as soon as you can."

He turned towards her. "I've said this a few times already, Tina, but it's getting serious now. You need to dump this guy. I'm working on a solution, but it would be easier if I wasn't dealing with a couple."

Tina said nothing but sat back and exhaled.

Joyce also leaned back. "I spoke to my man in Belfast and gave him those van registrations and the address of the house in Banbridge. Turns out the vans are owned by a building company in Lurgan. It's a front for MI5. If they want to spy on a particular guy, then they start a building job in his street. Their other trick is to offer work to builders who they suspect of being connected to the IRA. Once they have them on the inside, they work on them to extract information.

"The point is that we're not just dealing with the RUC here. If MI5 are involved, they will stop at nothing. They are more ruthless than a fullback in junior football. The house they brought you to in Banbridge is a secret interrogation centre used by all the spooks up north.

"Follow the logic, Tina. Oriel's real name is on that tape. We haven't exposed Oriel yet, so the Nordies will have to assume we either don't know about him or that we're playing games. That's why they went after you. So, the question they want to answer is whether Morgan has shared the tape with us or not. We have to give them the answer to that question, which is no, he hasn't shared it with us."

"And how do we do that?" Tina asked.

"You leave that to me, Tina. That's what I'm working on with my man in Belfast."

"But even if you succeed, it will mean that they will be even keener to eliminate Morgan. We're handing him to the wolves." Her mask of professionalism was slipping and she started to well up. She ran to the kitchen to get a tissue.

Joyce followed her and rested a hand on her shoulder. "Look, Tina, he doesn't have to face a firing squad. But he may need to disappear. To England or America or somewhere. You can get him a new identity and that sort of stuff. Eighty thousand Irish people are emigrating every year. He won't be noticed slipping out of the country. But for your own good, you need to start putting the brakes on before you get in too deep. You're a detective first, you know. And a bloody good one."

Tina blew her nose and nodded. "I know. You're right. We'll start packing up and I'll park him in a cheap hotel. There are bunks at Head Office and I might kip there for a few nights. I'll call up to your office on Monday and we can look at the next steps."

Joyce smiled. "Grand so, I knew you'd see sense. I'll let myself out."

———

After he left, Tina sat by the window. She could see the corner of the street and could just make out Morgan's head in the front window of the café. What was she going to tell him, she wondered? I'll figure that out when I get there, she decided, as she grabbed her coat and opened the front door.

Morgan was nursing a cup of tea and scanning the sports pages of the *Irish Independent* when she got to the café.

"How did it go?" he asked.

Tina flashed a thin smile and took his hand. "We're going to have to move again, I'm afraid. Our address here has been compromised."

"Where to? Not down the country again, I hope. I've had an enough of green fields and flies to be honest. I moved to Dublin for a reason, you know."

"I'll find you somewhere in Dublin. I need you close anyway." She smiled again and this time it seemed more genuine.

"But it might need to be a cheap hotel for a few nights while I sort things out. It seems that I've used up my quota of Garda safe houses."

"Are you going to stay with me?" Morgan asked with the desperation of a three-year-old who was struggling to sleep.

Tina looked away for a second. She was struggling to find the words to brook the chasm between her heart and head. She knew that Joyce was probably right. That having a relationship with Morgan was going to make solving this case a lot tougher. But she looked across the table and all she saw was a snorkel jacket filled with vulnerability.

"They have asked me to stay at Head Office for a few days so that I'm on hand if information comes in overnight. There are a couple of bunks there that we use for operational purposes."

"I don't suppose you could slip me in?"

Tina smiled. "I'd love to, but we're already breaking enough rules. That would definitely be a no-no. But look, the quicker I can focus on sorting this out, the quicker we can have a normal life."

"And how are you going to sort it out?"

Tina wasn't expecting that question and, in fact, she didn't have an answer.

She said, "Look, Joyce has a few ideas. I have to trust him. He's a bastard but a crafty one. He'll come up with something."

She took Morgan's hands in hers. "I think I'm falling in love with you, Morgan. It goes against all my training and professionalism. But I can't help myself. The last couple of weeks have been crazy but also the best time I've ever had. You have to trust me. I'll look after you and we can get out of this."

Morgan said nothing for a moment and took his hands away. His mind was flooded with doubt, as though every time he climbed the hill of trust, someone would push him back down again. He leaned back in the seat and then said, "There is a line from a song, I can't remember by who. People only tell you that they love you because it's easier than telling you what they really think. But I guess I have to trust you. I don't have any other choice."

Tina was hurt. This was the first time she'd ever told a man that she loved him before he had told her. She wasn't expecting roses and chocolates, but a bit of reciprocation would have been nice. But these were exceptional circumstances and she realised that a bit of slack would have to be afforded.

"Morgan, I know this isn't easy. I understand. Let's get back to the apartment and pack up and we'll find you a quiet guesthouse. Maybe you might let me stay the night."

McGuinness and Anderson drove into the car park of the Ballymascanlon Hotel outside Dundalk. They were dressed as casually as possible, which in McGuinness's case was a pink golf sweater and a pair of trousers that were last fashionable in the fifties.

Anderson was still bandaged from his altercation with Tina in Banbridge and he moved gingerly towards the hotel reception. They made their way to the bar which was empty apart from a heavy-set man busy reading the paper. McGuinness walked up to him and extended his hand.

"Good to see you, Oriel. This is my colleague Mr Anderson. I believe you have spoken to him occasionally by phone."

Oriel rose and shook hands with McGuinness and then offered his hand to Anderson.

"Good to meet you at last Mr Anderson. That looks like a nasty bang you got there. Was that the work of that little colleague of mine?"

Anderson sat down gingerly. "She's not too little I can tell you. And she packs a fair old punch."

They were interrupted by the waitress and after tea and scones had been ordered, they got down to business.

Oriel spoke first. "Lads, this isn't working out the way we originally planned. You offered me a few bob and I said I'd send you the sort of stuff we should be sharing anyway. Now you have soldiers running around the country and all sorts of shenanigans. And I don't agree with that young Tina girl getting kidnapped. She's a colleague of mine at the end of the day. You can do whatever you like with that Morgan chap, but leave the Guards alone."

McGuinness looked like he had just swallowed a wasp. "Look, Oriel, we're doing all this to protect you. What will happen if you're unmasked? You'll be drummed out of the police force for a start and you can kiss goodbye to a pension. And if they prosecute, well, I'd say that you'd be looking at a couple of years in Mountjoy. And I don't need to tell you what they do to ex-police officers in there!

"So, don't get all fucking moralistic with me now," McGuinness said as he thumped the table. "You're in this for the long game whether you like it or not. We can just walk away, hire another snoop in Dublin and get back to beating up Catholics in Belfast like we like to do. You'd don't have a choice, so shut the fuck up and start doing what you're told. And remember, Oriel, we still have those photos in a file in Belfast. The ones that Mrs Oriel would be very interested in seeing."

Oriel looked like a small boy who had been caught drinking the communion wine and was about to receive the priest's wrath.

Anderson stepped into the breach. "Look, Oriel, we're keen to clear things up as quickly as possible without any bloodshed. But as McGuinness says, this is mainly about protecting you. So, we need you to step outside your comfort zone. Do you know who this Tina woman reports to?"

Oriel nodded. "Fella by the name of Joyce. He runs one of the subversives teams in Special Branch. Sneaky bugger from what I can make out."

Anderson drew closer. "That's what we've heard too. You're still walking around freely, so we have to assume that the Guards don't know anything about you or that they are playing a little game. This Joyce fellow is at the right level to play those games, so we need you to do a little snooping. What time does everyone go home? Being the South, I expect it's around 4 pm?"

Oriel smiled. "The last people are usually gone by 7 pm. Earlier on a Friday. Why do you ask?"

"We need you to have a snoop in Joyce's office. We're guessing that if the Guards know about the tape, it hasn't gone any further than Joyce. So, there must be something in his office. Notes of a meeting and that sort of thing. Maybe even the original tape itself. I guess he has it locked up. Do you have the tools for breaking into safes and that sort of thing? If not, we can easily supply them."

Oriel nodded. "He won't have a safe. We're not that sophisticated in Garda Head Office. If he has something, he'll have it locked in his desk or a filing cabinet. I can easily get into that. I'll have a look on Friday night."

McGuinness stood up to leave. "Okay, you know the protocol. Give us a call on Friday night and tell us what you've found. If there is nothing there, then we can assume that this young Morgan fella is the only one who knows about the tape. So, we can concentrate our efforts on eliminating him. Any help you can provide in tracking him down would be appreciated."

"Grand so," said Oriel. "You don't fancy a little tour of Dundalk while you are down here, do you?"

Anderson rose slowly, using the table for leverage. "No thanks, Oriel. We'd stand out like tits on a bull if we drove around Dundalk. I think I'd rather walk around downtown Beirut dressed as a Hasidic Jew."

"There are some nice parts," ventured Oriel.

McGuinness was halfway to the door. "The only nice part is the road to Belfast. Pay for the tea and scones, will you Oriel? Like a good chap. We don't have any of that banana republic currency with us."

With that he was gone. Anderson shook hands with Oriel. "Sorry about that. The boss is a grumpy old bastard. Keep in touch, Oriel, and if you want any help, let me know."

McGuinness was sitting behind the driver's wheel when Anderson got to the car. He made no offer to help while Anderson cautiously opened the door and lowered himself into the passenger seat.

"He's just another Fenian prick, that Belton guy," McGuinness said. "Once this is all over, we're going to quietly sideline him. We'll find another pigeon in Garda Head Office to sing to us."

Anderson leaned forward and ran his hand under the console.

"What are you doing Anderson?"

"Just checking to make sure that there is no tape recorder down here. You know the trouble that caused us before."

McGuinness laughed and they talked about football for the rest of the trip. Referees still had it in for Glentoran, and

Cliftonville were secretly funded by the IRA. Anderson ignored most of the conversation and concentrated on the rolling dark green and granite countryside as they drove north. He was happy to be away from the potholes and boreens of Southern Ireland and its untended hedges. This was his countryside, the only one he knew. The one where he was born and his father and grandfathers were born. But he felt an overpowering urge to get away, to run as far away as possible. Northern Ireland had become a rotten and toxic place, and he was in a job that was at the heart of that rottenness.

———

Tina and Morgan had checked into a small guesthouse in Sandymount. The wallpaper was peeling in the corner and the shower had a strange fungus-like formation growing around the taps.

The bed wasn't any more welcoming. He threw himself on it when they arrived and it sagged so much in the middle that it almost sandwiched him. Tina was upset. She felt like she had given in too easily to Joyce and was letting him dictate the project.

"Just stay here tonight," she said. "I'll try and get us somewhere better tomorrow." But she didn't mean it. She had no budget for this and couldn't afford to pay for hotels indefinitely.

She picked up her coat and kissed Morgan. "I'm going to head into Head Office and spend the night there. I'll call over tomorrow. And I'd suggest you sleep on the edge of the bed. If you sleep in the middle, we night have to ask Mountain Rescue to save you."

Morgan smiled. It was the first time he'd done that since the café. "Thanks, Tina, I really appreciate everything you're doing for me. I might be a bit smelly tomorrow though. I don't fancy battling the Loch Ness monster in the shower."

They kissed again and then she was off. She got to the office around 7 pm and it was empty. She checked her desk for mail and then headed across the car park to the gymnasium. There were a couple of camp beds in the cupboard and she pulled one out and set it up underneath the basketball hoop. Tina had stayed here a couple of times before when she was working on big cases and needed to be close to the action. But Guards liked their own bed and the gym was hardly ever used for sleeping so she was confident she wouldn't be interrupted.

She turned out the lights and climbed into a sleeping bag. She could hear traffic on the nearby North Road but other than that it was quiet. She lay there thinking about Morgan and how he was faring in the bed with the stained sheets and clapped-out springs. She replayed in her head the conversation she had had with Joyce. It was clear to her now that he wanted Morgan out of the way as much as the RUC did. And that he wanted Tina to dump him because otherwise she could become collateral damage. But she was damned if she was going to let Joyce decide who she should be sleeping with. She turned over to try to find a comfortable spot on the lumpy camp bed and started planning how she would get Morgan back to his old self and solve the case.

Tina turned and twisted on the bunk, running the case around in her head. She didn't like the fact that Joyce knew more than he was telling her. Without access to the full facts, she was at a serious disadvantage. She decided to head back to her desk to pick up her notes. She slipped on a tracksuit and headed across the car park to the main block.

The building was in darkness but a small light on the second floor caught her eye. It was darting around, which made her think it came from a flashlight, and it was coming from Joyce's office. Tina froze in her tracks and pondered the possibilities. The British Army and RUC would like to know what was in Joyce's office but, surely, they would not be so brazen as to break into Garda Head Office?

She opened the ground-floor door quietly and carefully climbed the back stairs. The second floor was silent apart the occasional sound of filing cabinets being opened in Joyce's office. She tiptoed her way along the corridor until she came to the office door.

She could see that there was only one person inside, which came as a relief. He was huddled over a filing cabinet with a flashlight clenched between his teeth. The light created a halo around his face.

Tina reached her hand inside the door and found the light switch. She turned it on.

"Detective Belton. I think it's time that you and I had a full and frank conversation."

12

BELTON DROPPED THE TORCH AND STARED AT TINA LIKE A bear that had been caught with his arm in a beehive.

"Reynolds. What are you doing here?"

"I was just about to ask you the same thing."

Belton scratched his head and bit his lower lip. "Look, I'm following up on a tip I got from a confidential source. Seems we have a spy here in Head Office and my source tells me that it is Joyce. I was just having a look to see if I can find anything incriminating."

"Is that right?" Tina said. "And you didn't think to bring this to the commissioner or go through the normal channels?"

"Are you mad? You don't march into the commissioner making claims like that about a senior detective, unless you have some evidence. But look, I just found this file when you walked in. Looks pretty interesting to me."

He indicated to Tina to move closer and handed her a manila folder with 'RUC contacts' written in large felt pen on the cover. Tina took it over to Joyce's desk and started leafing through its contents.

She said, "This is standard operational stuff. You'd expect Joyce to have contacts in the RUC. We are dealing with the same subversives, after all."

As she said this, she noticed a page marked 'Carson'. It had a Belfast phone number at the top and a list of dates. She noticed that the most recent date was the day she had called into Joyce's office and he had told her about his RUC-based spy. She memorised the phone number and then closed the file.

"This is rubbish, Belton. Or should I say, Oriel."

Belton's mouth dropped and he had to step backwards to lean against the filing cabinet.

"I know who you are, Oriel. I know who you work for. Do you get a kick out of betraying your colleagues? Do you get paid well for it?"

Belton moved towards her and Tina flinched. He was much bigger than her and he was between her and the door.

"I'm not going to hurt you, Tina. That's not my thing. I knew this would come out eventually. Let me explain myself. As soon as I found out that soldiers were involved and people were being shot at, then I tried to stop it."

Belton was stuttering, his face drooped and he ran a panicked hand through his thinning hair.

"This has gotten completely out of hand, Tina. I got caught in a trap. I thought I'd be able to feed Belfast bullshit, low-level stuff, but they kept coming back for more and they had me over a barrel."

Tina relaxed and they both sat down with Tina taking Joyce's chair behind the desk. "How did they trap you?"

He sank into a chair and studied his shoes. "I did something stupid, Tina. I'm married with three kids but I've never been normal. Not in the married with kids way anyway. I've always felt a bit the other way, you know?"

Belton's forehead was peppered with sweat globules and his face, which was steadfastly staring at the ground, was reddening with every sentence.

Tina nodded slowly. She felt as though Belton was saying things he had never said to anyone before.

"It's not easy being gay in Ireland, Tina. You live this life in the shadows, being dishonest to your family and yourself, spending a lifetime in piss-stinking public toilets and fumbling with strangers in the Phoenix Park."

Tina coughed and Belton looked up as though he had been summoned from a trance.

"Ah, I'm sorry, Tina. I don't mean to be crude. I'm not myself at the moment. Those bastards in Belfast have really spooked me."

Tina pulled her chair around to the other side of the desk and placed it next to his. She placed her hand gently on his knee. "That's okay, Seamus. We're detectives. I've heard a lot cruder stuff in interviews. How did Belfast compromise you?"

"I was in a bar in town one night. I'm sure you know which one; there aren't many gay bars in this town. I just wanted a drink. It was a Tuesday night and I'd just come off a shitty shift. Then this young fella sidled up beside me and started chatting. I'm not the flirty type. Guys don't normally hit on me like that. I'm fat and fifty and I normally end up with other guys who are as desperate as me. This guy was different. Young, fit and self-confident. He wore his gayness with pride. Told me all these stories about San Francisco and Paris and the good times he had there.

"I was suspicious. Why would a hot young thing like this be interested in me? I guess as a cop you are trained to be. Then he came up with a story about his last boyfriend. Apparently, he was going out with some Spanish lad in the States and the boyfriend caught that Aids thing that is going around and died. Your man started crying and leaning on my shoulder and some stupid fucked-up part of me thought that he just wanted a father figure. Someone strong and secure.

"Anyway, we ended up back at his place. He was staying in the Westbury. Gorgeous room. Best I've ever been in. It even had one of those bidet things in the bathroom to clean your arse with. It was the best fucking night of my life. To be with somebody you were actually attracted to and in a proper bed to boot. With clean sheets and a radiator. When you're used to having sex in a car in the park, you've no idea how good it feels to do it in a bed.

"Anyway, like most things in my life, it was a big fucking lie. Two days later an envelope arrived here at work. It was all at a set-up; the young fella was working for the RUC. There were five full-colour photos and they didn't exactly show me in the best light. Believe me, you don't want to see this body without a flabby shirt covering it.

"They had a camera in the feckin bedroom Tina; can you believe that? I've been a cop for years and we're trained to be suspicious. I should have been that night. Everything was just working out too well for me. I should have known that my life is never that lucky.

"There was a draft letter to my wife enclosed, telling her about my secret life. Then there was a phone number. I called it and it was this prick in Belfast telling me I now worked for him. That's how it started, Tina. Just a stupid old drama queen too vain to see he was being screwed."

"What was his name?" Tina asked.

Belton looked up as though surprised that there was somebody else in the room. "Who, the young fella? I honestly can't remember. Isn't that shameful?"

Tina smiled. "No, the guy in Belfast. The one who you called."

"McGuinness. He's a bad bastard and the one behind all this

shooting. There is also a chap called Anderson who deals with me. He seems like a decent skin. But it's all out in the open now. My little secret.

"Look, Tina, if you're going to tell Joyce, can you give me a day or two to clear my desk and tidy up a few things? I think I need to have a long conversation with my wife."

"I'm not going to tell Joyce," Tina said. "But you're going to do a few favours for me."

"I don't get you, Tina, why wouldn't you tell your boss?"

"I might have to, at the appropriate time. But I don't want to hang you out to dry either, Seamus. If we can find a way to make the RUC call off their manhunt, then we might all be able to get back to whatever it is that we used to consider normal."

"Thanks, Tina. I don't know what I consider to be normal. What do you want me to do?"

"Meet up with McGuinness and Anderson. Tell them you've been through Joyce's office and found nothing apart from a memo from me to Joyce. I'll type it up for you. It will say that I'm calling off the case, that after extensive interrogation, Morgan said that he destroyed the tape and he can't remember any of its contents. I'll say it was all a waste of Garda time and that we're moving on. Then you keep tabs on those two RUC guys and see if they take the bait. If it works, we might all be able to get back to normal soon."

"Okay, Tina. Drop the memo down to me when you have it typed up and I'll make sure they get it. And thanks. It means a lot to me that somebody would listen to my story and not think I'm a freak."

"You're not a freak, Seamus. You just live in the wrong country at the wrong time."

Tina went back to her desk and typed up the fake memo to

Joyce. She found Belton at his desk staring at a picture of his family. He looked up and smiled weakly but sympathetically.

"Thanks for listening to me, Tina. I've never spoken to anyone about my secret life. It feels good to get it off my chest. And look, I don't want to work for those bastards in Belfast. If I can help you, it would be so much better."

"Here's the memo. Make sure Belfast see this and hopefully we can get them to call off their hunt. Then we'll figure something out. Maybe you could put in for a transfer and then tell Belfast that you don't have access to any sensitive information, that you're working in traffic or something like that."

Belton nodded. "To be honest, Tina, I'm thinking of getting out completely. I've a brother in Boston who says he could get me into the force over there. But I'll stay as long as I need to in order to help you out. I feel responsible for these guys going after you in the first place and, to be honest, you've shown me more kindness than anyone else here."

Tina put her hand on Belton's shoulder and squeezed it gently. "I'll see you on Monday. Let me know what you hear from Belfast."

She crossed the car park and returned to the camp bed in the gymnasium. Her mind had cleared and she slept soundly until the eastern window filled with a magnificent orange light.

———

Morgan also woke when the early sun screamed through his window. But the sleep angels hadn't been so kind to him. He braved the shower, which to his horror had only two settings. Ice-block cold or skin-melting hot. He endured it for about twenty seconds before retreating to the see-through towel provided.

He left a note for Tina and headed out into spring air. It was one of those rare days when the soft breeze from the south-west came without its usual companion of rain. Daffodils were sprouting in front gardens and sunglasses had been ferreted from the bottom of hallway drawers.

Morgan found a Pass machine and checked his bank balance. He was down to his last hundred punts. So, he decided to shun the bus and set off on foot across town. Without thinking about it, he found himself walking towards his old flat in Ranelagh. His battered Toyota Corolla was still parked outside, gathering dust and bird shit.

He stood at the end of street, scanning the parked cars for Northern registrations or drivers hidden behind newspapers. The street was quiet with no obvious sign of anything strange. So, he slipped quietly across the road and quickly opened the front door of his flat.

A musty and acrid smell met him in the hallway, and he remembered that his hasty exit was on the day before bin day. He opened the back windows and curtains to let some air and light in and then threw himself onto the sofa. A copy of *Hot Press* sat on the coffee table beside an empty pizza box. Nothing had changed since the night Tina had removed him from his old life, and he lay there embraced by the comfort blanket of familiarity. He picked up the magazine and read through the concert listings and regretted the fact that he wouldn't be able to go to any of them, when the truth was that he hadn't been to a gig in years. But that didn't matter as there was a difference between being lazy and being barred from doing what you want.

Eventually, Morgan got up and walked into his bedroom. He had brought only the bare essentials with him when he left with Tina and so he was keen to pick up a few home comforts. He pulled a sports bag from the cupboard and threw in some clothes. A battered paperback copy of First World War poetry was on his bedside table, and he thumbed through it before throwing it into his bag. The Walkman that his mother had bought for him the previous Christmas was also there, and he flicked it open to reveal the mixed tape he'd made for Orla but never worked up the courage to give to her.

Tales of Melancholy was written across the tape and Morgan winced as he remembered its contents, which was dominated by Janis Ian and the sort of country song where everyone in the song was dead by the end of it. He dug out a few more cassettes from the drawer and threw them and the Walkman into the bag.

He carried it into the living room and was about to leave when his attention was drawn to the small metallic object on the mantelpiece. It was the recording device that had caused all the trouble in the first place. Morgan stopped for a second in the doorway and then walked over and slipped the device into his bag.

He let himself out quietly and walked briskly to the corner of the street. Then he looked back to see if any cars had pulled out of parking spaces behind him. The street was quiet, so he pulled up his hood and headed back towards Sandymount. He fumbled in his bag and dug out the Walkman. He donned the headphones and pressed the play button.

The mournful sound of Leonard Cohen's 'Suzanne' filled his ears. Morgan smiled. Maybe Orla would like this after all.

———

Tina got to her desk at 7 am and was pleased that there was still tea in the staff kitchen and a packet of Mikado biscuits. It was Saturday morning and the office was deserted. She wrote down Carson's number on a pad and then went hunting for a Belfast phone directory. She found one and looked up the area codes at the front. The number was from Holywood, so she figured that it was his home rather than a work contact.

She went back to her desk and despite the early hour she decided to call the number anyway. A grumpy voice grunted "Hello."

"Good morning, Carson, I hope I didn't wake you."

There was a long pause and then the grumpy voice said, "Who is this?"

"I'm a colleague of Detective Joyce's. He asked me to give you a call."

"So, what's your name then?"

"I think the fewer names you know down here the better, don't you?"

Tina heard a long slow exhaling of breath that spoke to how pissed off Carson was.

"Alright, you want to play tin soldier games. Don't tell me your name. So, what the fuck are you doing calling me at this time of the morning?"

"Well, we need a bit of help from you. So, I was wondering if you were up for a meeting."

Carson laughed. "A meeting? You don't want to tell me your name but you're happy for me to see your face? What do you think this is, the boy scouts? I've never met Joyce. What makes you think I should meet you?"

Tina had to think on her feet. She wanted to meet Carson because she wanted to be on the same level as Joyce, but she hadn't really factored in pushback.

"Things have changed, Carson. We have a suspicion that RUC special branch in Belfast are aware that they have a mole. They might be on to you. I won't go into the details but the IRA killed some RUC guys recently and they stole a briefcase from the RUC car. Through certain back channels that I can't explain, that suitcase has come into our hands. I need to show you some documents. I think you'll find them interesting, so that's why I need a face to face."

"You are joking. I told Joyce that if there was a sniff of trouble then our deal was off. They take things seriously up here, honey. There are more spooks in the security services in Belfast than in Milltown cemetery. One hint of scandal and I'll be in a shallow grave on Cave Mountain before you can say a Hail Mary."

"There is no indication that they know about you, Carson. That's why I need to meet you. Show you the stuff we have and see if we can nip this in the bud."

There was a pause and she could hear heavy breathing.

"Okay, Mullen's Café on Glen Road, 11 am on Tuesday. I'll be wearing a checked jacket with elbow pads."

———

The phone went dead and Tina sat back in her chair. She had three days to come up with documents that didn't exist and a tale that would convince Carson to disclose his life story to her. She smiled, picked up her handbag and headed for the door. This was the part of the job she enjoyed, having to adapt to changing scenarios and to tease out information. Plus, she was heading back to Sandymount to see Morgan and that put an extra spring in her step as she jumped into her car and headed out of Phoenix Park.

Morgan wasn't home, however. He passed a phone box on the way home and on a whim, had called Orla at her house. She suggested meeting in Lamb Doyles pub at the foot of the Wicklow Mountains. "They'll never think of looking for you there, particularly if you change buses a couple of times," she said as though she was an expert in international espionage.

Morgan did as he was told and after a torturous journey,

eventually got to the pub around 3 pm. A couple of hillwalkers in brightly coloured rain jackets and mud-splattered boots were perched at the bar, watching English football on TV. For once, Orla had arrived first and was seated in a corner booth nursing a hot whiskey.

She rose and kissed him gently on the lips. "I'm dosed with a cold, Morgan. So, there will be no snogging tonight."

Morgan smiled and wondered if she was teasing him. She usually was but that didn't stop him from hoping it was something else.

"What can I get you to drink?" he asked.

"Just a Club Orange. I'm driving. This hot whiskey is enough alcohol for one night."

Morgan headed to the bar and got himself a Guinness. He thought about letting Tina know where he was but didn't have any way of contacting her. He guessed she might be still at work, but she had deliberately avoided giving him her work number. Then he looked over and saw Orla smiling at him and immediately forgot about making phone calls.

"So, what's been happening in your world?" he asked. He figured he'd get this out of the way first as she'd quickly turn the conversation around to her own life anyway.

"Oh, nothing much. I finally got rid of that guy at work. There were a few tears but it will teach him right for cheating on his wife. What about you? Is Tina still dragging you around on a lead?"

Morgan smiled. He could sense a little jealousy in Orla's voice and could only think that it could play to his advantage.

"She's been really good to me, Orla. She says that they have a plan to get these Northerners off my back and that I can then get back to a normal life. The only thing is, she has put me up in this god-awful hotel in a room that would not be out of place in a famine workhouse. I tried sleeping there last night and had to curl up on the floor. There are brown stains on the sheets that I'm not sure were put there by man or beast."

Orla leaned in and smiled. "You could stay at my place tonight if you wanted. My folks are away for the weekend and I could make up the spare room. But there would no peeking through the keyhole into my room," she said with a mischievous wink.

Morgan gulped. In all his years of chasing Orla he'd never received an invitation back to her house, never mind one that involved staying the night.

"Emm, I'd love to Orla. But I should tell Tina what I'm up to and I've no way of contacting her. She's not staying at home at the moment. I said I'd see her back at the guesthouse in Sandymount."

Orla took his hands and rubbed them gently. "She doesn't own you, Morgan, does she? We can have a bit of fun, maybe rent out a good spy movie on video. I'm at a loose end tonight. I was supposed to go into town with a friend, but she's just broken up with her long-term fella and I haven't got the energy to listen to all that moaning."

Morgan's mind was racing. He'd been waiting for this opportunity for so long that he would never forgive himself if he didn't follow up on it. And, in any event, he could always ring directory enquiries when he got to Orla's house and get a number for the guesthouse and leave a message. That's if the guesthouse had a phone. By the state of their rooms, they may still be communicating by carved writing on rocks.

"Okay, let's do it. I get to pick the movie though."

Orla smiled and picked up her coat. "My dad has a decent drinks cabinet, so we can raid that."

They walked to the car park hand in hand. Morgan felt a tang of guilt but it was diminishing with each passing moment. He slipped into the passenger seat of Orla's car and she reversed out and then pointed the car towards the city. They exchanged smiles and seemed lost in each other's gaze so they didn't notice the dark blue Vauxhall Cavalier that pulled out behind them and followed them down the hill.

Tina was still excited at how she had turned Oriel when she got back to the guesthouse in Sandymount. She was keen to see Morgan and to spend the day with him. She fancied a trip to the mountains with maybe a bowl of chowder in Johnnie Fox's to finish things off.

Her joy was short-lived, however. She opened the bedroom door and spotted Morgan's scribbled note on the bed. See you later, it effectively said, with no indication of where and when. Tina liked order, whereas Morgan seemed to favour chaos. She wondered if this was what attracted her to him in the first place. That old chestnut of opposites attracting each other. That may be fun at the start of a relationship, she thought, but ultimately it would drive her crazy.

She threw herself on the bed and it enveloped her as it had Morgan. She'd give him an hour, she thought. Then she'd start searching the usual haunts. She thought she'd use the time trying to sort the loose ends of the case in her head but found it hard to concentrate. Her annoyance was increasing with each passing minute. Why didn't he realise that she was just trying to keep him safe? Why couldn't he just check in every now again like any sane person would do?

In the end, she grabbed her keys and headed back to her car. She would try his flat first to see if he was there and, if not, she would call into the two or three pubs in town that he had mentioned favourably.

His flat was locked, but when she went around the back, she noticed that all the windows were open. She remembered that the day she had evacuated Morgan they made sure that everything was locked up. She called his name through one of the open windows but there was no reply.

She climbed up on a ledge and opened the window wider and climbed in. The flat was cold and quiet and after a quick inspection, clearly empty. She was about to leave when she noticed a green leather-bound book under the bed. She opened it and quickly realised it was Morgan's diary. The last entry was before his initial visit to Newry so it wasn't particularly relevant to the case. But curiosity got the better of her. She flicked through the details for the previous six months. It was full of self-pitying morbidity and the occasional witty observation on life as a lowly insurance clerk. But one word kept popping up and that was "Orla".

Tina closed the diary and placed it carefully back under the bed. Then she locked all the windows and left via the front door. She had a good idea where Morgan was and she wasn't the least bit happy about it.

Morgan and Orla stopped at a video shop in Blackrock. Morgan had an eclectic taste in film. He liked an action movie but was also fond of European cinema, where nothing much happened apart from a lot of long mournful stares over a windswept horizon. And of course, they always had an unhappy ending.

But in the end, Orla chose the movie. "Let's get *Terms of Endearment*. It won the best movie at the Oscars," she said as she studied the front cover. Morgan couldn't think of anything worse, but the chance to share a sofa with Orla made him swallow his priggishness.

They brought it home and Morgan set up the video player. Orla brought two ice-filled tumblers from the kitchen and then fetched a bottle of Baileys from the drinks cabinet.

"We only drink this at Christmas, so it will be months before

Dad notices that any is missing." She giggled and slipped onto the sofa beside Morgan.

They watched the movie in virtual silence, Orla edging closer as Emma's cancer got steadily worse on screen. When Emma eventually passed away, Orla was in tears and Morgan felt compelled to take her in his arms. Their faces met and he could taste the warm, salty tears. He had waited for this moment for years and in the end, it snuck up without him noticing. He thrust his tongue deep into her month and gently pushed her back on the sofa. His hands searched greedily for her breasts as she lifted his shirt and racked her fingernails along his spine.

They fell onto the rug and Orla ended up on top, straddling Morgan with her long, blonde hair swooshing across his face like a horse's tail. Morgan struggled to get his belt unbuckled while searching in his pocket for a condom. Orla, who seemed to have more experience in these matters, was already undressed and ready for action.

He finally unbuckled his belt when their passion was interrupted by the sound of a window smashing. They froze and then Orla instantly grabbed her clothes and disappeared behind the sofa.

"What the fuck was that?" she whispered as Morgan redid his belt buckle and crept towards the living room door.

"I don't know. I think it came from the back somewhere. Should we go and look?"

"You go and look. I'll call the Guards," Orla said as she slipped past him and headed for the phone on the hallway table. Morgan thought he heard the crunch of boots on glass coming from the kitchen and edged towards the door. He fumbled for the light switch and turned it on. The room suddenly lit up to expose a large man that Morgan vaguely recognised but couldn't place. He tried to speak but couldn't get any words out. Then a blunt object hit his head and he slumped to the kitchen floor.

———

Orla finished the call and headed back towards the kitchen. "The Guards said they'll be here in ten min...." She stopped as she noticed the back door swinging open and the pool of blood on the floor.

Then she heard the sound of a car engine coming from the front of the house and she raced through the front door and out to the road. She saw the car reverse out and head left towards the N11. As she stood there half-dressed and shivering, another car appeared from the right and stopped.

Tina jumped out. "Where's James?" she screamed.

Orla pointed up the hill. "He's in that car. It's a dark blue Cavalier. Somebody took him."

Tina said nothing but jumped back into her car and sped off. It was suddenly silent and Orla stood there in her bare feet, knickers and tie-dyed T-shirt. She was scared and her tough exterior was cracking. It exploded in a mixture of tears and snot as she stood there and watched the two sets of taillights disappear over the hill.

Tina followed the Cavalier as it sped down the N11 and then took a right turn at Kilmacanoge. They slowly climbed into the Wicklow Mountains and the traffic thinned out. Tina tried to stay as far back as possible and gambled on the other driver not suspecting that he was being followed.

Eventually, the Cavalier pulled onto a dirt track and Tina turned her lights off and followed. The Cavalier stopped in a clearing and the driver got out and opened the boot. She saw the prone body of Morgan being lifted out and carried towards a dark tarpaulin that lay on the ground, partly hidden by leaves.

She abandoned her car and crept closer. Morgan still lay motionless on the ground and she wondered if he was already dead. Then she saw him stir and she breathed a sigh of relief.

The Cavalier driver pulled back the tarpaulin to reveal a pre-dug shallow hole. Then he bent down and rolled Morgan's body into it.

It was late but a full moon bathed the forest in a shimmering light. Tina crouched behind a fallen log three metres from the Cavalier. She saw the driver reach into the glove box and retrieve a pistol. He then walked back towards Morgan's lifeless body and raised the gun.

"I wouldn't do that if I were you, Joyce," Tina said as she stood and pointed her own gun at her boss.

"I wouldn't have the slightest qualm about putting you in the same grave as James."

"Miss Reynolds. You'd do well to fuck off if you have any sense. You're in over your head. This is big-boy stuff and you girls should get back to making tea. I told you to stay away from this guy, but you wouldn't listen. Now if you want a career in the Guards, be a smart girl and get back in your car and let me deal with this."

"Why shouldn't I just shoot you now, Joyce? You're a piece of shit and I don't want to be in the Guards if it has scum like you in it."

Joyce laughed. "Because you haven't got the balls, or the ovaries in your case. If you were up to playing at this level, you would have dumped this waste of space long ago. He's toxic. But you let your fanny rule your head. Now fuck off and let me do my job."

Joyce cocked his gun and pointed it at Morgan.

"I wonder what Carson will say to you when I give his name to the RUC?"

Joyce froze and walked slowly towards Tina. "What did you just say?"

"Carson. I know his name and where he lives. See, I can play at the big-boy stuff too, Joyce. I know all about your little spy games, and if you do anything to James, I'll be happy to sing my pretty girl head off."

"You fucking bitch," Joyce shouted as he lunged at Tina. Her gun flew out of her hand and disappeared into the undergrowth. Joyce tried to free his pistol-wielding hand but Tina clung to it with all her might. Then she leaned up and bit deeply into the soft underside of his wrist. He screamed and dropped the gun and in the same motion punched her with his left hand. Tina could feel the crack of breaking bone and an electric shock of pain shot through her.

Joyce was on all fours searching for the gun and Tina snuck up behind him and aimed a sharp kick between his legs. He slumped in pain as his testicles disappeared into his body cavity.

She stood and examined her face. Her nose seemed to have taken most of the damage and she gingerly put it back into place. Then she stumbled towards the pit that Morgan was in. Before she got there, however, Joyce crept up behind her and smashed her across the head with a heavy piece of wood. He found his gun and then stepped over her body and stood over the pit. He slowly pulled back the trigger. But there was no target. The grave was empty.

Joyce scanned the forest. It was silent, apart from the occasional shallow breath from Tina. Shit, he thought. Then he climbed back into his car and drove off.

Morgan had woken moments earlier. His head throbbed and he could feel a sticky substance on his forehead that he was sure should be on the inside and not the outside. He could hear shouting and could vaguely recognise the voices. He gingerly pulled himself up and saw Tina and Joyce rolling around on the ground. His instinct was to run but he also felt an urge to help Tina.

Discretion ultimately got the better of valour and he snuck over to the nearest tree and found a thick bush to hide behind. He watched as Joyce whacked Tina with the branch and then as he climbed into his car and drove away.

Morgan raced over to Tina's side. She was groggy but awake. He held her in his arms for a few minutes and said nothing. They rocked gently as the sound of Joyce's car disappeared down the forest track.

"Bet my head hurts more than yours," Morgan ventured.

Tina returned a weak smile. "Let's just go home, James. I'm not sure I can drive but I'll try. We can go back to my place. I'd say Joyce will hang low for a few days. But I dropped my gun in that bush. Maybe you'd give me a hand to find it. I've just threatened to shoot my boss. I'm in enough trouble without having to tell the office that there is a Garda gun missing somewhere in the Wicklow Mountains."

They got down on all fours and after a few minutes, Morgan put his hand on the gun. He lifted it carefully and handed it to Tina.

"Should I avoid getting my fingerprints on it?" he asked.

"I think that's the least of your problems," Tina said. "Come on, let's go."

They drove back to Dublin without exchanging any more than small talk. Adrenalin still coursed through their veins but they each had other questions to ponder. Morgan thought back to where he was the moment before he heard the glass smash. He was about to do the thing he'd been dreaming about for two years. And yet, here he was in a car with the woman who always seemed to be around when he needed help most. A wave of guilt overcame him and he reached across to rest his palm on Tina's thigh. She flinched when he did so and pulled away.

Tina was thinking about her arrival at Orla's house. What was Morgan doing there in the first place and, more importantly, why was Orla half-dressed when she got there?

"I suppose you'll be wanting to call Orla and tell her you are okay?" Tina asked with an edge that would cut through butter.

Morgan looked across at her. Tina's face betrayed a hint of sadness. "Maybe. She was going to call the cops. So, we might want them to call off the hunt."

"Oh shit. I'd better call her and see if she gave them your name. If she did, we'll have the whole bloody force out looking for you. We don't need that hassle. Look, maybe we'll call in there on the way home. It's pretty close. I want to say hello to my cousin anyway." Tina threw Morgan a look when she said this that left him wondering who was more in the shit. Him or Orla.

They pulled into the driveway of Orla's house, just as the Garda squad car was leaving. Orla was better dressed than the last time Tina had seen her and she ran straight to Morgan and flung her arms around him. "Thank God you're okay, Morgan. I was so worried about you."

Morgan looked over Orla's shoulder and stared into Tina's eyes. She was standing feet apart with her right hand firmly placed on her hip. She had a face that suggested thunder, with the risk of forked lightning to boot.

"Thanks, Orla," Morgan whispered as he pulled away. "I think Tina has a few questions for you. Can we go inside?"

Tina dispensed with the usual air kisses and got straight down to business. "What did you tell the uniforms? Did you mention James's name? Cause if you did, we'll have a shit storm to clean up."

"Tina, I know you think I'm a bit of an idiot, but I know that Morgan is caught up in this nest of international espionage that you are playing at. I'm not going to start shouting his name out. I just told them that there was a break-in and that I chased a guy out of the house."

"Did they ask if anyone else was here?"

"Yeah, they did. I told them I was on my own, necking a bottle of Baileys and watching *Terms of Endearment* because the love of my life had run off with my cousin."

Tina and Orla stared at each other and Morgan stared at his shoes. Women are like buses, he thought. You wait ages for one and then two come along together. But so close together, that they end up crashing into each other.

13

"ANDERSON, GET INTO MY OFFICE," MCGUINNESS BARKED AS he arrived at work on Monday morning. Anderson smiled at his colleagues. He'd won the weekly mood guessing game again but felt that he wouldn't get an opportunity to enjoy his prize.

"What's up, boss? I see Glentoran blew it again on Saturday."

"Fucking Linfield. I think I'd rather lose to the Taigues from Cliftonville. Anyway, I need to talk to you. Take a look at this."

Anderson sat and read the paper McGuinness had passed to him. "Interesting, did you get this from Oriel?"

"Yeah, he called me on Saturday. Said he'd been through the top guy's office and that he came across this. What do you think of it?"

"Hmm, well, it would explain why Oriel is still free to operate. I guess it's good news. We can call off the hounds and start chasing the really bad guys like we're supposed to."

"I'm not so sure, Anderson. This all seems too neat to me. Like it's all been tied up with a neat bow. And something about Oriel makes me suspicious."

"What do you mean?"

"Well, he's normally a dour old bastard. This time he was dancing around like a foal at Toomebridge horse fair. Either the old puff had his cock sucked by a young fella the night before or he's not being honest with us. Basically, he's never liked working for us. I can understand that. Why is he looking pleased about it now?"

Anderson read the memo again. He hated to admit it, but McGuinness might be right. It looked too straightforward. Everything you'd expect if you were trying to lure a dog off the scent.

"Okay, boss. Do you think they might have turned Oriel? We'd better find out, I guess. Should I head south and keep an eye on him? See what he's up to?

"I think so. He told me he was working till 3 pm today. So, wait for him outside their headquarters. Follow him around for a day or two and if you don't pick up any intelligence, pull him into Banbridge and see what information you can get from him. He's a big nancy boy so it shouldn't take too long with the pliers to get him squealing. And if he has been turned, make sure you finish him off. Bring a couple of those army goons with you if you need help."

Anderson sat back. He'd been planning to bring up his faltering enthusiasm for this project for some time and this seemed as opportune a time as possible.

"Look, boss. I've been thinking a lot about this. I'm not comfortable with the screwdriver and bullet in the back of the head part of this job. I'm a detective. I like solving puzzles and putting bad guys away. Torture isn't really my thing. You've got all those Loyalist contacts. They'd be more than happy to push lit cigarettes into the eyes of Southern cops."

McGuinness slammed his fist on the desk. "You think you can

just walk away from this, Anderson? Do the stuff you like and then turn your nose up at the smelly work? I've let you into the inner circle. The circle of trust. You know enough stuff to send me to jail for a long time. Do you think I'm going to let you sit on the sidelines fiddling with your conscience? You seem to forget that I know all the dodgy stuff you've been doing too. And if it comes down to it, who do you think the brass will believe? Me, or a low-ranking detective like you?"

McGuinness got up again and struck his Napoleonic pose as he gazed out onto Knock Road. Dark clouds were gathering over Black Mountain and tumbling down towards the city like a mediaeval army.

"Don't you realise this is a war? Do you think the IRA are down there having a meeting where some young fella says he doesn't want to blow up pubs any more; he'd rather just make the tea or look after the bookkeeping? How do you think the Provo commander would deal with that request? You're in this up to your neck."

McGuinness was leaning over Anderson with a twisted scowl on his face.

"There's no going back until I say so. We're going to wrap this business up and then you can fuck off to traffic duty in Fermanagh."

Anderson shook his head. He figured that he'd have to find some way out of this using his own wit and McGuinness wasn't going to help him.

"Alright, boss. I'll head down to Dublin today and let you know what I pick up." He got up and slouched out of the office. McGuinness was still staring out the window and said nothing.

"What's up with the boss?" Anderson's workmate asked.

"Same old shit. He's dug a sewage pit and wants me to fill it in." Anderson grabbed his car keys and wallet.

"I'll see you in a couple of days," he said. "I have to go and buy a shovel."

———

Tina called Oriel and arranged to meet him by the Wellington Memorial when he finished his shift. She hadn't spoken to Morgan since Saturday night. She called in a favour with a friend of hers and had dropped Morgan there and parked him in the spare room. Her parting words were to lie low for a few days and they would catch up during the week. She needed that time to get her head around Saturday's activities. Her professional and romantic futures were on the line and her head still ached from the whack Joyce had given it.

Morgan sat on the bed in Tina's friend's house, staring at the wall, with his small luggage bag at his feet. He didn't have the energy or enthusiasm to unpack, or even the curiosity to check out his new lodgings. He had a nagging ache in his heart that told him that he'd blown things with Tina. He had held back on telling her how he felt, because part of him still thought that Orla was his true desire. He now saw the difference between love and lust. Orla was the one he held dark sexual thoughts for. But Tina was the one he felt most comfortable with, the one who cared about him and the one whose body sank into his when they hugged.

And now he felt as though he'd blown his chances with both of them. He thought back over the previous nights. How Tina had been sleeping at Garda Head Office and shipping him off from one sad spare room to another. Was she getting fed up with him, just like every other woman he ever knew? Had she finally grown tired of his forced humour? He needed to know.

He fished out his copy of First World War poetry and headed down to the bus stop. He had no fixed plan but thought he wanted to confront Tina and tell her what he thought. But he needed to immerse himself in some maudlin verse first to match his mood.

Oriel finished work at 3 pm and drove out of headquarters. Anderson was parked just down the road and he pulled out behind. Two hundred metres later, however, Oriel stopped the car and got out. Anderson assumed he'd been rumbled and he also pulled in and slunk down below the steering wheel. But Oriel walked in the opposite direction towards the memorial. Anderson grabbed an anorak with a hood and got out and followed him. He could see a figure ahead and, as they got closer, he realised it was Tina.

Those fuckers have turned him, he thought as he hid behind a tree. He couldn't hear what they were saying but by the hugs and kisses on display, they clearly weren't mortal enemies.

They parted with another hug and Oriel went back to his car. Anderson wondered which of them he should follow. Tina might bring him to Morgan. But his instructions were to follow Oriel and there was no mileage in annoying McGuinness any more than was necessary. So, he pulled out behind Oriel's car and followed him across the river to the south side.

Morgan's bus had passed through Phoenix Park as all this was going on. He was about to jump off when he saw Tina. But then he saw her smile as she met Oriel and watched the hugs and kisses they exchanged. A wave of jealousy and anger overcame him. Was this why she wanted to stay at Garda Head Office and not with him? He was trying to come up with the appropriate words to say to Tina when the bus swept out of the park and into Castleknock.

In the meantime, Oriel had driven into the city and parked and made his way down a laneway strewn with overflowing bins. Anderson watched from the road as Oriel entered the side door of a pub, illuminated only by a single red bulb above a nondescript door. Anderson found a parking spot and waited a minute before following Oriel into the pub. He pushed the door open to be met by a thick floor-to-ceiling curtain. He found the parting and an aroma of stale cigarette smoke and cheap aftershave wafted over him.

It was dark and it took him a moment to become accustomed to the light. A jaunty, British-style jazz song was playing over the hushed tones of the twenty or so patrons, all of them men. They were huddled in groups of one or two but lifted their heads en masse to study Anderson as he entered. He felt like a cowboy who had just walked into a sleepy and out of the way saloon.

Oriel was sitting alone at the bar, cradling a large whiskey in his hands, with his back to the door. Anderson slipped past the crushed velvet-backed armchairs and slid into the empty bar stool beside him.

"Not the friendliest pub in Dublin, is it?" Anderson ventured.

Oriel looked up in shock. "What are you doing here?"

"Just thought I'd drop down and see how things are going. Is Maurice Fitzsimons here?"

"Who's that?"

"You know the Irish gay guy and his partner Simon Fitzmaurice?"

Oriel looked bemused.

"You know, Maurice Fitzsimons and Simon Fitzmaurice?"

The joke went down like a lead balloon. Oriel looked around to make sure they weren't being overheard. He leaned closer. "Shouldn't you call me first and arrange to meet on neutral ground?"

"So, is this a pick-up joint for your sort?" Anderson asked.

"And what exactly is my sort?"

Anderson laughed. "I'm just winding you up, Oriel. I'm not one of those Pentecostal Northerners. I couldn't give two shits where you want to put your willy. I just wanted to have a chat with you about this memo you found. It looks a bit fishy to us."

Oriel's face darkened and his eyebrow twitched. "What do mean, fishy? I found it in Joyce's office. Why would I make something like that up?"

Anderson caught the barman's attention and ordered two more whiskeys.

"So, how did you end up in Special Branch, Oriel? You don't strike me as the sort of hard-nosed bastard that usually joins the branch."

Oriel shrugged. "I was just a normal cop, popular with the locals with a good nose for the business. You end busting the same guy for stealing cars or fighting in pubs and you think you can do better. The top brass were always pushing me too. Making me do sergeant exams and that sort of thing. Then a place came up in Special Branch and I thought what the hell. It's a chance to catch bigger criminals. Then you get there and you realise that it's nothing to do with criminals at all. We spend all day bugging politicians and looking for communists in RTE.

"But, I kind of reconciled myself to that. I was holding out for the pension, to be honest. And then your fucking boss comes along with his hidden camera and suddenly I'm a spy, an enemy of the state. I haven't actually caught a criminal in years. I've ended up working for them."

They sat silently for a minute, nursing their drinks.

"My story is not dissimilar," Anderson said. "Look it's different up north, as you know. We have a real war going on up there. I've lost count of the number of funerals I've been to or body parts I've picked up in bombed-out bars. There is no such thing as a normal cop up there, so that's how I ended up in Special Branch. I figured I'd be doing the same job but at least targeting bigger fish. Getting at the leadership guys in the IRA and not just the foot soldiers.

"But every time I'd pick up a bad guy it would turn to shit. I'd work him hard for seventy-two hours and get him to sell out his own mother. Then I'd get a phone call from some stuffed shirt in MI5 telling me to let him go because the wee Provie was an important 'asset'.

"Everyone seems to be working for two bosses in Northern Ireland. I honestly don't know who are the good guys and who are the baddies any more. And if you're a cop, that's a dangerous place to find yourself in. I woke up one morning and realised I wasn't a policeman any more. I'm what they call a player. An actor in some geo-political drama. I joined to catch burglars and terrorists. Not to be James Bond.

"Now, we're running spies like it's Berlin in 1945 and chasing a young fella all over the country because he had a nerve to accidently leave a tape recorder in a car. I'll be honest with you, I don't think you've given us one decent piece of information in the last three years. That's not your fault. You guys just don't have anything that we don't know about already. I mean, MI5 are probably tapping all your phones anyway.

"We get most of our best info from picking up wee Provies and bending their wrists back until they scream like a child. It's as simple as that. You're a vanity project. Something to make McGuinness feel like he's George Smiley."

They ordered more whiskey and swapped tales of deering-do in their careers.

"So, without being rude, Anderson," Oriel said, "what are you doing here anyway? I doubt if you're down here to investigate Dublin's underground gay scene."

Anderson swirled the whiskey in his hand and stared into the distance. Nina Simone came on the speakers and he hummed along gently.

"I don't know Oriel. I was sent here to keep an eye on you. To see who you were talking to and so on. But on the way down, I started to re-evaluate things. I want out of all this shit. I've got a chance to move overseas and, to be honest, I think I'll take it. But I'd like to tie up a few loose ends before I go. You, for example. I never liked the way McGuinness dicked you around and I'm not proud of my part in it. So, I'd like to figure out a way of getting you off the hook."

Oriel's face brightened. "That would be fantastic, mate. But how are you going to do that while McGuinness still has those pictures."

Anderson sat and lowered his glass. "That's the thing, Oriel. As long as those pictures are the only thing he has on you, I think we'll be alright. McGuinness is a bully, a bigot and a bigmouth. But he's as thick as a short plank. He has a combination lock on his filing cabinet at work where he keeps all his dodgy shit, including the negatives for your little romantic tryst."

Anderson put his arm on Oriel's shoulder. "I was only on the job a week when I worked out that the code was his Orange Order lodge number."

Oriel smiled for the first time in years. "That would be magnificent," he said. "But you might want to take your arm from my shoulder. I think you've just crushed the dreams of half the patrons here."

Anderson drained his whiskey and grabbed his coat. "I'll be in touch soon. Don't tell McGuinness we had this conversation. I'll spin him a yarn and I'll let you know if I get my hands on those photos. Mind yourself, Oriel, and keep your eye on the barman. I think you're in there."

Morgan had spent the night tossing and turning. His jealousy had distilled itself into a deep and dark paranoia. In his dreams, Tina was in league with the RUC. That it was all an elaborate plan to suck him in and blow him out in bubbles.

He woke at 6 am feeling as though he had spent the night on a treadmill. He needed to have it out with Tina, so he packed his bag and headed over to her house.

Tina was on her way out when she met Morgan on her doorstep. He looked like he'd been standing there for hours trying to work up the courage to ring the doorbell.

"James, what are you doing here?" she asked as she scanned the streets. "Are you sure you haven't been followed?"

Morgan mumbled an apology as he desperately searched for the words he really wanted to say.

"I left my toothbrush here. I feel like I've got fur growing inside my mouth. Can I go and get it?"

Tina was flustered. Her plan with Oriel and Carson was coming to fruition and yet she had a puppy dog on her doorstep to deal with.

"I'm sorry James, I have to run. Grab your toothbrush and head back to my friend's place. It's not safe around here."

She rushed past him and jumped into her car, leaving Morgan alone on the doorstep like a birthday cake that had been left out in the rain. He eventually went inside and found his toothbrush. As he was leaving, he noticed a notepad on the hall table with a note in Tina's writing scribbled on it.

"Mullen's Café, Glen Road, Belfast, 11 am."

Morgan held the note in his hand. He wondered what the meeting was about, but in his sleep-addled state he couldn't make sense of it. Then he looked at his watch and figured that if he got a bus to the station, he could make it to Belfast for 11 am, and he didn't really have anything else to do.

Tina found the café on Glen Road and spotted Carson straight away. He was the only customer there.

He looked like a typical washed-out policeman, clinging on desperately for his pension. His hair was greased back and his dark eyes shifted menacingly around the room, as though he was expecting a gunman to barge in at any moment.

She slipped into the seat opposite him and pushed an envelope across.

"Carson, I presume. I'm Detective Reynolds. But you can call me Tina."

Carson took a slug of tea. His nicotine-stained fingers trembled as he lifted the cup. "What can I do for you, Tina? This better be quick."

Tina nodded towards the envelope. "There are a couple of names in there. Colleagues of yours, here in Belfast. We've picked up intel that they have been asking questions about a Garda spy in RUC headquarters. I've included a few interview notes and dialogue from some phone taps that we've picked up."

Carson picked up the envelope and peeked inside. "And is my name mentioned in any of this?"

"No, that's why I wanted to see you today. We have a chance to nip this in the bud before they find out."

"So, what do you want me to do? Like I said on the phone, they take things a bit more seriously up here, sweetheart."

Tina picked up the envelope. "There are a few names in here that we'd like to learn more about. You'll see in one of the phone tap extracts that they talk about a guy called Morgan. We think he might be the key to all this. We want you to see what information you can find internally at the RUC. Check out what records have they got on this Morgan chap."

Carson put his cup down and leaned in. "And how do you figure I'm going to do that, sweetheart? If this is a guy tied up in a spying network, do you think they are going to type everything up in a nice memo and file it in the middle of the office with a come and get me sticker on the outside? I'm already risking my fucking neck for Joyce. If you think I'm going to start messing with this craic, you've another think coming, honey. I promised a wee bit of photocopying to Joyce. Maybe a copy of the tape of an interview or something if it crossed my desk. I'm not getting paid to be fucking James Bond?"

"And how much exactly is Joyce paying you?" Tina asked.

Carson lowered his cup slowly and stared suspiciously into Tina's eyes.

"That's none of your fucking business, sweetheart. You're not in on this, are you? How did you find my name and phone number?"

"Look, Carson. I'm trying to save your fucking life here. I don't expect it will be easy. But McGuinness will have some information in his office. You just have to break in when he's not there and have a snoop around."

Carson leaned back and let out a snorting, sarcastic laugh. "Let me get this right. You want me to break into a Special Branch inspector's office and go through his filing cabinets? Do you know what would happen to me if I was caught?"

Tina folded her arms and leaned back. "And what do you think will happen to you if they find out about you before we get a chance to clear things up?"

Carson picked up the envelope and headed for the door. He stopped and looked back at Tina. "Maybe I'll give Joyce a call. See what he has to say about this?"

Tina had to think on her feet. "Look, he wants to take a back seat on this. He's worried that the RUC may be monitoring him, knowing that he's the probable conduit. So, he wants it all to go through me. I've left my number on a page inside that envelope. Call me if you find anything. I'm not at my desk much these days so leave a message and I'll get back to you."

Carson snorted and turned and left without saying goodbye.

Morgan watched all this from a bus stop across the street. His jealousy had abated as he saw that Tina was clearly not at a romantic meeting. The hostility between her and Carson was palpable from across the street. He suddenly felt foolish and wanted to slip away and get back to Dublin before Tina saw him.

A bus arrived with Central Station as its destination written on the front. Morgan got on and bought a ticket. Just as the doors were about to close, another passenger jumped on. It was Tina's meeting companion, and he angrily sat down and scribbled furtively in a notebook. Morgan watched him carefully as the bus trundled its way towards the station.

They both alighted and Morgan hid himself inside his anorak as they entered the concourse. The train to Dublin was due in twenty minutes so he found a bench and dug out the Walkman from his backpack and slipped his *Tales of Melancholy* mixed tape into the machine. A chill wind crept along the platform, so he huddled against a pillar as Sade's "Smooth Operator" flickered through his headphones.

The bench was separated by a half-length partition and the man Tina had met sat at the other side of this from Morgan. He was joined a moment later by a heavy-set man in a dark overcoat.

"The Dublin train will be here soon. So, this better be quick, Carson. Tell me about the meeting you had with Reynolds. Did she say anything about our spy in Dublin?"

Morgan's ears pricked. He recognised the voice from that fateful night in the Wicklow Mountains when he found himself lying in a shallow grave waiting to be dispatched. It was Joyce, and Morgan couldn't help thinking that he was on this platform in Belfast for no good reason. He pulled his anorak closer and turned his face away. Then he quietly opened his bag and took out the recording device. He pressed the record button and carefully placed it between himself and the two men.

"No, she wants me to break into McGuinness's office in Belfast and look for information. She seems interested in some fella called Morgan. I humoured her and said I'd see what I could do. But I knew it was fishy. And if I got caught breaking into an inspector's office, I'd be dead before sundown. So that's why I called you."

"You did the right thing, Carson. This is where we're at. This Morgan fellow discovered some sensitive information about an RUC spy in Garda Head Office. The RUC are aware of this and they are keen to liquidate Morgan. So am I to be honest. He's a serious security risk. Reynolds and myself are the only other people in the South who know the spy's identity. But the RUC don't know that. As far as they are aware, Morgan is the only one with the knowledge, so if we can get him out of the way, we can maybe keep it that way."

"Right," said Carson. "But what about Reynolds? Isn't she a risk as well?"

Joyce scowled and shook his head. "She's a big disappointment to me, Carson. I had high hopes for her. But she let her heart rule her head. She's hooked up with this Morgan fella and thinks she can play games with the big boys. I'd love to get her out of the way, but that old cliché has never been truer. Women, you can't live with them and you can't kill them."

"So, what's your plans?" asked Carson.

"Look, this Morgan guy is a nobody. He was involved in an incident with the British Army last Christmas. I'm guessing he's probably on some file somewhere as a subversive. And if he's not, then maybe that's something you could help me with. Get his name into the system up the North, if it's not there already. Then, if we clip him, the authorities will think it was a subversive's job and the case will be closed in three days."

Carson nodded. "I can get you a gun if you want with a bit of history, if you want to tie it back to the IRA or UVF?"

Joyce smiled. "That would be excellent, Carson. I don't suppose you could put your hands on an ex-MI5 weapon? That would really fuck with the heads of the ballistics department and make them bury the case before they got back in their cars."

"I doubt it, Joyce," Carson said as he laughed. "Them boys don't lose weapons the way the terrorists do. I'll get you something that will do the job though. But what about this Polis woman? How will you keep her quiet?"

"A bullet from the same gun would do the trick. But she's a female Garda. If you kill a cop, the entire force would be out looking for the killer. And we can't afford that sort of attention. I'm confident that once Morgan is out of the way, I can bring her to her senses. And then put her in charge of traffic in Leitrim and hope to never set eyes on the fucking bitch again."

A blast from a train's horn interrupted them and they looked up to see the Dublin-bound train approach. Joyce rose and shook Carson's hand. "Let me know when you have that gun ready and I'll arrange to pick it up."

Joyce boarded the train and Morgan waited until the last minute before grabbing his recording device and darting towards the last carriage. He found a backward-facing seat and buried himself again inside his anorak. It would take two hours to get back to Dublin and sharing the train with a man who had just talked about killing him made for an uneasy journey.

Morgan made it back to Tina's friend's house as it was getting dark. Tina was in the kitchen and she said nothing as he walked in but threw him a look that could sour butter.

"Hi Tina, I'm so happy to see you. I need to show you something."

Tina stayed sitting with her arms folded. "You can't keep doing this, James. You have to stay in one place where I know I can find you."

Morgan pulled a seat up beside her. "I know, I'll explain all that later. But you have to listen to this." He took the recording device out of his bag and pressed play.

Joyce's deep-throated voice echoed around the kitchen. Tina said nothing until the tape finished. Then she stood and carefully pulled the curtains back and scanned the dark street outside.

"Okay, James," she said. "This highlights more than ever that you need to stay here and not go out on any adventures. Not even to the corner shop. We'll move you on tomorrow. I just need to figure out where. How did you get this, by the way?"

Morgan told her about the encounter at Belfast Station without fully explaining how he had ended up there. Tina took detailed notes. Then she picked up her coat and headed towards the door.

"I have to head into the office, James. I'll come back later and bring some takeaway. And, look. We need to talk about Orla. But maybe not tonight."

And with that, she was gone. Morgan sat in the silent kitchen and looked around. This was probably the sixth kitchen he'd sat in since Christmas and he hadn't felt comfortable in any of them. Somewhere, out there in the dark, the Dublin and Belfast police were both looking for him and both wanted to see him in a cold, shallow grave somewhere in the Wicklow Mountains. But he wasn't thinking about any of that. He was thinking about Orla and Tina. A few days ago, he felt like he had his choice of either of them. Now, there was a good chance that he had managed to piss both of them off sufficiently, that he would end up with neither.

He was overcome with feelings of loneliness, anxiety and sadness. So, he did what he always did when he felt like that. He made a cup of tea, took it to bed and tried to write a poem.

———

Anderson was waiting in the golf club bar for McGuinness to finish his round. The bar had a sweeping window overlooking the 18th green and Anderson watched as McGuinness approached and surreptitiously kicked his ball closer to the hole.

Anderson smiled. Once a cheat, always a cheat, he thought.

Twenty minutes later, McGuinness had showered and joined Anderson at the bar. "So, what have you got for me, Anderson? How did it go with our poof down in Dublin?"

"It's all good, boss. I followed him around for a couple of days. He didn't meet anyone he shouldn't. Then I pulled him in for a chat. He was quite offended that we would question his word. But he said that it's gone quiet in Dublin. Reynolds has been put on another, unrelated job. He's confident that nobody in Garda Head Office knows about him. And let's face it, if he had concerns, do you think he'd be sitting at his desk waiting for a tap on the shoulder?"

"That just leaves this Morgan chap then," said McGuinness. "Let's wrap things up and get rid of him once and for all. I had a call from the army top brass earlier in the week. They are keen to shelve the case of those three Scottish soldiers and their assault charge. I told them we'd help, if we could borrow them for a week for a wee job. They are waiting for you to contact them and then we'll head south with all guns blazing. I might even go myself. This could be a bit of fun."

Anderson frowned. The last thing he wanted was to be dragged into a glorified fox hunt. "Fair enough, boss. But how are we going to track him down?"

McGuinness leaned in closer. "I haven't been talking just to the army brass this week. MI5 have also been sniffing around. They are just as keen as we are that our assets in the South are protected. They have access to way more kit than we do, Anderson. They could tell you what you had for dinner last night. Anyway, they have identified three key people that Morgan contacts regularly and they have bugged their phones. If Morgan calls any of them, they reckon they can identify the place he's calling from within five minutes. They have a bunch of agents in Dublin and so long as he's not calling from the back of beyond, one of them will hopefully be able to get to him before the call finishes. Then they'll keep an eye on him until we can turn up with the cavalry."

McGuinness leant back with a chuckle. He was enjoying his role at the centre of all this security intrigue.

Anderson stood to leave. "Okay, boss. I'll call the Scottish soldiers and put them on standby. I'll go along myself to make sure that they don't fall on their arse again."

"Good man, Anderson. Good to have you back on the team as a committed player."

Anderson threw back a weak smile before leaving. I'll have to move quickly, he thought. Events are starting to overtake my plans. He drove back to the office and dug out his phone book. Then he checked his watch. It would be 7.20 am in Toronto.

He dialled the number and a groggy voice said, "Hello."

"Hiya cousin. It's Anderson here in Belfast. I was wondering if that job you mentioned with the Mounties was still up for grabs. I think it's time I got out of town. And I've always pictured myself on a horse!"

Tina stopped at the chipper in Ranelagh and picked up a couple of quarter pounders and chips. Morgan was watching TV when she got there and they ate in silence. Tina tidied up and came back into the living room.

"Okay James, I know you have two different police forces chasing you at the moment with murderous intent. But I'm sorry. I have to talk about Orla and what you two were up to in her house."

Morgan looked up sheepishly. "What do you mean?"

"I mean what was she doing in her underwear when I turned up?"

Morgan needed time to think, so he made a meal of tidying up the coffee table. Should he be honest, he thought, and admit that he was torn between the two of them. But honesty had never worked well for him in the past.

"I was bored that day so I called her and asked if she wanted to meet for a drink. She invited me back to her house to watch a movie and then we ended up having a few Baileys, so she didn't want to drive. So, I was going to sleep in the spare room when Joyce turned up. I guess that Orla had already gone to bed."

He threw Tina a quick look to try to gauge whether she was buying the story or not. The look on her face suggested that the jury was still out.

"Look, Tina. It's been a difficult few weeks. But I've found that you are the only person I can trust. I don't want to mess this up, but let's face it, it's not a normal relationship. I want to be able to take you to the pictures, to be able to stroll through St Stephen's

Green on a sunny day, to bring you down the country to meet my mother. But we don't do any of that. I sleep in more beds than Hugh Hefner."

Tina moved across and threw her arms around him. Salty tears fell onto his neck and he was engulfed with the sudden realisation that he too was in love. He had fought it for so long, but Tina had managed to find a key to a door that he had kept bolted for years. Her body melted into his as they hugged, and he was struck by how her shape fitted so comfortably into his.

He pulled back and carefully swept the tear-soaked hair from her face.

"I love you, James. I love you more than I ever realised that love could stretch to."

"I love you too, Tina."

She smiled and then turned away. He could hear her sobbing and went and gently placed his hands on her shoulders.

"What's wrong, Tina. This should be the happiest day of our lives."

She turned and stared at Morgan. Her eyes were bloodshot and shimmering with tears.

"It should be the happiest day of our lives but that's what makes this so hard for me. I love you dearly. But you have to go away and never see me again."

Morgan sat on the sofa. It had been five years since he had ventured over the parapet of love and now he felt like he'd been hit by a sniper's bullet.

"Tina, I don't understand. What do you mean?"

Tina sat beside him and took his hand. "I'm sorry, James. I really thought I could control all this. To find a solution that would stop those bastards chasing you. But it's bigger than I can control now. The RUC and the Guards both want you dead. MI5 may even be involved. And I don't think I can protect you from all of that."

Morgan's face drained of its entire colour. The enormity of his dilemma was finally seeping into his consciousness. He had delegated any anxiety about his current situation to Tina, allowed her to do all the planning, to rescue him whenever danger lurked and to scan the horizon for threats. Now he felt like she was casting him adrift on an ocean of peril and uncertainty.

"But I can't do this on my own, Tina. Skip from guest house to friend's house to God knows where. Sleeping on sofas and constantly looking over my shoulder. I'll be lost without you, Tina."

He looked like a little boy again with his lower lip trembling and about to explode into a full-on sob. Tina gripped his hand tighter.

"Look, you can't stay in Dublin, James. They'll track you down eventually. It's too small a city. And they'll play on your weaknesses. Wait for you to make contact with Orla or with me. They'll follow me to get to you and I wouldn't be able to live with that on my conscience. Your only hope is to go away, to London or New York. Start a new life and maybe someday things will change and we can get back together. But we have to assume that it may not happen."

"But won't they just track me down there as well? I mean the RUC will be able to talk to the British police and if MI5 are involved, I won't even be safe in America."

Tina leaned down to her handbag and took out a green and white form. "I've filled most of this in; you just need to sign it. But you'll be signing as Sean Walters. So, practise writing it a few times on this scrap of paper."

Morgan took the pen and paper from Tina. "Who is Sean Walters?" he asked.

Tina looked at him with sad eyes still reddened from her earlier crying. "You are Sean Walters. That's your new identity. We have access to the deaths register at head office. Sean Walters was born the same year as you in Dublin. He died from leukaemia when he was eight. I got a copy of his birth certificate and this passport application form. We just need you to sign it and to get a couple of headshots of you. I've already signed and stamped it as a Garda witness. I have a contact in the passport office. She does emergency stuff for us when we have a witness protection thing. If we drop this in today, she can turn around a passport in a couple of days.”

Morgan started practising his *Sean Walters* signature. Soon, he was able to come up with a consistent form and he signed the passport application and passed it to Tina.

“What do you need me to do now, Tina?” he asked.

Tina took him in her arms and hugged him so tightly he thought she would choke him. Then she whispered softly in his ear. “I need you to take me to bed and do something that will make me remember you.”

They climbed into bed and made love. As they climaxed, Tina gripped him tightly and yelled, “Yes, Sean, yes.” Morgan was dead and Sean Walters would have to continue carrying the flame.

The next morning, they travelled into Connolly Station and Morgan found a photo booth and had some photos taken. Tina smiled at the snaps. “That hair is going to follow you around for the next ten years like a police mugshot.”

Then she dropped him at his branch of Bank of Ireland and he closed his account and withdrew his remaining cash. He used that to book a flight to London under his new name for three days’ time.

They stood on Grafton Street and listened to a busker murdering ‘Summer in Dublin’. Morgan pulled Tina to him. “So, I’m leaving on Wednesday morning and trying to find a place where I can hear the wind and the birds and the sea on the rocks and where open roads always are near.”

She smiled. “I’ve always liked that line. But I don’t think there will be much sea on the rocks in London.”

“Tina, there must be some way we can keep in touch. Can I write to you? Sean Walters could be your long-lost pen pal.”

Tina nodded. “Send me a letter every few weeks. Put the envelope inside a bigger envelope and address that to my friend in

Blackrock. She'll pass it on to me. But don't call me. They'll bug my line, I'm sure of that. And don't turn up out of the blue at Christmas or anything like that."

"Do you think I could be a different person as Sean?" he asked.

"How do you mean?"

"Well, maybe I could take this opportunity to reinvent myself. To become self-confident. To cut my hair in the New Romantic style. To become a punk or a rocker. Or maybe wear cardigans and sit in draughty pubs in Camden writing poetry. I don't know this Sean chap. He could be anything. The only thing I'm sure about is that he's not me."

Tina ruffled his hair. "I wouldn't change a single thing."

Morgan smiled. "I thought when a man met a woman he loved, he wanted her to stay the same and never change. But when a woman met a man, she hoped he would never stay the same and she could improve him."

Tina pulled him closer and a lonely tear meandered down her cheek. "I told you, James, I'm not like other women. I want you to always remember that. It's a big world out there and I'm scared that I'll lose you when you see the bright lights of Soho and the lure of English girls who grow weak at the knees when they hear an Irish accent. I want you to remember me as I am. As somebody who loves you for who you are and not for who you might become."

They walked down to the bus stop and caught a 46A. Tina rested her head on Morgan's shoulder. "I have to go into work tomorrow. But I'll cook a nice dinner for us for us when I get home. Then we'll figure out a way of getting you to the airport without being seen on Wednesday. Because I'm sure that's one of the places they are watching."

The bus trundled its way towards Dún Laoghaire and Morgan stared out at the mudflats of Dublin Bay. Somewhere in the distance lay Britain and his new life. But he had a few loose ends to tie up before he left dirty old Dublin town. 'Summer in Dublin' rattled around his head like an ear worm.

———

Tina left early for work. Morgan spent the morning packing and then wandered down to the pier in Dún Laoghaire. He found a phone box and called Orla at work.

"Howya Orla. It's Morgan here. I was wondering if you fancied catching up? I've got a bit of news and wanted to let you know."

"Ah, it's my international man of mystery. How are you? Things are a bit busy at the moment. Maybe we could meet in a week or so."

"That's the thing, Orla. The news I wanted to tell you is that I'm leaving Dublin in two days' time. So, I wanted to say goodbye."

"Oh, are you and Tina running off somewhere together? Getting married in Rome or something like that?"

"Hmm, I'd rather talk about it face to face. That's why I wanted to meet up. Do you think you could manage something tomorrow afternoon? I'd just prefer to do it when Tina is at work. The less she knows about the two of us meeting the better."

Orla laughed. "Did my cousin give you a telling off about you being at my house? She always had a bit of a jealous streak that girl."

"Yeah, let's just say that I had to mend so many fences that I could claim to be a qualified carpenter at this stage. How about Dún Laoghaire? That's on your way home and is handy for where I'm currently staying."

"Grand, I'll tell the boss I have a dentist's appointment and leave early. How about I meet you on the pier at 3 pm tomorrow?"

Morgan agreed and then hung up. The ferry to Holyhead was just pulling out and he walked to the end of the pier to watch it leave. He thought about all his classmates and friends from home who had taken that ferry to seek out new and exciting opportunities in England and beyond. To be able to buy condoms freely, to lie in late on Sundays and avoid Mass, to eat food that wasn't stewed or fried, to fall in love with brown or yellow girls. He had never felt that urge to leave but now the choice was being taken out of his hands. That was how his life had happened anyway. He had never directed it. Doors opened and he walked through without question, oblivious to whether there was a cliff on the other side.

This was just another door, and he would open it and blindly see where it took him.

———

The restaurant in the Europa Hotel was quiet at lunchtime. Perhaps the reputation as the most bombed hotel in the world was enough to scare customers off. Or perhaps it was the prices.

Thankfully, MI5 had a generous budget. McGuinness always made a point of meeting his contact there and treated himself to a three-course lunch while he was at it.

Clive was waiting for him when he arrived and ordered a bottle of Châteauneuf-du-Pape, which he knew was McGuinness's favourite. He was a stereotypical Englishman, with a plummy Oxbridge accent and a tie with a bulbous knot that made him look like he was still being dressed by his mother.

He greeted McGuinness warmly and they took a table at the back out of earshot of the staff. McGuinness was paranoid enough to believe that the IRA had ears in all the city centre social establishments.

"What's up Clive, are you boys busy?"

Clive wiped his lips with the linen tablecloth. "Same as ever, McGuinness, trying to stay one step ahead of PIRA. Not always easy, as you well know."

"Anything we can help you with?" McGuinness asked as he studied the menu and pondered whether to order the fillet steak or the lobster.

Clive twitched his nose and twirled the glass of wine between his thumb and index finger. "Funnily enough, McGuinness, I think you might be able to help. I know you wanted to talk about this asset you have in Garda Head Office and the threat this young Morgan guy poses to him. Well, that asset might just have become more important to us, so I've been authorised by HQ to give you all the help you need in swatting your irritating little fly."

"Excellent, Clive. It's good to hear that we're on the same page. So, what makes our asset more valuable to you?"

Clive leaned in. "Our friends in MI6 have been creating a lot of chatter. They like nothing better than dressing up like Lawrence of Arabia and tramping all over the desert. Anyway, one of their chaps in Libya has got wind of another arms shipment heading towards our friends in PIRA. The ship is already on the high seas, by all accounts. Full to the brim with Semtex and anti-aircraft missiles from our old friend Mr Gaddafi. That's what the MI6 guys say anyway, although one has always been of the belief that they are prone to exaggeration.

"But the Foreign and Colonial goons in London are creating a lot of noise and putting pressure on us to come up with some local intel. I don't like to drop names old chap, but the Lady in Downing Street is showing a bit of interest in the case. She's keen as mustard to embarrass Gaddafi and she's putting a bit of a squeeze on us. Of course, she would also like to embarrass the Paddies in the process."

McGuinness didn't like to discuss politics. He was a simple Loyalist who believed in the Union while hating England and didn't have the time or temperament to consider the contradiction. But he knew that Clive needed to be humoured.

"I thought the Lady was trying to make friends with the Southerners. She upset a few people up here when she cuddled up with that Fitzgerald guy in Dublin. We thought she was selling us out, to be honest."

Clive chuckled. "Don't worry about the Lady old chap. She's on our side. She can be a bit two-faced sometimes. Mind you, if she is two-faced, she wouldn't wear the one you see on television." Clive laughed again and then lowered his voice and moved in closer.

"The problem is, the shipment is all being run by PIRA down south. None of our contacts in Belfast know anything about it. We have a few agents in Dublin, but they haven't come up with much. So, we reached out to the Garda Special Branch. But let's just say we don't believe that they are being fulsome with the truth. One always feels like a mushroom farm when dealing with the Gardai. They keep you in the dark and feed you shit. So, we were hoping that your mole in their head office might be able to help us. Take a little poke into their internal files and that sort of thing."

McGuinness smiled. He liked nothing better than having others depend on him. "We'd be happy to help, but as a matter of interest, shouldn't MI6 be looking after things in the Republic? I thought they looked after the overseas stuff."

Clive raised his eyebrows. "MI5 never really recognised the Government of Ireland Act, old chap. Or Eire getting all uppity and declaring itself a republic. We still see it as our patch. Don't tell your Loyalist pals. But we have always looked at this island as one country."

Their lunch arrived and McGuinness greedily tucked into his prawn cocktail starter.

"So, Clive, did your boys in Dublin find out the whereabouts of this Morgan chap?"

Clive gestured to his upper lip and McGuinness looked at him quizzingly. "Maire Rose sauce, old chap. All over your moustache. But, yes, I do have something on that Morgan chap."

He reached inside his Savile Row suit jacket and took out a piece of paper which he read with a pained expression.

"He is meeting a girl tomorrow at 3 pm at the pier in eh, Doon Logair."

McGuinness took the paper from him and studied the contents. "That's Dún Laoghaire, you eejit. It's no wonder you Sassenachs can't get any decent intel down south if you can't even pronounce the bloody names. Grand, I'll organise a posse and get down there tomorrow. I don't suppose you guys could help out?"

Clive smiled. "We're night creatures, old chap. We don't like being seen in the daylight. Doesn't suit our complexion. Anyway, we're not very good at this sort of operational stuff. We prefer to stay in the background and to leave the bang-bang stuff to the bang-bang boys. And God knows, there are enough of those in this godforsaken country. But if you need any kit, particularly weapons that are untraceable, then I'd be happy to help."

"Thanks, but I think I'm okay in that regard. I plan to use some Provo weapons that we have in storage, so that the ballistics will all point back to them."

"I like your thinking, McGuinness. With that level of deviousness, you are cut out for a career in the spy services."

"I'd think about it, Clive. But I believe the pay is shit and I just can't talk like I have a silver spoon in my mouth and walk around like I have a broomstick shoved up my arse."

They laughed and Clive ordered another bottle of wine as

McGuinness's steak arrived. The battle would commence tomorrow, and they were both determined to eat, drink and be merry today.

———

McGuinness got back to RUC headquarters just after 5 pm and was as merry as a town drunk. He hobbled up the stairs like a bag of springs loudly humming the 'Londonderry Air' as he went.

The whole office stopped and stared as he made his way to his office, colliding with the occasional desk or filing cabinet as he did so.

"Anderson, my office now," he barked as he passed Anderson's desk.

Anderson grabbed a pad and pen and wearily followed his boss.

"Good meeting with MI5, I take it," Anderson said as he sat down.

"Couldn't have gone better, Anderson. I went in with my cap in my hand expecting to beg. By the end of the meeting, he was practically licking my arse. Which thinking about it, would be right up his street, if you know what I mean. Turns out that they need us more than we need them, Anderson."

"And why is that, boss? Have they finally realised that we're the only ones who have a clue about what's going on here? That you can't drop an Oxford-educated spook into Ballymurphy and expect him to seamlessly slip into the IRA?"

"Not quite, Anderson. Those arrogant English pricks would never admit weakness. No, they are on the back foot over Libya. London expects them to come up with quality intel from Garda Head Office and they don't have an asset there. And we do. Which means that they are just as keen as we are to protect Oriel and to eliminate any unnecessary risks."

"That risk being Morgan, I assume?"

"Exactly. Morgan is meeting some young one at Dún Laoghaire pier at 3 pm tomorrow. I called the army CO and those three Scottish squaddies are going to meet us outside Lisburn barracks at 10 am tomorrow. MI5 are providing one of their builder's vans for the day and I've sourced a few captured IRA weapons from stores. You meet me here at 9 am and we'll travel down in my car. I want as many shooters in place as possible. This is our big opportunity to show the mandarins in MI5 that we can run the operation here.

"So, get a good night's sleep, Anderson. We have a big day ahead."

Anderson slouched out of the office and threw his notepad on the desk. He needed to call his cousin in Canada, and he didn't want to use his own phone. He headed to the canteen for some privacy.

Ten minutes later, Carson appeared at Anderson's desk. He said hello to the guy at the next desk. "Is he around?" he asked, nodding towards Anderson's seat.

"He was here a few minutes ago. I think he just nipped down to the canteen."

Carson sat in the seat and swivelled around. "What was all that shouting about earlier?" he asked.

"Just McGuinness, being a knob as usual. He got pissed at lunchtime and came back full of the joys of spring."

"Yeah, he likes an old lunchtime beer, does our friend McGuinness," Carson said as he idly flipped open Anderson's notebook to the most recent page.

Morgan, Dún Laoghaire pier tomorrow at 3pm. was scrawled across it.

"Can I help you?" Anderson asked as he appeared at Carson's side. Carson closed the notebook as delicately as he dared.

"Just came over to see what all the singing was about. Thought it might be a ceasefire. Peace in our time and all that lovely stuff."

"No such luck," said Anderson. "Just a drunk Super, sucking as much free booze out of MI5 as is humanly possible."

"Fair enough," said Carson. "I'll leave you to it."

Carson walked back to his desk and dialled a Dublin number. A gruff voice answered. "Howya, this is Joyce."

"Can you be at the call box in ten minutes? I have some information for you."

———

Tina called round to her friend's house after work to find Morgan in the kitchen peeling potatoes.

"In thought I'd make a start on dinner," he said. "Although, to be honest, peeling spuds is all I'm good at. I thought about adding a few spices, but I had a look in the cupboard and most of them looked like they were brought back from the Crusades."

Tina threw him a weak smile and started emptying the shopping bags she had brought. She was hunched over the fridge and Morgan came over and put his arms on her shoulders.

"Is something up?" he asked.

She turned and her eyes were filled with tears. "I'm sorry, James. Maybe you don't appreciate the enormity of what's going on. But these guys will stop at nothing to protect their intelligence assets. They will keep you on their radar forever. Which means the only way I'll be able to spend any time with you is to quit my job, change my identity and come and join you."

"So why don't you do that?"

As soon as Morgan said this, he regretted it. He knew that in that single question he was asking Tina to give up everything for him and in return she would have the rightful expectation that he would give everything up for her. And he wasn't sure he was quite ready for that.

She looked up at him with wide eyes. "Do you mean that, James? Do you want me to come with you?"

"Ah look, Tina. I'd love you to. But it's too much to ask. You have a job. You own your own house. I'm giving up everything I know and love. The city I've made my home. I can't ask you to do the same. I'd never be able to live with the guilt."

Tina laid her head on his shoulder. "That's the problem with being a Catholic, James. Guilt is our strongest emotion and stops us from doing anything."

"I must be a super Catholic then. I don't just feel guilty about the things I've done. I feel guilty about things other people have done."

Tina took his hand and led him to the living room sofa. "I'm a realist," she said. "I knew what I was getting myself in for when this started. You were already a target back then. Go to London or whatever and write to me as Sean. I'll keep on top of things at Head Office. You never know, Joyce could die peacefully in his sleep one night or get a posting outside Special Branch. Circumstances could change and if they do, I'd be happy to come and meet you. That's if you are still happy to meet me. London has the tendency to make eyes wander."

"I'd always be happy to see you, Tina. Particularly if you brought your uniform with you."

She leaned over and nibbled his ear. "I have a freshly laundered uniform in my car. Would you like me to put it on?"

Morgan nodded and smiled. "Give me five minutes," she said. "And then come up to your bedroom."

She raced out to the car and he could hear her footsteps on the stairs above the pounding of his heart.

Five minutes later, he heard a command from upstairs. "Can the prisoner please present himself for interrogation?"

He climbed the stairs and turned on the landing towards the bedroom. Tina was standing in the doorway in full uniform. Her peaked cap sat over her sparkling green eyes and her sky-blue blouse was crisp and tight. The dark blue skirt ended just below the knee, exposing sheer and gleaning black tights.

"I think you need to put on these," she said, holding up a set of handcuffs. "We can't be too careful."

She handcuffed Morgan to the bedpost and he lay spread-eagled on his back. Then she started slowly undressing. As she lowered her skirt, Morgan noticed that she was wearing stockings and suspenders. He groaned as though his birthday and Christmas Day had arrived together.

"I'm a sucker for suspenders," he moaned.

"It's not strictly the official uniform but I thought you wouldn't mind."

She straddled him, wearing only her stockings and cap, and started undoing his belt and trousers. He wanted desperately to touch her, to grope and to fondle. But his hands strained against the cuffs.

She leant down and whispered, "I'm in charge," as she gently took hold of his manhood and placed it inside her.

"I don't think you'll be in charge for long," he moaned.

Three minutes later it was all over. She collapsed on top of him and they lay there in a pool of sweat. Tina undid the cuffs and they lay side by side, warm and cosy in a post-coital embrace.

"Penny for your thoughts," she asked.

"You don't want to know," he said.

She raised her head from the pillow and looked at him with a worried expression. "What do you mean?"

Morgan smiled. "I think I left the spuds on the hob."

———

Tuesday was bright and sunny with the first signs of the approaching summer. McGuinness drove through East Belfast on his way to work and admired the Union Jacks and pictures of King Billy that were being put up for the approaching marching season. This was his favourite time of year and he had a good feeling about this afternoon's plans in Dublin. Having MI5 beholden to him would be a major feather in his cap and finally putting this Morgan business to bed would allow him to progress with his ambition to further infiltrate Garda headquarters.

He whistled as he made his way upstairs to his office. He didn't notice that Anderson's desk was empty, with all the photographs and mementoes that had previously adorned it now gone.

As he opened the door to his office, he was greeted by a uniformed gentleman and a sharply dressed middle-aged woman.

McGuinness paused and tried to take in the scenario.

"Chief Constable. To what do I owe the pleasure?"

"McGuinness, you might want to take a seat. This is a delicate matter that we need to discuss. This is Shirley Robinson, by the way. Our head of Human Resources."

"Grand," said McGuinness. "It's just that I have a major operation planned for today. I haven't really got time for a chat."

He moved towards the door and shouted, "Get in here, Anderson. We need to leave soon."

The Chief Constable stood and closed the door and pointed

towards McGuinness's chair. "Sit down, Stanley. Anderson won't be coming in here. It's him that we need to talk about."

McGuinness slumped in his chair, convinced that he was about to hear that Anderson was in the City Morgue after an early-morning booby trap.

Shirley took a manila folder out of her briefcase and placed it on her lap. "Detective Anderson approached us last week and made some allegations. We have been investigating these allegations and we have to say that we think there is an element of truth to them."

McGuinness leaned across the desk. "Look, you're from Human Resources, so I assume that these allegations are staff related and not security issues. Well, just to let you know, Shirley, we run a tight ship here and if there are any staff issues, we deal with them in-house. Frankly, I'm disappointed that Anderson saw fit to tell tales rather than come to me with his problems. But rest assured that if somebody has been giving him trouble, I'll root the fucker out and deal with him the way Special Branch have always dealt with these issues."

Shirley's mouth hung open as she struggled to come up with a reply. The Chief Constable stepped in to save her embarrassment.

"He made the allegations about you, Stanley. And they are of a sexual nature."

McGuinness stared in disbelief for a second and then said. "Are you fucking serious? Is he saying that I'm a queer?" He glanced at both of them. "What did the fucker say?"

Shirley consulted her notes. "He alleges that in recent weeks you have made several advances of a sexual nature, mainly in the changing rooms of your golf club. He claims that you invited him there to engage in, hmm, homosexual activity. He says that he repulsed these advances and that you started leaving lewd and abusive messages on his phone. He taped some of these messages and provided us with a copy."

McGuinness jumped from his chair and raced to the door. "Where is the fucker? I'll kill him."

"Sit down, Stanley. That's an order," said the Chief Constable. "Look, I've heard this tape that Shirley is referring to. It's pretty damning stuff. It's definitely your voice, Stanley."

"It's bullshit, Chief. Do I look like a poof? What sort of stuff is on this tape?"

The Chief nodded to Shirley and her face reddened as she read, "*I own you, Anderson. I own every part of you and I'm going to enjoy owning it. And we're going to have a good time on Tuesday, Anderson. I can feel myself getting a hard-on just thinking about it.*"

"And there was another one," she said as she rifled through her notes. "*I'll see you at the golf club at 2 pm on Thursday. I'll finish my round around then but it's important I see you. So, bring a towel and meet me in the showers.*"

She looked up at him as she finished. "Did you say those things, Mr McGuinness?"

"Yeah, I probably did but not in a gay context, I was discussing operational issues. Anderson must have spliced different messages together. He's a clever fucker that way. We did that once on a supergrass case. Spliced different phone calls together to make this IRA guy sound like a nonce. Then we threatened to release the tape to the IRA. He became a supergrass overnight. That's where Anderson learned that trick."

"I understand you are upset, Stanley. And you may well be right. But these things need to be investigated. The last thing we need is a homosexual scandal within the RUC. Our reputation is shaky at the best of times. I have to ask you not to make any contact with Detective Anderson."

"Where is the little fucker? I suppose you've put him on long-term sick leave."

"Detective Anderson has actually resigned. We couldn't tell you beforehand for obvious reasons. Due to the nature of his complaints, we decided to forego his notice period and he has already packed up and left. I believe he is heading overseas, but I'm not at liberty to say any more."

The Chief stood up. "We'll see ourselves out, Stanley. But can I ask that you keep your head down while Shirley completes her investigation? She may need to speak to some of your team and clearly we'd like to keep this as confidential as possible."

McGuinness stayed sitting so they passed up on handshakes and left. He turned and stared out the window onto Knock Road. The marching season banners seemed less attractive now.

Then he noticed a file on his desk marked *Oriel*. It was empty apart from one handwritten note.

Hi boss,

By the time you read this, I'll be gone. Away from this god forsaken nation of small-minded bigots with oversized egos. I never wanted to be a part of your illegal and immoral schemes but I went along with it for a while because I foolishly believed your bullshit that we were in a war. It's only a war if you choose it to be.

I'm off to do something positive. To fight crime and not innocent bystanders. And by the way, you might be wondering why this file is empty. I've taken all the incriminating photos and negatives of Oriel and all your file notes. They are now in the incinerator out the back. I'll let Oriel know that you no longer have any blackmail material.

And finally, I'd just like to say that I've always hated Glentoran. And go Fuck Yourself.
M

McGuinness tossed the letter aside and grabbed his car keys. Fuck Anderson, he thought. Fuck the lot of them. If you want a job done right, do it yourself.

———

Morgan and Tina woke up on Tuesday morning in each other's arms. The sun was streaming through the window and Tina remembered that in their haste to tear each other's clothes off, she had forgotten to close the blinds.

She watched Morgan wake up and wipe the sleep from his eyes.

"So, lover boy. This is your second to last day in Dublin. What do you have planned? Please tell me you'll be careful."

Morgan turned around, yawned and stretched his arms out. "Finish packing, I think, then I'll find a call box somewhere and call my mother."

He saw the worried look on Tina's face. "Don't worry, I won't tell her anything about Sean. I'll say that I've quit my job and I'm going travelling. That I'll head to Germany first to earn some money on the building sites and then I'll go to Australia. That should throw them off the scent for a while."

"Good idea," Tina said. "In fact, why don't you call your work and give them the same story. And maybe some friends too like..."

Her voice trailed off. "Like Orla, you mean?"

"I don't like talking about her, James. But, yes. You should call her. At home and at work. That's where they bugged you before so the likelihood is that they'll do it again."

She got up and headed towards the shower. "I'm going to pick up your new passport today, James. I'll bring it round later and maybe we could watch a video or something. I'll get a bottle of whiskey and we can have what they used to call an American wake."

Morgan pulled the blankets up and tried to snatch another few minutes of snoozing. It felt like a wake alright. He had an overwhelming feeling that his old life was dead and a new one was about to begin.

McGuinness pulled up outside Lisburn army barracks. The three Scottish soldiers were waiting for him beside a white van with the markings of 'McCloskey Painters and Decorators' on the side.

"Right lads," he said as he parked his car. "We'll leave my motor here and travel down together in the van. We'll just have to transfer the kit first."

He opened his boot to reveal three Armalite rifles and an AK-47 as well as several balaclavas and overalls.

"This kit all came from a wee IRA arms dump in South Armagh. They don't know that we found it, so they think the guns are still there. When we finish this job today, the Irish cops are going to be chasing the IRA."

"Good thinking," said Hastie. "Needless to say, we don't want anything traced back to us. And like I said to Anderson, this is our last job. When this is done, we're quits. Where is he by the way?"

"Anderson is on long-term sick leave. So, you're dealing with me from now on, and let me tell you Sargent Hastie, I decide when we're quits."

They transferred the contents of McGuinness's boot into the van. Hastie climbed into the driver's seat and Burr moved towards the passenger seat.

"And where do you think you're going, Private?"

"I sat here on the way down. I just assumed it was my seat."

"Well, just assume a position in the back of the van then. If you think I'm sitting back there then you obviously don't understand the chain of command."

Burr slumped towards the back of the van and McGuinness climbed into the front seat. "Point her for Dublin, Hastie. I'll give you more directions as we get closer. And if we hit any checkpoints, north or south of the border, then let me do the talking."

Burr and McMillan sat crouched in the back, admiring the guns that McGuinness had brought along. "Fucking IRA have better weapons than we do," Burr said as he picked up an Armalite and balanced it in his hands.

"Yeah," said McMillan. "But we have the helicopters and a ticket out of here after six months. They have to spend their whole life in this miserable shithole."

———

Joyce got to work early on Tuesday morning. Carson had given him the time and place of Morgan's meeting and now all he had to do was find a suitable weapon. Like McGuinness, he was concerned about traceability, but he had less access to captured weapons.

He headed down to the storeroom. The store's manager didn't start until 9 am and Joyce knew that at this early hour, it would be locked up and he knew where he could find the key. Once inside, he knew what to look for. An evidence bag from a 1982 post office robbery was down the back and it contained a very workable gun. Joyce knew that the case was going nowhere so the evidence bag was unlikely to ever be needed or disturbed. He removed the gun and ammunition and wrapped them in a towel he had brought with him.

Joyce left by the back door and headed towards his car. He'd left a message to say that he would be out all day meeting a potential informer. Instead, he drove to Dún Laoghaire and parked beside the pier. Then he pushed his seat back and fell asleep.

15

Morgan arrived early at Dún Laoghaire pier, but Tina's warnings were finally sinking in. He knew that it wasn't smart to stand in the open for long. So, he found a bus stop that overlooked the pier and buried himself inside his hooded jacket. He had brought a couple of homemade tapes along and slipped one into his Walkman.

Ballads and Bodhráns was a tape he had made for his exgirlfriend when she was in college. He hadn't listened to it in years but now that he was leaving Ireland and taking the well-worn path across the water to England, it seemed that ballads about emigration and the cruelty of the security forces was just what he needed. He pressed play on his Walkman and the sound of The Wolf Tones drifted in.

He had almost fallen asleep when a bus pulled up and a single passenger alighted.

"Hello, spymaster. Is Tina still dressing you like a reject from *Top of the Pops*?"

Morgan stood up and greeted her. "Thanks for coming along, Orla. You are looking well."

"Thanks," she said as she sat on the bench beside him. "Now, what's all this about you moving away."

Morgan took her through the latest developments, the fact that both the Northern and Southern police wanted to kill him. He also told her about his new identity.

"Sean Walters! Couldn't she at least come up with a name to suit your new persona? Like something with Bond in it."

"I don't think she had a choice, Orla. She needed to find a real person who is my age, but dead."

Orla said nothing but stared out at the Irish Sea. A summer storm had appeared and the rain lashed against the water. The dark clouds seem to reflect their mood.

"It's been a crazy couple of months, Morgan. I thought it was all a bit of fun at first. But now it feels like you are going away forever. I'll miss you."

Morgan could see the tears welling in her eyes but was helpless to say anything useful.

"And why there?" she said nodding out to sea. "To that godforsaken nation of child molesters."

He smiled. "Funnily enough, that's the exact thing my mother said. The truth is that I emptied out my bank account. A plane ticket to London was all I can afford."

"I feel bad, Morgan," she said as she groped for his hand. "I played you along. I knew you were interested in me but I held you at bay. The truth is that I've only ever gone out with guys that I don't like. I've been scared to get into a relationship with somebody like you. Somebody I really like. Because I think if I let you inside me, you'd find that it's empty in there. That there is nothing to hold onto."

"It's strange," he said. "All I ever wanted was to be inside you. I never gave any thought to what I'd find when I got there."

"Why don't we go for a walk down the pier like in the old

days?" she said. "We can pretend that we are an old married couple. We can dream about what might have been."

He took her hand as they set off down the pier. On the way, they passed a white van with Northern registration plates. But Morgan was so focused on the softness of Orla's hand that he never even noticed it.

Tina called into the passport office and picked up Sean Walter's new passport. She smiled at the photo. Morgan looked like he was having his balls squeezed when the photo was taken, and it amused her that this shot might follow him around for the next ten years. She drove from the passport office to her friend's house. As she half expected, Morgan wasn't there. Instead, she found a handwritten note on the coffee table.

Hi Tina,
Just gone out to say goodbye to a friend. Should be back
around 6ish.
Love
James

Tina threw the note down. She struggled to maintain her frustration. She was pretty sure the friend was Orla. In all the time she'd known Morgan he had never mentioned another friend. But she was also worried. She had warned him that Orla's phone was likely to be tapped and she could sense the dark forces that would have listened to their conversation.

She jumped into her car and drove to Orla's house. Uncle Frank answered the door in his wellies and gardening gloves.

"Tina, what brings you here? Is everything okay?"

"Everything is grand, Uncle Frank. I just wanted to speak to Orla about a house I was thinking of buying. I thought she might be able to help."

"Ah, well, she did come home early but she headed out again. Said she was meeting a friend on Dún Laoghaire pier."

"Thanks, did she say who the friend was?"

"No, but I expect it's another one of those temporary boyfriends of hers. I do wish she'd settle down and give your aunt and myself a day out. But she doesn't seem keen on domesticity. Mind you, a little birdy tells me that you are courting these days, Tina. Are you going to introduce him to the family? We could organise a Sunday lunch or something."

Tina frowned and shook her head. "We're going through a bit of a rocky patch, Uncle Frank. I don't think I'll be organising any lunches any time soon."

Uncle Frank nodded knowingly. He had enough experience of turbulent relationships to know better than to ask awkward questions.

"Grand so, Tina. If you don't see her, I'll let her know that you called. See you at Mass on Sunday, God Bless. I must get back to my roses."

Tina raced to her car and drove towards Dún Laoghaire. If Orla's dad knew they were meeting at the pier, then others would know that as well. Her heart was racing as she ran through red lights and pushed the accelerator to the floor.

———

McGuinness watched as Morgan and Orla set off hand in hand down the pier.

"Right lads," he said. "Park in that alleyway over there and we'll get the kit on and get ready. That sports bag in the back has overalls and balaclavas. Put them on. This is a broad daylight operation and we don't want any eyewitnesses."

They parked up and Hastie, Burr and McMillan went around to the back of the van and started putting on the overalls. Suddenly McGuinness appeared from the side of the van carrying an Armalite rifle that was pointed at the soldiers.

"I'm sorry about this, lads. But today is about tidying up loose ends. And you lot fall into the loose-end category. I blame Anderson. I always wanted to keep my distance from you. To leave no trace that you were connected to me. Well, Anderson pissing off has ruined all that. I can't afford to have three Scottish squaddies floating about telling tales about this mission next time they get pissed.

I run a professional operation. It's nothing personal."

He pressed the trigger repeatedly and the three soldiers fell. Two into the back of the van and Hastie in a dishevelled heap on the roadway.

McGuinness replaced the magazine in his rifle and set off for the pier. As he got to the end of the alleyway, he had a clear view of Orla and Morgan. He pulled a balaclava from his pocket and slipped it on. Then he stepped out onto the roadway and placed the Armalite against his shoulder. He looked through the sight and focused on Morgan's head.

"I have you now, you Fenian bastard," he muttered as his finger searched for the trigger. A single shot rang out. But McGuinness hadn't fired it. Back in the alleyway, Hastie was on his knees, blood flowing freely from wounds in his abdomen and legs. He dropped the rifle he was holding and winced with pain. He could see McGuinness's body on the road, with crimson blood seeping from his head and spilling into the nearby drain.

Hastie pushed himself back against the side of the van and pressed against the wound in his side. "Take that, ya cunt," he shouted. "If ya were as professional as ya think ya are, you would have made sure we were dead."

Then the pain subsided and he closed his eyes. His mind brought him back to a hill outside Port Stanley with his two best friends beside him. And then it all went dark.

———

Joyce was woken by the sound of gunfire. He sat up in his car and the first thing he saw were two figures on the pier, looking scared and confused. As his eyes cleared, he recognised that one of those figures was Morgan. He reached into the glove box and pulled out a revolver. I've got you now, he thought.

Morgan and Orla had heard the gunfire too. They froze momentarily before Orla took control of the situation. "Let's go," she said. "We're out in the wide open here. If we get to the main road, we might be able to get a taxi at least."

They started running back towards the main road when Joyce stepped out from his car and pointed his gun at them. That stopped them in their tracks.

"And who is this little lady, Morgan? Does Tina know that you're going for romantic walks with other young ones?"

"Orla, you go on. I'll deal with this," Morgan said with a bravado he had never seen in himself before.

"You're going nowhere, Orla," Joyce said. "But it's a pleasure to finally meet you. I've had the pleasure of listening to a lot of your phone calls. You really should just pick one fella. I was finding it hard to keep up."

"Fuck you," she said. "Why don't you leave us alone? Morgan hasn't done anything wrong."

Joyce laughed. "When did right or wrong ever come into the equation? This is just business. Morgan here has got himself involved in something he shouldn't have. But it's convenient that you happen to be here too, missie. Because I'd say my friend here has been whispering a few things over the pillow at night. I'd say you know more than you should about this business. So, I might be able to kill two birds with the one stone, if you can excuse the pun. You're just in the wrong place at the right time."

Orla was indignant. "You won't get away with this. Tina will track you down. She's ten times smarter than anyone else in the Guards."

"Do you think so? I'll deal with Tina in my own way. Now say a prayer to whatever God you believe in."

Suddenly a car screeched to a halt behind them. Tina jumped out, her gun already in her hand.

"Drop it, Joyce," she said. "Or so help me God, I'll fucking kill you and not lose a moment's sleep over it."

Joyce looked over his shoulder. "Ah, Tina. I was wondering if you'd show up. You're like a fucking bad penny. But put the gun down, love. I know you haven't got the balls to shoot another cop. If you did, you would have topped me already."

"Do you really want to take that chance, Joyce? Do you remember my score from that target practice course you sent me on? Probably not, as all you did was complain about wasting money on having to send a girl on a course to learn how to fire a gun. Well, I beat all the guys that day, Joyce. I could hit that snot in your left nostril. So, I'll tell you again. Put down the gun or I'll show you that the money you spent on that course wasn't a waste."

But Joyce ignored her and turned and aimed his gun at Morgan's head. A shot rang out and Joyce fell to the ground, clutching his knee and screaming in so much pain that even the seagulls circling Dún Laoghaire pier stopped in mid-flight to stare.

Tina coolly walked towards the prone figure of Joyce. His gun had fallen from his hand and lay on the edge of the pier. Tina casually kicked it into the tide and watched as it sank beneath the murky brown water of Dublin Bay.

"I hope that wasn't a Garda-issued gun, boss. You know that Paddy in stores will make a song and dance about a missing weapon."

She leaned down and stroked his hair. Joyce was clutching his left leg as blood slowly oozed between his fingers.

"We had some good times, boss. And you taught me a lot. So, I'm sorry it had to end like this. If that shot was as accurate as I think it was, it will have gone through the back of your knee and taken out your kneecap. That's probably what those three seagulls are fighting about over there. They like nothing better than some fresh patella. I thought it would be appropriate if I hit you with the traditional IRA punishment shot. I don't know if you remember but the first job you sent me on was a kneecap job in a pub in Finglas. Two IRA guys had dragged a punter from the pub and took him into the toilet. They were using an old rifle which was always a dumb thing to do in an enclosed space. They put him face down on the floor and then aimed at the back of his kneecap. But the shooter must have been shaky because he missed from six inches away. The bullet hit the tiled floor and then bounced off the tiled wall before ending in the belly of the shooter himself. I found him dead when I got there. Funny how those things stick with you."

"You fucking bitch, Tina. I'll get you for this. Whether I have to kill you or drum you out of the Guards, I will fucking get you."

"No, you won't, boss. This injury means you'll be on crutches for a long time. Then you might want to go to Belfast. Apparently, the surgeons up there can do marvellous things with false kneecaps. I guess they get a lot of practice. Then, I'd suggest that you take early retirement on medical grounds. You see, you taught me too well, boss. I've taken precautions. If I hadn't that bullet would have been aimed for your head and those seagulls would be enjoying the remains of your skull now.

"We taped that conversation you had with Carson in Central Station in Belfast. I typed up a deposition with his name, rank, et cetera. I also have a signed statement from Oriel. All that stuff is in a safe in my solicitor's office. If anything happens to me, he is authorised to hand it all over to the Garda Commissioner and the Chief Constable of the RUC. But I'm happy to keep this as our little secret, if you are."

While all this was going on, Morgan and Orla were huddled together by the pier wall. Tina put her gun back in her holster and went to them.

"You should get out of here as quickly as possible," she said. "All that gunfire will have the uniformed guys here quickly and I'd prefer if we didn't have to explain everything. It's going to be hard enough explaining why a senior detective is lying there with a bullet wound."

"Where will we go?" Morgan asked in his old squeaky, uncertain voice.

Tina turned towards Orla. "Do you have any money on you?" Orla nodded that she had.

"The Holyhead ferry is waiting over there," Tina said. "It will be leaving soon. Orla, can you take Morgan over and buy him a ticket as a foot passenger? I'll call an ambulance and call in this shooting from my car radio. Then I'll meet you at the ferry departure gate."

She ran back towards her car while Orla and Morgan tried to regain their composure. They walked past the groaning body of Joyce without looking and headed towards the ferry terminal. They noticed a large crowd gathered around a white van and smaller crowd fifty metres away circling a lifeless body in the middle of the road.

———

Orla bought a single foot passenger ticket and handed it to Morgan. She also emptied her purse and gave him the contents. "It's only about eighty punts, but it might get you by for a day or two."

Morgan took the money and ticket and hugged Orla. "I don't know what to think, Orla. I always thought you were the woman of my dreams. But Tina has rescued me so many times that I feel that I owe my life to her."

Orla patted his hair. "You don't have to say anything today, Morgan. Not after all this madness. Go to England. Start a new life and let the future take care of itself."

They hugged and then heard the sound of somebody clearing their throat.

"We don't have time for that," Tina said. "The ferry leaves in five minutes."

She reached inside her pocket and took out a passport and handed it to Morgan. "Your name is Sean now. Remember that and start practising. I've no doubt that word about today's events has already made its way back to MI5 and they'll have people waiting in Holyhead. So, think about a back story while you're on the boat. Where does Sean come from? What sort of work does he do and why is he heading to Britain? It doesn't matter what the story is, just make it believable and be consistent."

Morgan nodded that he understood, and he slipped the passport and ferry ticket into his jacket pocket.

"What do I do when I get to Holyhead?" he asked.

"Get some new underwear and some deodorant," Orla ventured.

"You'll need some new stuff, alright." Tina replied. She handed him some notes. "This is all I have on me, but get the first train down to London. You'll stick out like a sore thumb in Holyhead but London is the best place in the world to go if you want to disappear. And believe me, James. You need to disappear. They won't stop hunting you as long as they think there is a secret to protect."

Morgan welled up and crudely wiped the tears from his eyes with his sleeve. "I don't know how to thank you two. I'll repay this money as soon as I can. And I'll be back as soon as you give me the green light."

Tina shook her head. "Don't expect that green light anytime soon. And even if you have the money, hold off on contacting either of us for as long as you can. It's just not safe."

She turned and spoke to Orla. "Do you think I could have a minute with James on my own?"

"Sure, Tina, I'll just say goodbye."

Orla stepped forward and kissed Morgan gently on the lips. "Travel safely, my gentle tiger," she whispered. "I'll be waiting for you when you get back."

Orla turned and walked away and Morgan's eyes followed her as she stepped out of the terminal and the wind caught her blonde hair.

Tina put her hands around his shoulders and lay her head in the nape of neck. "You drive me crazy, James. I know you still think about Orla. But it doesn't stop me loving you."

"I love you too, Tina. A few weeks ago, I was a gormless insurance clerk whose biggest thrill was reading claim forms for chicken factories that have burned down. Now, I'm an international man of intrigue, being chased by the security forces of two countries. And through all of that, you've been at my side. Making sure I'm okay. That's what scares me about moving to London, Tina. You are my safety blanket. It's like you are casting me naked out into the world."

He could feel Tina's warm tears trickling down his neck.

"I know, James. I wish you didn't have to go too. But I can't see another way."

The ship's foghorn sounded and the tannoy announced that the doors were about to close.

"You'd better go," she whispered. "Don't look back."

Morgan kissed her on the forehead and started up the walkway to the ship's door. When he got there, he turned. Tina was still waiting and she waved with one hand while she wiped away tears with the other. Behind her, the streetlights of Dublin were flickering on. He could see the stands of Lansdowne Road in the distance and the dark brooding Wicklow Mountains.

He turned and walked into the bright lights of the ferry's interior and headed straight for the bar.

Adrian Chapman grew up in Dundalk, on the east coast of Ireland. He has a keen interest in history and particularly the events that are euphemistically called the 'Troubles'.

Writing is also his passion and his musings can be found at manwhokilledmy-mojo.blogspot.com

Adrian now lives in Auckland, New Zealand with his wife and daughter.

Email: adrianchapmanauthor@gmail.com